A SHELL ISLE MYSTERY

RED, WHITE, & Boom

TONYA PENROSE

This is a work of fiction. Names, characters, places, and incidents are products of the author's imagination or are used fictitiously and are not to be construed as real. Any resemblance to actual events, locations, organizations, or persons, living or dead, is entirely coincidental.

World Castle Publishing, LLC
Pensacola, Florida
Copyright © 2025 Tonya Penrose
Hardback ISBN: 9798286015962
Paperback ISBN: 9798891264144
eBook ISBN: 9798891264151
Second Edition World Castle Publishing, LLC, July 21, 2025
http://www.worldcastlepublishing.com
Licensing Notes
Cover: Cover Designs by Karen

Dedicated to: Page and her inklings. Keep them coming!

CHAPTER 1

The eclectic beachfront town of Shell Isle did one thing really well, celebrate the fourth of July. While a tepid greeting met most tourists, on this particular day, the locals made an exception. Everyone felt welcome as long as they brought an appetite for Bailey's Barbeque and an appreciation for lavish fireworks. However, one celebratory tradition trumped all others, the required energetic clapping before the firing of the town's beloved Revolutionary War cannon at the stroke of nine p.m. That upcoming event held a worrisome portending for sleuth Page Wright. She'd received one of her intuitive inklings earlier that morning.

Hearing the jingle of Honey Bees Shop's door meant her cousin, Betsy, had turned the sign to open. Page pushed the concern away and hurried to the kitchen. Peering through the oven's glass door at the flat popovers, she sighed. The batter needed to swell and pop over the muffin pan. It hadn't. Maybe the fussy, full-of-air breads required a few more minutes of her watchful eye before the drizzle of cinnamon honey.

An anxious Betsy appeared at the kitchen's door. "Well? How's my new recipe behaving? Have they popped? Ina Funk's waiting on her dozen. Remember, she's hosting the bridge club at her house."

"Nope. They're still sitting low in the cups. Tell me again why we added popovers to our menu? We're still novices at this baking business." Page's delicate features and cornsilk hair skimmed her shoulders. A petite frame and a sprinkling of freckles across her cheeks presented the image of someone much younger than fifty-one.

Celebrating having the same birthday, along with their moms being twins, had helped Betsy and Page forge an early bond. That bond had brought them back to Shell Isle to heal from personal losses. Page, as a widow, and Betsy, as a divorcée, reclaimed their joy by opening Honey Bees and embracing the beach lifestyle. Smiles had replaced tears as they had set about writing new life chapters.

Page stole another glance inside the oven. "They're not feeling it."

Ina materialized next to Page. "Let me look." She released a breath and shook her head. "Ladies, nothing's going to pop in those muffin tins. You've got what I call flat tires."

"I was afraid you'd say that." Page's oven mitt brought out the pans and tossed the contents into the trash can. "Oh, Ina, we're so sorry. Is there something else you'd like for the club's meeting? It's on the house."

"How about a dozen of our honey cake donuts? They've become quite a favorite with the cops," Betsy chirped. An abundance of wavy auburn hair framed her heart-shaped face. Her tall frame, once called willowy, spoke now to a passion for food. She embraced flamboyance in the way she lived and dressed. The now-signature brightly-colored beach muumuus testified to her latest style interpretation.

"Donuts won't work. I promised the girls popovers." Ina's expression brightened. "Listen, you two get out front and take care of the customers, and let me whip up some popovers. I've got a couple of hours free before bridge. As they say, what are friends for?"

Page hugged Ina. "You're aces and our best friend, too. Our kitchen is your kitchen." Page made a grand sweeping motion with her arm. "Right, Bets?"

"Right. And, Ina, would you bake an extra batch of those

popovers for Honey Bees?"

Ina grinned. "I like your confidence in me. You got it. An extra batch coming up. Now, get out there and kibitz with the customers. Leave this to me."

Page led the way. "Are you thinking what I'm thinking?"

Betsy halted. "Probably not. What are you thinking?"

"Ina lost her job when we busted her boss for insurance fraud," Page reminded.

"Yeah, I still feel bad about that, but what does—"

"Stay with me, and don't interrupt. Ina loves to bake. Ina needs a job that taps into her creativity. Ina's husband wants her busy. And, we need someone who can take our ideas and transform them into something edible." Page stopped to gauge Betsy's reaction, fearing she'd gone too far, stating the obvious. Betsy was a lousy cook, and choosing the word *lousy* was her being kind.

A frown settled on Betsy's face. "Hold on. Are you saying my baked goods and such aren't edible because—"

Page grabbed Betsy's hand. "No, no. I'm saying your gift lies in coming up with a menu of baked items using all the variety of honeys that you've discovered. Why not let Ina bring your recipes to life? Of course, you can and must oversee things."

"But I enjoy baking and combining ingredients." Betsy looked away, pondering.

If Page could shift Betsy from unsupervised baking to supervised baking, the kitchen debacles would end. She could focus on growing Honey Bees' business and not resetting the smoke detectors countless times a day. Vistas might open for new honey items to sell. Page tapped Betsy's shoulder. "Guess what? I'm feeling another inspiration bubbling that I promise to share with you later."

"Yeah?" Betsy's tone sounded hopeful. "Inspirations are good."

"Yep, and I predict you're going to feel super jazzed. Come on, Betsy. Let's grow this business. What about adding Ina?"

Betsy tilted her head, pondering. "Well—"

Page jumped in. "If you agree, I think you should make the proposal." Page needed to empower Betsy.

"You want me to—"

"Yes, you're better at pitching," Page replied, sensing a win. "Since Ina's the one who invited you to join the Mermaids' bowling team, I bet she'd love to hear the proposal from you. You're bowling buddies. What do you say?"

Betsy preened and smoothed her unruly mop. "I say—go greet that guy coming in the door while I hire us a baker."

"You're sure?" Page asked.

"I'm sure. You're right. Ina's the perfect addition. We need her. Scoot. I got this." Betsy grinned, while her hand made scurrying motions.

Page went to greet the man waiting at the counter and felt the strange inkling return. She'd observed him only yesterday in a heated exchange with Jake, the town's favorite charter boat captain. Another unwelcome foreboding washed over her as they made eye contact.

CHAPTER 2

"Thank you. Enjoy." Shutting the cash register drawer, Page watched the man leave with a box of lavender honey cookies. His Scandinavian good looks didn't pair with his intimidating demeanor. However, his stinginess with words did pair with the way he ogled her and made her feel uneasy. Page paused, sensing that another more troubling encounter would happen soon.

Betsy came alongside her. "He looked familiar. Handsome rascal." She shrugged. "Maybe he's a repeat customer?"

"Um, I don't think so." Page relaxed her frown. *No point in worrying Betsy, yet.* "So? What happened with hiring our Ina?"

"Oh, I left her doing a Yiddish jig and calling Abe with the happy news. Honey Bees now has an official baker, and she's even starting work tomorrow. Isn't life at Shell Isle grand? Didn't I tell you this was the perfect place to start fresh? And, wasn't my idea to open our shop perfection?" Betsy delivered an enthusiastic high-five to Page.

"Yes, you did, and more than once, as I recall," grinned Page. "And, to celebrate the firecracker holiday and your snagging Ina, I propose we close early and enjoy an afternoon on the beach." Page rearranged the cookies on a tray.

Betsy smiled. "Dare we cut out?"

"Yes, we dare. We're the owners. Besides, all that's left to do is bake and decorate the cupcakes for the delivery tonight." Page grabbed a cloth and wiped the counter.

"That's a plan to love. I'll go bake the cupcakes." Betsy retied her apron and scurried toward the kitchen, humming a patriotic tune off-key.

"Hey there, tuneful?" hollered Page.

Betsy turned back. "Yes?"

"Maybe Ina can lend a hand with the cupcakes before she takes off? We'll get to the beach sooner. *Plus, we'll have cupcakes that won't need forgiving in looks.*" Page mumbled the last sentence to herself.

~*~

Page and Betsy dragged their lounge chairs down to the water's edge, claiming their spot and getting things set up. Colorful umbrellas dotted the beach, testifying to the sun's devotion to shun the few cumulus clouds. A retreating high tide left shells and other treasures for the curious. The teenage lifeguard's whistle sounded while his arms motioned a couple to swim closer to shore. Sandcastles appeared under children's moving hands, giving parents a respite. The scene painted a typical beach day that Page's spirit never grew tired of experiencing. Since she was a young girl, Shell Isle Beach had become her Siren song. Summer vacations spent at Aunt Tilly's Hibiscus Cottage held nothing but happy memories for Page—and Betsy, too. Now flying solo, she'd answered Shell Isle's call to return. She glanced at Betsy, who was pulling a cold soda from the cooler. "You can't possibly feel thirsty this soon?"

"Oh, yes, I can." Betsy popped the tab and rolled the chilled can around her face. "I'm experiencing one never-ending hot flash this afternoon. I can promise you one thing."

Page chuckled. "This ought to be good. What's the promise, hot mama?"

Betsy took a long drink. "I, Betsy Ross, possible ancestor to the sewer of our flag, promise to reincarnate next time as a man if there's no draft. That's right. You heard me. I'm coming back as a guy."

Page laughed, as her police detective neighbor and quasi-beau materialized next to them.

"Reincarnate as one of us? That's scary," said Steve. He planted the yellow surfboard next to the two women and winked at Page.

Betsy twisted in her chair toward the voice coming from behind. "If there's no draft. These feet don't march." She wiggled her scarlet-painted toenails. "What's new, Detective Steve? Chasing down any bad guys?"

"Not today. I gave them the holiday off." Steve removed his *Live to Surf* t-shirt and draped it over Page's lounger. "May I?"

"You may. Don't forget to leave your phone, too." Page enjoyed hanging out with Steve. However, she'd been experiencing one growing complication. If she focused on his tall, dark, and too handsome looks, she'd feel all flushed and bothered in an instant. At her age, such an intense physical reaction was troublesome and most unwelcome. Lately, being around Steve Tanner was turning her traitorous body into a nuclear reactor. Page forced her mind to the present and made eye contact with his forehead, a part of his body that she had yet to succumb to. "The waves look well-formed. Bet you get some good rides."

Steve nodded. "Let's hope." He grabbed his board and headed toward the water.

"I say again, no man our age should look that fine." Betsy pulled out her hand fan. "He's not helping this flash."

Page released a laugh. "Hand me something cold."

"See? The guy's irresistible." Betsy peered into the cooler. "Grape fizz or cherry crush? Never mind, I choose crush, 'cause girl, you have got a big one."

"Shut up and read your historical romance. You're allowed those. It's getting into any new male relationships that are a no-no for you, Betsy Ross." Page took a sip of the soda. "I don't know why you buy these flavors. They're for kids."

"I like anything cherry. It elevates my mood, which I need since agreeing to be placed in this man moratorium. I don't know how much longer I can hold out." Betsy plopped her straw bonnet atop her head and opened her novel.

Ignoring talk of Betsy's much-needed exile from the opposite sex, Page leaned over to see the book's cover. "Ah, I see you're still with the Dowager Gertrude and her family of wannabe aristocrats." No reply came from Betsy. Page knew her cousin had already time-traveled to eighteenth-century merry ol' England.

Page watched Steve ride the first wave, effortlessly staying ahead of the whitewash. He grinned and motioned for her to swim out. "Um, Betsy, if you can hear me, I'm going for a swim." Page yanked off her beach coverup.

Betsy lifted two fingers in a wave, her eyes never leaving the book.

The coolness of the water against her skin worked in Page's favor as she swam out to Steve. She instructed her mind to ignore his tan, well-developed muscles. "Hi. Thanks for the invite. I needed an interruption from Betsy. We're together so much right now, at least until she moves into her bungalow."

"You're welcome. Give me your hand so I can pull you aboard." Steve reached down and hoisted Page to face him.

His brief touch ignited familiar sensations, proving again her mind was no match for her body's response. She'd run her mouth as a distraction. "Listen, mister. You'd better not let a surprise ginormous wave dunk me like last time. My stomach sloshed saltwater for hours after that," Page declared.

"I like that you think me capable of controlling the ocean's movement. You know, since you and Betsy opened Honey Bees, I've missed seeing you on the beach." Steve maneuvered to miss a wave break.

"Yeah, we're putting in long hours to get established. We've been looking for more help. You almost got us dunked." Page's fingers gripped the side of the surfboard.

"Nah, we're good. Have you found anyone interested in working at the shop?"

"As a matter of fact, yes, we hired Ina Funk today as our baker. That means Betsy's unique honey recipes might actually develop a following under Ina's care. And, with another person working, that should afford Betsy and me more flexibility in our hours." Page sighed, anticipating some spontaneity returning to her life.

"That's great news, Page. And don't you have Detective Koch's daughter working part-time, too?"

"We do. Daisy graduated from college with a double degree in business and marketing, so she's going to prove a valuable addition to Honey Bees as we grow." Page adjusted her bathing suit strap and took stock of Steve's last words. "You know what? I appreciate your interest. That's nice. You're nice when not badgering me about my sleuthing." Page beamed a smile.

"Why, thank you. And since you acknowledged how nice I am, perhaps you'd like to spend more time in my company? You've been avoiding me lately." Steve tucked a strand of Page's blonde hair behind her ear.

She sucked in a breath. Blast the man for kindling her hormones. "I'm working, not ignoring. What did you have in mind, sir?"

"I thought since Honey Bees is closed on Sundays and Mondays, why don't we take *Carpe Diem* for a sail Monday? If I ask nicely, would you be willing to pack us a picnic lunch? Nothing fancy," Steve added.

Page adored sailing, which made his offer irresistible. "You've got yourself a deal, detective, and thanks for the invite." Page extended her hand for a shake. "Now, it's my turn. Let's chat about your work."

"Sure. Hang on, we've got a big swell coming." Steve

turned the board to face the wave and paddled quickly past the break line. "You can look now."

Page opened one eye and breathed. "Anymore rogues out there?"

Steve laughed and pulled her closer to balance the board. "Yes, but not for a while. You were asking about work?"

She twisted her ponytail elastic tighter. "Yes, I was wondering if you missed the FBI job since you agreed to work part-time for Shell Isle's Police Department? That's a huge change in action for an ex-Seal guy." *Why must he look at her so intently?* Her fingers dipped into the ocean, making swirling patterns, mimicking her emotions.

"You're right about the change, but I was ready to notch down. I live at Shell now, and commuting to DC had become tiring. Fifty-three is knocking on my door, and going part-time as a detective to help Koch felt timed right. It's only been a week, but I can tell—"

"You're where you belong?" finished Page.

"Exactly, Miss Drew," replied Steve, drawing on his favorite nickname for Page from the author, Carolyn Keene's Nancy Drew books. Steve pointed toward shore. "Ah, it appears Betsy has abandoned her latest romance book and wants to tell us something."

Page looked over her shoulder at a waving Betsy. "She looks like a human windmill. I guess it's time I abandon ship."

"Sit tight. Let me catch this next wave and save you the swim."

Once they were close to shore, it became evident whose attention Betsy wanted. She held up Steve's cell phone.

"Guess you're the winner, and I can tell you that I'm not the least jealous," Page said, as they walked toward Betsy.

Steve chuckled. "And, I lay you odds it'll be me that gets cheated out of beach time and the perfect waves." Steve glanced over his shoulder longingly at the water.

"Your cell keeps ringing and annoying my reading. Here." Betsy passed the phone to the detective and returned to her chair.

"Sorry, Betsy. I know how you and the…who is it again, Page?" asked Steve.

"The Dowager Gertrude. It seems she's made an impression on you, too," Page laughed.

"Would you two please stop disparaging Gert and me and leave us alone? I have a fancy ball to attend." Betsy adjusted her sunbonnet and put her nose back in the book.

Steve stared at the phone's screen. "Okay, ladies, duty calls. Maybe I'll see you later at the fireworks?"

"Could be." Page watched him jog toward his bungalow and wondered what needed his attention. Another inkling came to her. She sensed sinister forces were contriving to do harm.

CHAPTER 3

"Betsy, will you please hurry up? I hear them testing the fireworks. We're supposed to have these trays of honey cupcakes delivered to Bailey—" Page paused and glanced at her thin, gold watch. "Five minutes ago." Double parked in front of Honey Bees, she popped the tailgate on her vintage British SUV.

"I'm here already." Betsy's free hand made a swipe at her damp forehead. "I can't help that the shop's humidity caused the cupcakes' frosting to act all drippy. We need to have that AC checked. Anyhow, dashing them into the freezer for a minute did the trick. See?" Betsy lifted the lid on the top box.

Page took a peek. "Wow, they look scrumptious. Well done, Bets, but we're still late. Since Honey Bees has only been in business for a short time. We need to—"

"I know, exceed all customer expectations. Don't worry. Bailey is so laid back that I guarantee you he doesn't even own a timepiece. He'll never know we're a touch behind schedule. Close the hatch." Betsy hopped into the passenger seat, tossing the ever-present straw hat in the back. "I keep trying to protect this perpetually flushed face from more freckles since we moved to the beach."

"You do an excellent job with that enormous hat," grinned Page.

"Thanks, but don't get me started about my wardrobe of brightly colored muumuus that have grown with my waistline since we opened Honey Bees."

Page broke into laughter. "Actually, I have noticed a lot of deliveries in the past month. Now I know."

Betsy grabbed the armrest. "Hush yourself. I need camouflage. Listen, we'll hand this order off to Bailey in a snap. Could you please take that next corner with all four wheels touching the pavement? We aren't toting upside-down cakes back there."

Page laughed. "Sorry. Running late unsettles my qi."

"As long as we're only dealing with your unsettled qi and not one of your inklings again, I'm sympathetic." Betsy sighed and stole a glance at her cousin, waiting for a reply that didn't come. "Fine. Don't tell me, but you've acted aloof this afternoon. I'm suspicious." Betsy crossed her arms. "Besides, I'd rather not know. I'll just sit back and try to enjoy the wild ride."

"Go with that plan," Page agreed.

"I don't like it when you ignore my inkling questions. It usually means I'm about to get mixed up in some mystery-solving something." Betsy released a huff. "I don't like it."

Page reached over and patted her cousin's shoulder. "I know, Betsy, but we make such a good sleuthing team. After the last case, we've proven our value to Shell Isle's Police Department."

"Listen up, Sherlocka. I like us better as Honey Bees. We sleep a lot better and work regular hours. No more tailing the baddies."

Page opened her mouth.

"Don't say it. Let me finish. Starting our new life at Shell meets our needs. After my last testy divorce and your loss of that wonderful husband, Jeff, the stars have finally aligned for us to do more than summer vacation here. Besides, our kids are settled in their careers, and that frees us to have new adventures. Plus, your inheriting Great Aunt Tilly's beach cottage, and my idea of opening Honey Bees cinched things. We're meant to call Shell Isle home. So, can we please be purveyors of all things honey and not all things curious?" Betsy grabbed her flowered hand fan.

"A hot flash? Don't you hate them?" Page grinned.

"You're deflecting. Now, I am nervous." Betsy's fan picked up speed.

~*~

The two Honey Bees, wearing smiles, grabbed the cupcake boxes and headed for Bailey's tent, anticipating the fun festivities. The darkening indigo-painted sky provided the moon a stray cloud to hide behind. Page noted the sea breeze carried an unseasonably damp chill, but the silent voices of frogs and insects were what unsettled the overall ambiance.

Page paused, taking in nature's subtleties. The inkling returned. She realized that she could no longer pretend it away and exhaled a long breath. For now, she'd act engaging, join the celebration, and hope Betsy didn't notice the shift. "Hiya, Bailey, here we are, as promised, delivering six boxes of honey buttercream cupcakes with red, white, and blue sprinkles."

Betsy placed her boxes on the table. "And, just so you know, I'm the Queen Bee cake froster extraordinaire."

A wiry-built Bailey scratched his bald head and smiled at Betsy. "Froster, huh? That's a word I've not heard before. Must be some baker lingo."

"It's Betsy speak. It means she's fishing for a compliment," Page explained, smiling.

Betsy tried and missed swatting Page with her fan.

"Give the woman her due, Bailey, so I can snag a cupcake from that box that she's got a death grip on," Detective Koch said, coming alongside the two women. His grin stretched wide across his weathered face.

"Yes, sir." Bailey delivered a mock salute and activated his southern charm. "Why, Miss Betsy, I do believe these frosted cakes look extra purdy this evenin'."

Betsy shook her head in mock displeasure and handed Koch a cupcake from the extras she'd brought. "Stuff that in your yap trap. Your daughter, Daisy, sure doesn't take after you. She's mannerly and so well-spoken. And, I might add the ideal employee for Honey Bees."

Koch smiled. "Is she now? That's nice to hear. Not the doesn't-take-after-her-father part, but the rest. Damn, if these aren't good. Give me another to take to the Mrs."

Page handed him one on a napkin. "I'd like to second that Daisy's wonderful and a most needed new addition. She brings great energy and ideas. That college degree you paid for is proving valuable. We hope to make her a full-time offer soon, but keep that under your cop's cap."

"Can do. My girl's always been an achiever." The detective's face showed pride in his daughter. "Listen, I need to mosey around. Catch you ladies later. Oh, and stay out of any mischief."

Page sent a warning glare toward Betsy to keep her retort inside. "We hear you, detective." She added a lilt to her voice.

Koch's brow furrowed as he studied Page. He shrugged off his concern. "Thanks again for the dessert."

"Just sweetening you up for any future mystery-solving interactions," Betsy hollered back. "Geez, what made me say that? I declare that man has a way of drawing out...oh, forget it."

Page winked at Bailey. "Please excuse us. I need to find blabbermouth a time-out seat." Page pulled her cousin's arm.

"Yeah, I need a time-out to sit. All this baking and heat. Is anyone else melting?" Betsy released her fan.

Bailey waved, hiding his mirth from Betsy.

"Here's an unoccupied bench with our names on it." Page released her tote bag from her shoulder. "What ya think of this find, mouthy one?"

"I say major bench coup. I'm ignoring the 'mouthy one' remark, partly because it's true," Betsy declared. "What's in that tote? Pray, something cold to drink?" Betsy tugged at her shift, trying to cover more of her legs.

"Here's an iced green tea." Page settled next to her cousin and gazed over to the point where the cannon waited. "Look, I see the torch. Captain Jake must be close to firing. You know he got tapped for the honor this year?"

Betsy swallowed a gulp and pressed the cold bottle to her cheek. "Actually, I hadn't heard that. He's a swell fellow. Every time I see him around town, he says hello and offers me some of his latest catch."

"Well, isn't that an interesting tidbit? That explains the fresh flounder you tried to cook—?"

Boom!

"What do you mean tried to cook?" shouted Betsy over the sound of the cheering crowd.

Not able to call her words back, Page shrugged and pretended she couldn't hear. "Two more booms to go." She held up her fingers, avoiding more talk about Betsy's eclectic culinary skills.

"That cannon sound is so loud. I feel it in my chest." Betsy gave a little shake.

"Yeah, it's a real attention-getter." Page felt the nudge to act. It was time to coax Betsy along. She grabbed a breath and pitched her cousin the first volley. "Fireworks come next. While they're setting up for the show, let's walk to the point, give Jake a cupcake, and congratulate him on a perfectly timed cannon firing." Page stood.

Betsy wavered. "I don't know. He's probably busy cleaning the cannon or something."

"Cleaning the cannon? He's not cleaning the cannon." Page paused, assessing Betsy's demeanor. "Betsy, why don't you want to go see Captain Jake?"

"I'm flashing." Betsy pushed her damp curls away from her forehead.

"Betsy? Have you been naughty?" Page took in her cousin's all too familiar look. "You've broken the man-free zone rule. You promised not to get involved with any guy until your picking skills improved...a lot."

"Hush." Betsy glanced around and lowered her voice. "I haven't broken the rule. I've been dabbling, is all—some harmless flirting with Jake when he handed off a fish last week. I don't know the man that well. Besides, I need to keep my wiles sharp—"

"Come on and bring your wiles. Even though we aren't well acquainted with Jake, he's earned a sweet, and that's not you, Betsy Ross." The moon reappeared as if assigned to light their way out to the point. Page took advantage and hurried her steps, knowing Betsy languished behind. Catching sight of Jake stretched out on the ground. Page broke into a run. "Hurry, Betsy."

CHAPTER 4

"No, not you." Page choked back a sob. The inkling and nudge proved reliable again.

"Is he?" Betsy knelt and took in the scene.

"I'm afraid so."

"I knew it. I knew it. Here we are, standing over another dead body. Now, it's poor, Captain Jake. Oh, and—lucky us—here comes Detectives Koch and Steve."

"Stifle yourself, Betsy, and let me handle this." Page turned toward the two approaching detectives.

"What's going on here? Steve and I came to help Jake secure the cannon." Koch squatted. "Hey, buddy, you okay—" Pain took over the detective's features.

Steve assessed the scene and tossed his rain parka over Jake's body. "I'm sorry, Koch. I know you thought highly of him. Want me to call it in?"

Koch managed a nod and found his handkerchief.

Steve turned his focus on Page and Betsy. "Of course, I find you two at the scene. Don't move. Don't touch anything. You've got questions to answer as soon as I talk to—"

Detective Koch took the cell phone from Steve's hand. "I'm okay. Let me handle this. See if you can get some straight answers from our two busybodies." Koch's shoulders drooped as he walked away.

Page lifted her chin up a notch, temporarily stowing her sadness at Jake's death and attraction to Steve Tanner. "Listen up. You and Koch know very well that Betsy and I solved Catherine Lange's murder, and all thanks to my inklings and nudges. I thought we'd gained your respect. And, P.S., I resent the busybody name tag."

Steve's hands rested on each hip. "Okay, one last time, let me spell this out nice and neat. Yes, you did solve Catherine's case and thank you. Yes, you did put yourself in jeopardy to do so, which still has me chapped. And yes, I do respect your intuition and those tinklings of yours."

Page looked heavenward. "Inklings. I get inklings. And they're always right. Always."

"I stand corrected. Inklings. But you forget the most important—"

Betsy sashayed over. "I'm not forgetting. We promised never to interfere in anything that looks like police biz. I keep reminding Sherlocka that we're in the biz of honey baking now." Betsy looked away from the still form and saw the first fireworks light the sky.

Steve rubbed his face. "She doesn't appear to be listening, Betsy."

"I know," sighed Betsy. "It's not her strong suit."

"You do know I'm standing here witnessing this personal blasphemy while Captain Jake's lying over there? Don't you want to ask us discovery questions?" Page sent a warning glare toward her cousin.

Steve pulled Page close and whispered, "Does she know, 'cause I'm sure you do? Your keen eyes don't miss much."

"Ask her."

"Um, Betsy, I'm going to start with you, so could you put the candy bar away for a moment?" He watched and waited as she shoved the last piece in her mouth.

Betsy swallowed. "Sorry. I needed something to make me feel better."

Page took a few steps back, seizing the opportunity to survey the ground nearby.

"So, Betsy, do you happen to know how Jake died?"

"Are you daft? The poor man has a bullet hole in his ticker. Maybe I should be the one asking the questions?" Betsy cocked an eyebrow.

"It seems your observation skills have improved," Steve replied with a smirk.

"I'd like to think so," Betsy affirmed. "Do you have any real detecting questions for me?"

"I do. So, we all agree Jake was shot. Any ideas? Did you see him talking with anyone this evening? Perhaps a person visiting him on the point before he fired the cannon?"

"No, no, and no." Betsy waited.

"Okay. Do you know someone who possibly held a grudge against Jake? Didn't like him?" Steve pulled out his notebook.

"Maybe and yes."

"Ms. Ross, I've never known you short with answers before. It makes me wonder why you're holding back?" Steve stepped closer. "It better not be because you and Page have any ideas about snooping around this case."

An irritated Page came alongside her cousin. "Ignore his taunts and answer the questions so we can get out of here. I feel a migraine coming."

"Okay, fine. I might have seen Jake's niece throwing a hissy fit yesterday when he refused to give her money for a trip to the Amalfi Coast. I love that place. My second husband and I ate the most incredible—"

Steve's lips tightened into a fine line. "Please, stick to the subject. None of your side trips, and that pun was intended. So, his niece acted chapped. Anyone else come to mind?"

Betsy took a moment to ponder. "I did hear Ralph and Buck act all agitated with Captain Jake over his proposal to limit fish catches, whatever that means. Do you know those two creepy guys? We see them around town and at the marina. They run fishing charter boats for tourists. Page, you were there with me. Remember the other day on the dock, you wanted to see if Steve's sailboat was docked and—"

"Hush, Betsy." Page felt the embarrassment rush to her face. She didn't dare sneak a look at Steve, as she knew his *gotcha* face all too well. She turned her attention toward rectifying the mortifying moment. "As usual, Betsy tends to flaunt the absurd. I wasn't actually—"

Steve cracked a grin. "I'm not sure which piece of information interests me more. The part about Ralph and Buck being at odds with Jake over a county proposed fish ruling or your interest in my whereabouts."

"Easy, stay interested in what matters," Page managed to get out. She'd deal with her big tattletale cousin later.

"So, Betsy, your thirst for gossip has given us a few possible suspects. Anything else?" Steve clicked his pen.

"Well, gossipy me will miss Captain Jake and his gratis flounder. He seemed like a nice bloke. Didn't he, Page? I can't imagine any person wanting him gone. Can I sit on that bench and sip my warm tea? I'm suddenly feeling out of sorts." Betsy pointed toward the seat.

Steve's face shone sympathy. "Of course, go park yourself, and thanks for the help. Let me have a few minutes with Page, and then you both can head home."

Betsy nodded and walked toward the nearby bench.

"Page, you get the same questions, but before you reply, I have one that's even more vital. "Did you get any of those inklings before this happened? If so, I want to know. I learned the hard way from the Lange case not to doubt your gifts. Though I remind you again, I do not want you and Betsy to go clue gathering. Your curiosity gene and intuition needs to lay dormant. Are we clear?" Steve's gaze was intense.

"May I answer now?" Page's words didn't wait. "Yes, the

inklings came a few times today, and tonight, I got the nudge to go check on Jake. I sensed trouble brewing but didn't want to worry Betsy. She tends to overreact when a new case—I mean, we were bringing him a cupcake." Page course-corrected and sniffed.

Steve wrapped his arms around Page. "Look, I know your intuition thing carries a burden. I'm sorry you're involved again in someone's death. I meant what I said about you and Betsy steering clear of this investigation." His thumb wiped a tear away from Page's cheek.

"You know I can't ignore my inklings in good conscience, but I can promise you I won't chase trouble." Page's face grew somber as she watched the fireworks light the sky with gold and blue orbs. Jake was getting quite the sendoff, and the irony went unwelcomed. "Listen, if it's okay, I'd like to answer those questions and get Betsy and me home."

"Okay, start anywhere." Steve flipped a page in his notebook and nodded.

"So, my interaction with Jake has been minimal, unlike flirty Betsy." A little humor helped lift Page's spirits. "My answers come more as observations. As a business owner and someone who is naturally curious, I'm interested in town doings and who plays a dominant role. You get my drift?"

"I think so. Go on," Steve answered.

"Um, it's like I'm making an investment in Shell Isle and those who cross my path. Opening Honey Bees has helped introduce the islanders to me. Forget it. Look, I've observed Captain Jake on a few occasions in a heated discourse with his brother. I don't recall his name."

"Don't worry. That's easy enough to find out. Elaborate more on their talks."

"I think the last time was the most significant. Betsy and I were lunching at The Bistro. I swear that place is a magnet for putting me in the middle of a fracas," said Page, reminded of her initial sighting of the murdered Catherine Lange there. "To continue, it sounded like Jake's brother owed him money, and they exchanged words over the lack of payback. The brother threatened to tell something if Jake didn't forgive the debt."

"Any idea what that something was?"

Page shook her head. "Captain Jake laughed and said whatever his brother thought he had on him was probably fabricated, and he wasn't the least concerned. At that point, his brother puddled and slumped in his chair, but Jake didn't let up."

"Why not if his brother had backed down?" Steve adjusted his ball cap.

Page grinned. "Jake had more in his craw that came up. It seems he suspected his brother of some shady doings and threatened to get someone to check it out. His brother's face turned redder than a tomato, and he stormed out. If you ask me, Captain Jake won that round."

"Okay, that brother qualifies as suspect number four. Please don't tell me you've identified anyone else?" Steve scribbled some notes.

"Sadly, there's one more who needs to go in that notebook." Page stared off. "You and Koch aren't going to like this part, but for now, I'm only sharing the name. And, detective, that's non-negotiable or explainable."

Steve turned his focus on Page. "I suppose this tests my trust and belief in you and probably a lot more." His voice grew husky. "Who is it?"

"The mayor's wife."

CHAPTER 5

The cousins climbed into the SUV, bringing their plethora of emotions. The last big ta-dah of fireworks ended, and so did any chance for a sound, untroubled slumber. Rain clouds gathered, blocking out the stars' nightly show. Not even pondering the universe's vastness could break the spell of Captain Jake's death and what it meant to Page and Betsy's world. Another mystery to solve had found them. Page started the engine. "Let's go home. I've had enough fireworks for one day. You?"

"Me? Had enough? You might say that and a whole lot more. For now, drive us to the cottage at warp speed whilst I shut my eyes and pretend what happened tonight was a dream." Betsy inhaled and slammed her eyes shut.

Aunt Tilly's gift of Hibiscus Cottage had proven the catalyst for bringing Page back to Shell Isle. For the most part, Page had made a success of creating a fulfilling and happy lifestyle in a short time. Living on the beach and enjoying the ever-changing ocean's mood fed her spirit like no other place before. With her inner peace restored, Page had managed to refresh the cottage's interior space despite Betsy's presence. Even Honey Bees was turning a profit, which proved she'd made the right decision to start a business with her cousin.

Once inside the cottage, Betsy spoke first. "Since I fear sleuthing has claimed us yet again, it's good that my bungalow's completion date got delayed. We can work on this case so much more easily under the same roof. Mind you, that's if I can convince myself to do this. My staying here is also a definite bonus for you." Betsy headed to the kitchen.

Page followed. "A bonus? Really? I love bonuses. What's this bonus?" She nodded yes when Betsy held up a bottled iced coffee.

"Why, you get to enjoy my fantabulous cooking genius a bit longer." Betsy splashed lavender syrup into her glass and poured the coffee over it.

"Yes, there's that." Page grinned and snatched her glass, avoiding the genius's latest concoction. She moved to the aqua sofa's cocooning cushions and collapsed. "I guess we need to chat about things before we call this night *finito*."

Betsy opted for the printed swivel chair. "I suppose. I can't stop seeing Captain Jake lying there. I mean, moments before, he'd been firing the cannon, and then someone put a bullet in him. I realize we weren't really well acquainted, but he gave me a flounder, for pity's sake." Betsy nabbed a tissue and dabbed her eyes.

"It's terrible. Beyond terrible, and that's why we must find out who did this to Jake." Page took a sip of her coffee and decided not to wait to share the first clue with Betsy.

"Ah, Page, must we get involved this time? For once, can't you ignore the inklings? We've got our shop to run and no time for snooping. I want to conjure more recipes for cakes. I want to conjure more knowledge of honey's magical properties. I want to be a conjurer of all things honey and not a sleuth or a busybody." Betsy's voice took on a pleading tone.

Page decided to mellow with her cousin. "I understand how you feel, and I'm supportive of your conjuring for Honey Bees. You can still do that because we're fortunate to have Daisy and Ina working with us. They can fill in the gaps when we're —"

"Knee-deep in gathering clues. The one thing Steve warned us not to do. Be warned. I may feel inclined to squeal on us," Betsy interjected.

Page burst into laughter. "You will not squeal on us if you

want to keep our partnership going and stir that potion cauldron. Say you're with me."

Betsy's resigned expression came before her words. "Honestly, like I ever had a choice. I'm in. What's next?"

"For starters, we've got five suspects to learn more about." Page held up five fingers.

"Five?" Betsy screeched. "How did we go from my three to five?"

The corners of Page's mouth turned up. "Because observant me added two more suspects for Steve. Number four is Jake's brother. Then, I blew Steve's mind, naming the mayor's wife. I'll explain why those five tomorrow when we're fresh."

"Yeah, please don't enlighten me tonight. Geez, Page, five maybe murderers for us to scrutinize?" Betsy shook her head. "What other tidbits do you want to share? Spill it fast. My bed wants me, and I want it."

"Duly noted. So, I offer you one juicy tidbit before slumber." Page paused for effect. "I happen to hold our first clue." Page took the empty glasses to the kitchen, allowing Betsy's curiosity to awaken.

Betsy spun the chair in Page's direction. "What clue? Why do I always miss things? Get back in here and tell me."

Page returned to the sofa wearing a mischievous grin. "It's a pretty significant clue and probably worthy of investigation. You tell me why it's worthy and prove what I appreciate about you the most."

"Keep going. I'm hooked." Betsy tried and failed at tucking her legs.

"While Steve questioned you, I let my eyes wander around the area and struck gold. I spied a smoldering cigarillo a few feet from Captain Jake. That was troubling me. And, I bet you can—"

Betsy's face lit. "Ah, I've got it. You appreciate that I'm ever so observant of men...all men. It's one of my gifts."

"Bingo," chuckled Page. "Help me figure out why that cigarillo has me vexed."

"Easy. Jake didn't smoke," Betsy answered. "I know my men."

Page nodded. "He didn't, huh? I'm not going to ask how you know this. I agree. Thinking about Jake with a cigar doesn't fit his image. Which begs the question, who came calling on Captain Jake smoking a cigar? That answer might lead us to the person who shot him. First thing tomorrow, after Daisy gets to work, we go—"

"Nosing," finished Betsy. "Hold the fort. Did you tell Steve about the cigarillo?"

"What do you think?" Page's eyes twinkled.

Betsy tapped her forehead. "I think no, and instead, you brought the clue home for us. Your turn. What do you think about the cigarillo?"

"Oh, I think where there's cigarillo smoke, there's fire."

CHAPTER 6

The next morning found Betsy buzzing around the kitchen with a skillet in hand. The refrigerator door stood open as she deposited an array of ingredients on the island. Her flushed face demonstrated a growing eagerness for the coming breakfast. That's the scene that greeted Page and caused her to bypass the words of good morning.

Flour and eggs waiting didn't worry Page, but glancing at the assortment of jars and spices did. She lifted the bottle of turmeric. "I see you're busy making us one of your...savory breakfasts. What's it going to be? Chili pepper French toast with goat cheese?"

Betsy opened her mouth.

"No, let me guess. How about last week's waffles with jalapeños and honey mustard?" Page recalled it had taken six antacids to put out the fire after one bite. In desperation to protect her digestive system from attack, a clever Page had found ways to dispose of Betsy's cooking, though she could no longer count on Barnacle, Steve's dog, to help her cause. Tossing him some of Betsy's spicy French toast had once sent the poor animal into coughing spasms, forcing Page to confess her deed to his owner. Steve still held that secret over her head.

"I'm here waiting. You get one more guess." Betsy grinned as she grabbed the hot pepper sauce and closed the fridge's door.

Page panicked. "Um, could you hold the fire starter off my portion? Okay, I give up. What's my fate? I mean, fare?"

Dropping a stick of butter into the skillet to melt, Betsy turned back. "Today we're having Bright Eyed Hashers. The name for this recipe just came to me."

Page gulped. "Catchy title. What goes in it?"

Tapping her chin with a wood spurtle, Betsy considered her answer. "Let's see. Of course, there are potatoes, shallots, olives, finely chopped mango, and, for flavor, turmeric and cinnamon. Two sunny-side-up eggs make for the bright eyes. Clever, don't you think?"

"So clever." Page felt her stomach flip over. "If you don't mind, I'd like to savor those hashers in the den while I do a fast search on our five suspects. You know, see if I can discover anything of interest?" She'd save herself from a day with antacids by sneaking a garbage bag and a cup of yogurt into her den.

"That's some impressive multi-tasking. Give me ten minutes, and I'll have your plate loaded, sans the fire starter." Betsy returned to the stove, activating her never-in-tune humming.

~*~

Later, Page found her cousin swinging in the porch hammock. "Let's go, kiddo. Saturdays at Honey Bees is a beehive."

Betsy grinned at the funny and made two failed attempts to extricate herself from the hammock. "Take my hand. I'm telling you this thing lives to trap me. I feel like the middle of a taco." Once upright, she followed Page outside.

"Quite the visual. I may never see a taco the same." Page scrunched her face.

"Forget the taco. When are you going to apprise me on the dastardly five? What did your sleuthing uncover?"

"Apprising happens as soon as you get into the vehicle."

Betsy stole a glance at Steve's bungalow. "Look, there's your hunk of burning love pulling out. Or do you prefer dreamboat? I sort of like dreamboat more."

Page refused to steal a glance. "Will you please give it a rest? Steve and I are friends—"

"With unlimited possibilities," supplied Betsy. "About those five?" she asked and buckled her seat belt.

Page engaged the gearshift. "Yes, those five. First, Jake's brother made my list. I overheard him and Jake arguing at the Bistro. They each threatened to blab something on the other. It got nasty and loud."

"I don't remember any altercation at the Bistro. Where was I that day?" Betsy asked.

"You were at Honey Bees. It was the day I treated Daisy to a celebratory lunch for saying yes to employment."

Betsy bobbed her head. "Oh, that day. Go on."

"Nosing a bit more, I determined Jake's brother owns the Plant Hugger. You know the garden shop on Maple?" Page flipped off the radio.

"Yeah, the place where we bought your hibiscus. That's his brother? Life in a small beach town sure does connect a lot of people. What else?" Betsy sipped her bottled water.

"His name is Bert West. And, his daughter, the one hankering for tripping the Amalfi Coast, works at the nursery. I think she goes by Rosa. At least that's what it said on the store's website. Later, we can check out social media and maybe glean more on them. I can tell you Bert isn't a nice man. The word slimy comes to mind." Page waved to a friendly jogger crossing in front of her SUV.

"So, that's two of the bunch. Anything of interest on Ralph or Buck?" Betsy popped a mint in her mouth and offered one to Page.

"I'll pass. As for Ralph, his website acts more like a brochure luring tourists to book a fishing trip."

Betsy groaned. "Luring. Almost clever."

"I try. Anyway, once I found out Ralph's last name, a door opened. Upon further investigation, it seems our Ralph Owen has gotten smacked a few times for price-gouging tourists and failing to deliver on the guaranteed best fishing spots. There are plenty of bad reviews posted by the people who booked him and came home with a full bucket of bait and not much else." Page shook her head.

"Bad business practices. And, Buck?" Betsy's expression held concern.

"Buck Lester looked good at first blush, but not when I dug deeper. Most customers rate his excursions with five stars, and I saw a multitude of tourists posting photos holding impressive catches, including sharks." Page paused. "Aren't sharks protected from overfishing here in North Carolina? They creep me out. Who'd want to pose next to a shark? Sorry, I digress."

"Geez, I don't know about sharks. Ask me about food. On that, I'm an expert. Speaking of, how did you find my Bright-Eyed Hashers?"

Page felt her stomach tighten. "Out of this world." And she meant it. Those hashers belonged on a planet far, far away.

"Hurry and finish with Buck. We're almost at Honey Bees."

"I'm trying. You're the one who wanted to talk about your self-proclaimed expertise with food. So, get this. I stumbled upon Buck's record for domestic violence. The charge was a decade ago but was dropped for some unknown reason." Page shrugged.

"I'd label Buck as someone with anger management issues. Anger can sure push someone to hurt another. I bet we'll find more on this guy. The few times I've seen Buck interacting with other fishermen, he behaved like a bully, and I detest bullies," Betsy added.

"When were these Buck sightings of yours?" Page braked for a red light and turned her focus on Betsy.

"You're not catching me on breaking my no new men vow." Betsy gave a guffaw. "My observation happened twice when you left me idling at the marina. Remember? You saw

Steve on his boat and simply had to say hello," Betsy huffed.

"Hold up. I invited you to go on board with me both times. As I recall, you refused to walk the plank." Page couldn't resist a chuckle.

"Whatever, a tightrope walker would feel challenged on that rickety piece of wood. I say again. Buck's a bully and a know-it-all. I wager Ralph is, as well. Birds of a feather and all. Take that parking place." Betsy pointed to where a sedan had pulled out.

"Good parking karma, Bets." Page turned toward the empty spot and tried to position her SUV. A frown found her face when she realized the space size wasn't welcoming enough for her vehicle. "Listen, we're here. So, I guess we'd better take off our sleuthing caps and become Honey Bees."

"Yes ma'am, Honey Bees, we be. Look, Ina is waiting at the door. I've got three new cookie recipes for her to—"

"Hop out. Go to Ina. It's going to take me a few tries to parallel park my big buggy."

~*~

When Page finally entered the bakery's kitchen, she found two mixing bowls being used by beaters. "What did I miss?"

Ina laid down her whisk. "Betsy and I were discussing the dreadful news about Jake. It was only last week that Abe and I attended a town hall meeting where Jake spoke about the critical importance that local fishermen limit their hauls. According to Jake's statistics, the fish aren't as plentiful nowadays. Things got plenty hot when he included captains of charter boats in his proposal."

"Why?" Betsy asked. She mopped her brow with her apron skirt.

Ina returned to her ceramic bowl, adding flour. "I think the major concern revolved around Jake wanting them to stop the jackpot fishing competition and promote more environmentally friendly catch and release style fishing. Who knows? I'm pretty clueless on this subject. I eat them, but I don't catch them. Anyway, Abe and I decided to cut out and go for egg creams."

Page smiled. "I adore chocolate egg creams. Out of curiosity, do you recall which charter boat captains acted the most upset over Jake's ideas?"

Betsy winked at Page, acknowledging their info score.

Ina stopped moving the cake batter and stared out the window. "Yes, besides the mayor's wife, who had a few choice words about stifling the tourist business with such limitations, I remember two men asserting this proposal would destroy their livelihood. I think one guy was the owner of Out Cast Fishing Charter." Ina thumped the counter, pondering.

"Good memory," said Betsy. "Can you identify the other man?"

Ina's expression changed. "Ah, and the second guy's name was Ralph something. I've seen him around town often enough and heard he's a bit of a shyster. That description doesn't fit with Shell Isle's reputation. His type we don't need around. Anyway, that's what I've got, ladies. Why all the interest?"

"You know us. Curious to a fault," Page answered.

"Some might say we're busybodies, but that's a stretch," interjected Betsy.

Ina took a read on her friends. "You almost had me convinced." She placed two cake pans in the oven. "Oy vey, I'm staring at two snoops on the hunt for Jake's murderer, aren't I?" Ina pointed at the cousins, not hiding her amusement. "Don't deny it. I know what I know."

Betsy and Page exchanged looks.

"Tell me the truth, if you want to keep this baker in a good mood—"

Page jumped to answer. "You're right, Ina. We do want to find the person who took Jake's life. You see, Betsy and I were the ones who found him. Besides, you know we've got this sleuthing thing we do. You helped us with our last case without realizing it. You're doing it again."

Emotion played across Ina's face. "My gosh, this news is worse than I imagined. You two discovered Jake West last night? How awful for you. The newspaper didn't give details, but that's probably because the police held a lot back." Ina paused and found her humor. "By the way, forget trying to butter me up. I'll help you both."

"Thanks, sister baker. Now, you understand more why we feel led to poke around. Please keep our involvement to yourself. Staying safe is near and dear to my heart," chimed Betsy.

"And my heart, too," said Page, tapping her chest. She chose to keep her inkling gift from Ina.

"Not one word will escape these lips." Ina made a pretend zip of her lips. "My Abe tells everyone that I'm multi-talented and can read people like nobody's business." She handed Page a filled muffin tin ready for baking.

Betsy hooted. "So, multi-talented, read me."

"Easy. You're going to ask that I keep an ear open for any anti-Jake chatter. This assignment I accept. You got a talented baker and a—"

"A talented observer," Page and Betsy chorused in unison. Both cousins bestowed a hug to their friend.

Page squinted at the yellow bumblebee clock. "Ten on the dot. Time for me to sell what you talented bakers bring out." As Page scurried to unlock Honey Bees' front door, a new inkling came to her. From the display window, two unwelcome faces stared at her.

CHAPTER 7

Ralph and Buck entered Honey Bees wearing unconvincing friendly expressions. They approached the checkout counter.

Page felt a chill wrap around her. "Good morning, gentlemen. We've got some warm honeybuns fresh out of the oven. Would you care to sample—"

"No, thanks. Give me one of those cake donuts." Ralph's seedy looking appearance peered at the tray. His stained finger banged on the glass. "You want one, Buck? I'm buying."

"Yeah, throw in a couple of extra donuts." Distracted, Buck stepped back and typed something on his phone. His face, lacking any attractive features, rested on a large frame. The man's barrel-shaped chest complemented his blow-hard reputation.

With the bag on the counter, Page rang up the sale. She waited while Ralph fumbled for his money.

"Here you go. Keep the change." Ralph stuffed a couple of napkins in the sack. "Is this shop making any money? You haven't been open long." His eyes, void of warm-heartedness, assessed Page.

Taken aback by his abrupt shift, Page scrambled to find an answer fitting the questioner. "My cousin and I feel grateful for the town's support. We're meeting our sales goals." She wanted these two suspects gone. The time wasn't right to question them. "Is there anything more you'd like?"

"Matter of fact, there is. Buck, hand me your clipboard." Ralph pivoted toward Page. "What's your name? I'm Ralph Owen."

Page forced a smile. "Nice to meet you. I'm Page Wright.

How else may I help?"

"We've got a petition that we're asking merchants and business owners to sign. You probably haven't heard, but there's a group of crazy environmental types around town that want to ruin things for all of us with their proposal to limit the fish we catch. The ringleader has, let us say, recently stepped down."

Ralph's words and sinister-sounding laugh put Page on alert. "I can tell you're passionate about this cause."

"That's one way of putting it, ma'am," interjected Buck. He tucked his cell phone and joined his friend.

"Anyway, Buck and I mean to nip this little problem in the bud. So, if you'd sign this, we'll be on our way." Ralph shoved the paper and pen across the counter.

"Sign what?" echoed Betsy, carrying a tray of honey almond tea biscuits. Surprise registered on her face, seeing the two customers' faces.

"Um, Betsy, this is Ralph and Buck. They've brought a petition for us to consider signing—"

"Count us out of signing any petition." Betsy arranged the biscuits and covered them with a crystal dome. "We're new at Shell Isle and not educated yet on the town's doings. No thanks, fellows."

Buck snagged the petition. "You might want to reconsider that no. Take a look at the names who agree with us. Being new and all, you don't want to offend certain ones."

Page sensed the atmosphere changing. "Listen, guys, maybe you could leave some information on this proposal? I'm sure my cousin and I—"

"Forget it, Buck. Let's go. These two aren't cooperative types." Ralph moved toward the door.

Buck gave a terse nod. "I expect they'll act more agreeable next time we stop by. See you later."

"Holy smokes, Betsy Ross, you just ticked off two of our

main suspects. Have you gone bonkers?"

"Bonkers." Ina appeared, sipping an iced coffee. "I haven't heard that term in an age. Who's bonkers?"

"Your Mermaid bowling buddy who's standing next to you. In one sentence, she managed to ignite Ralph and Buck. The same Ralph and Buck who are going on our suspect board. She's bonkers," finished Page.

Betsy chuckled. "You're so wrong. What I am is a brilliant strategist. I set up those two lowlifes for an encore visit. When they show up and—trust me, they will—we shall be armed with our trusty objective. That's how we work, Ina."

Ina peered at the two women over her glasses. "I see."

Page's mouth opened and closed several times. No words came forth. Throwing her arms in the air, she escaped to the back.

"Perhaps she's gone to work on that objective? I'm happy to take care of any customers if you want to hurry and help Page," offered an amused Ina.

Betsy stood considering. "Nah, I'd better stay out here with you. She seemed unsettled. It's better if we give her space and let her mind the ovens."

"If you're sure?" Ina cast a glance toward the kitchen.

"Don't fret. Once I tell Page what I'm preparing us for dinner, she'll perk up and find her gratitude voice."

~*~

Page entered Hibiscus cottage with murder on her mind, and it had nothing to do with the five suspects. She'd managed to keep focused and smiling during the workday, allowing the good energy of Honey Bees to carry her along. She loved Betsy to pieces, but not what had come from her cousin's lips that morning.

Betsy dropped her tote bag on the kitchen island and faced Page. "Okay, go ahead and dress me down. I realized later that I messed up engaging with Buck and Ralph. I have an explanation of sorts. Want to hear it?" Betsy folded her hands in a beg. "Please?"

Page hid her grin behind the open refrigerator door. Betsy's sense of humor always took the detonator out of her anger. She handed Betsy a bottle of green tea. "Lay it on me."

"There are times that I can't help feeling protective of you. I mean, you're petite, and…well, there's me. I take up more real estate. With those two clowns, I saw my stature as a good thing." Betsy popped the lid on her tea before continuing. "They were intimidating and bad to the bone. I felt it. Don't you agree?"

"Give me a moment." Page's expression showed appreciation. Betsy had always acted as a protector and with ironclad loyalty. She'd been steadfast when an inkling had presented Page with a mystery to solve. The essential supporting role Betsy played was key to their sleuthing success. Understanding her cousin's earlier motivation for the outspoken behavior called for a whole different response. Page sat on the barstool next to Betsy. "First, I agree, those guys are bad to the bone. Next, I owe you an apology for acting frosty this afternoon. Thank you for reminding me how much you care. I can't imagine this life without you in it. I love you to pieces, Betsy."

"Geez, Page, you're getting me all weepy. Still, I shouldn't have butted into that conversation you were having with Buck and Ralph. You're the clever and smart cousin and always able to handle people intelligently. Did I mess up things?"

Page shook her head, smiling. "Truthfully, they caught me off guard showing up at Honey Bees. I couldn't gain the offensive, but you accomplished that for us."

Betsy's face registered surprise. "I did that?"

"You sure did, and thank you for rescuing me…this time. However, in the future—"

"I hear you. You always tell me to *pause, observe, and then react*. POR is my acronym, right? Slipped my mind, but I promise it won't while we're on this case. POR will define Betsy Ross. Hey, I should use that when bowling with the Mermaids next week."

Page patted her cousin's arm. "That's an excellent idea."

"So, am I forgiven?" Betsy waited.

"If you forgive me, too." Page offered her hand to shake. "We're good, and I'm famished. Let me toss a frozen pizza in the oven before we resurrect the suspect board. I'm ready to divulge details on the five unsavory ones."

"Absolutely no pizza. I've got dinner all planned." Betsy rose and headed for the pantry.

"Nope. You're off KP duty tonight." Page didn't bother to hide the panic in her voice, seeing Betsy lay a box of raisins and canned anchovies on the counter. "Cooking will eat up too much of our discussion time."

"Listen, Sherlocka, let me do what I do best while you get that suspect board resurrected." Betsy held up the raisins and anchovies. "See? Sweet and salty. They'll marry nicely with the chicken thighs and poblano peppers. The way I see it, I owe you another mouthwatering dinner."

"Oh, that recipe definitely will cause mouthwatering." *Before the nausea sets in,* worried Page. Resigned to her plight, she rallied her indulgence again for Betsy's sake. "It so happens I have an observation from this morning's Ralph and Buck encounter that I think you'll find noteworthy once we start laying out clues."

~*~

Betsy pushed the dishwasher button. "Alrighty, the kitchen is spotless, and I put the rest of your uneaten dinner in the refrigerator. This case sure zapped your appetite tonight."

Page laid the marker in the board's tray. "Yeah, sorry 'bout not doing tonight's supper justice. I'll polish it off later." She'd polish it right into the outside trash can at the first opportunity. Poor Betsy and her eclectic menus, but at least her cake baking angels stayed close. "So, suspect board time, and you can see I've written the names. We're ready to fill in what we know."

Betsy remained standing. "Um, Page, could we go for a nice bike ride before tackling that board? I overate on the poblanos and need to settle things." Betsy patted her stomach for effect.

"Work before play. That's the rule," Page answered. "As luck would have it, I've got exactly what you need to settle your things. Back in a sec."

"Okay, guess I'll soldier on and look forward to the bike ride later. What's that?"

Page dumped two extra-strength antacids into Betsy's palm. "Call it two settlers. Start chewing while I talk."

"Yuck. These taste like chalk." Betsy pulled a face.

"Chew and listen." Page used the marker as a pointer. "We've got Ralph, Buck, Bert, Rosa, and the mayor's wife. Do you happen to know her name?"

Betsy swallowed. "I think it's Eleanor." She paused. "Never give me those settlers again. I'd rather bloat."

Page rolled her eyes. "So, I've added Eleanor's name. Let's move to identifying motive, means, and opportunity. First, that charmer Ralph, whose company we enjoyed today. What's his motive?"

"I'd say the same as Buck's. They don't want to lose charters because of Jake's fish limit proposal." Betsy paused. "Which means less moolah and—"

"Yes, and from what I understand, the charter fishing business operates on slim profit margins," Page added.

"Whatever that means." Betsy grinned. "That's why you're the expert on running Honey Bees, and I'm overseeing the...what exactly am I overseeing?"

Page grabbed a breath, scrambling for the best answer. "Why, Betsy, you're overseeing Ina, the kitchen operations, and, of course, creating recipes to delight. Remember the enchanted honey cakes recipe you discovered and the role they played in me getting the confession from Catherine's murderer? That was because of your enchanted honey cake."

"Yes, my magical cake did make that happen, but we're not selling those. Though I am adding new recipes, and I take care of our customers when you need me. All in all, I'm a real asset to Honey Bees and our partnership." Betsy fluffed her ever-damp hair.

"So true," Page agreed, smiling. "Now that your ego's sufficiently inflated, might we get back to Ralph?"

"Sure, unless you want to inflate me more by discussing my talent for—"

"Ralph. We've moved to personable Ralph and another clue." Page picked up the marker, poised to write. "Today, when he showed up, I noticed a stain on two of his fingers."

"What does that mean? A stain?" Betsy leaned forward.

"The stain was the exact shade of tobacco in the cigarillo we found. Guess what else I noticed?" Page waited.

"Tell me. This is good stuff." Betsy's tone grew impatient.

"Ralph smelled of smoke, which begs the question—"

Betsy clapped her hands. "Of course. Does he enjoy a cigarillo? That's what you saw next to Jake. Geez, we got to find that answer, Page."

"We do. And, if he does, that puts Ralph at the top of the list of suspects." Page wrote the information beside his name. "Next up is Buck. We know his motive is likely the same as Ralph's. Don't mess with his livelihood. Right?"

"Right, and as I said earlier, Buck's got anger management issues based on his past." Betsy took a breath. "After interacting with him today, what's your take?"

Page allowed Betsy's words to linger in the air. "My take is Buck's passive-aggressive, which makes him more cunning than Ralph, who's a straight-out intimidator. Both men trouble me. They're not upstanding members of Shell's community. Agreed?"

"Agreed." Betsy pointed to the next suspect on the board. "So, moving on to Bert. You observed him and Jake arguing at the Bistro and each threatening the other. Correct?"

Page nodded. "Yep. Bert owed Jake money and wasn't paying up. Bert threatened to blab something if Jake didn't stop harassing him about the loan. Jake fired back that whatever Bert had couldn't be of any significance. Then, Jake said he suspected his brother was involved in serious shady doings."

"He threatened to spill the beans on whatever that was, correct?" Betsy watched Page add the motives to Bert's side of the board.

"Yes, ma'am. And my intuition tells me whatever Bert's involved in, we need to uncover because that's a strong motive for murder." She chose not to tell Betsy that Bert had visited Honey Bees. Page turned back to her cousin. "That brings us to the ladies. Let's go with Rosa since she's Bert's—"

"Spawn," Betsy laughed. "I don't like that girl, and I don't even know her."

"Since we saw her at the marina having the hissy fit, the word 'spoiled' comes to mind." Page twirled the marker, considering Rosa.

"That was the day Jake gave me that flounder," Betsy sniffed. "What's Rosa's motive? I don't get it."

Page shrugged. "It's clear the girl wants what she wants. A trip to the Amalfi Coast, but does that qualify as a motive to take out her uncle? I don't think so. We're missing pieces around this suspect. We need to snoop."

"I'm with you on all points with Rosa. Let's mess with her. That'll prove fun." Betsy grinned.

"You're a mess." Page bopped Betsy on the arm. "Last is the mayor's wife, Eleanor."

Betsy's head bobbed up and down like a cork on the water. "She's your suspect, and I can't wait to hear how she made the cut."

"As it happens, I had to get my driver's license renewed at City Hall a week ago. Remember you wanted to stay home and—?"

"Work on more amazing recipes," Betsy supplied.

"Yes, anyway, I stood in the hallway, waiting for my turn. Jake and Eleanor were in conversation. He told Eleanor she should consider mending her ways before they destroyed her and the mayor's reputation. She didn't like his meddling and told him so. I understand she's all about living the good life. Anyway, I heard Eleanor say a few nasty words before she walked away in a huff."

"Her motive being that Jake knew something that Eleanor wouldn't want out there for public consumption?" Betsy tapped her temple. "Yes, and if that something is bad enough to ruin one's reputation, it might that qualify as a strong enough motive for murder?"

"Absolutely, if one's wired to maintain their standing in the community above all else. We must determine Eleanor's secret. Did you hear something?"

"Someone's knocking on your door." Betsy frowned.

Page went to look through the peephole. "It's Steve. Quick, go ditch the suspect board."

CHAPTER 8

Page opened the door to Steve, waving a bag. "Evening," he said. "It's a hot one, so I thought you two might enjoy a cool treat." He winked and leaned in to whisper. "Did Betsy cook dinner for you?"

Page rolled her eyes and nodded. "Come inside and give me that sack."

He followed Page into the kitchen. Seeing Betsy parked on the sofa, Steve ventured over. "Hiya, Betsy. You doing okay?"

"Sure, why wouldn't I be?" Betsy craned her head, peering at Page.

"Oh, I don't know. Maybe you have a bee in your bonnet? In fact, I see them swarming around the one in the kitchen who's dishing our ice cream." Steve turned his grin toward Page.

Betsy sniffed. "No sleuthing bees in our bonnets, Detective Tanner. Honestly, why do you always assume we're meddling in police business. Jake's murderer —"

Page groaned, which stopped Betsy from saying more. She placed three desserts on the tray and served the blabbermouth a glare and a dish of peppermint mocha. She handed Steve his bowl and took a seat, knowing what was coming.

"Um, Betsy, I never said what bee was in your bonnet. Thanks for confirming the obvious. I can always count on you." Steve nodded.

Betsy's expression changed to chagrinned. She shoved a spoonful of ice cream into her yap. "I can't believe I already forgot about my pause, observe, react."

"Ignore her. So, Tanner, you showed up with ice cream

along with an ulterior motive. I think you're worried that our exceptional sleuthing will once again best you detectives," taunted Page.

"Not exactly. I doubt you've progressed that far, but I am worried that you've pulled out that suspect board." Steve did a fast glance around the room. "Where did you hide it?"

Betsy hurried to swallow her last bite. "You're not getting any help from us. Do your own detecting, mister. We've got— I've got POR."

"You've got POR? Is this POR thing contagious?" Steve scooted further from Betsy. Merriment found his eyes.

"Steve, will you please forget the POR?" Page tried and failed at making eye contact with Betsy.

"I forgot POR. My brain is the size of a mosquito. A baby mosquito," mumbled a contrite Betsy.

"Betsy, eat your ice cream. What she means is we're confident you and Koch will button this case fast." Page sent a dagger look toward her cousin.

Steve burst into laughter. "Flattery never works on me. Are you going to share those clues? I brought ice cream. That's gotta be worth something."

Page jumped in before Betsy could rally another response. "It's worth a thank you. So, thanks, Steve, for the ice cream. Nod your thanks, Betsy."

Betsy bobbed her head, still avoiding eye contact with Page.

Steve stood, ready to leave. "Maybe we could trade a clue for a clue, that is, if you've gained any of value."

Page reached over and clamped her hand over Betsy's mouth. "I'll walk you to the door. Thanks again for the peppermint mocha. Mint helps digestion. You made an excellent choice," said Page, pointing to her stomach.

"I'm a detective. I know about a lot of things," he stated

cryptically and closed the door.

Page dismissed Steve's words and went in search of the magpie.

"You found me." Betsy sat swinging in the hammock.

"It wasn't hard," Page grinned.

"If you're still speaking to me, can we go for that bike ride? I can do penance while we pedal."

"Give me your hand so I can hoist you and your mosquito brain from Tilly's hammock. Your penance awaits." Page tugged her cousin to standing. "I'm going to grab my cell phone. Would you mind getting the bikes out of the shed?"

Amiable, Betsy replied, "Why, it's my pleasure to de-spider and prep your bike for a lovely ride on the beach. Princess, might I make you a lovely mint julep to take along?"

"Your penance just grew longer," threatened Page, going inside. An inkling came calling. She'd been expecting more of them. It was the way her gift worked. Inklings often lead to nudges. Page hurried to find Betsy in the backyard.

"Here you go." Betsy released the handlebars to Page. "Notice how it's all spiffed. Does that help reduce my penance?"

Page chuckled. "It does. Did you bring me a water? Why, yes, you did."

"Less penance?" asked a remorseful yet hopeful Betsy.

"Would you chill? Let's go ride. I think you're closer to absolution."

"Is that good? It sounds good." Betsy began pedaling on the hard sand.

Before Page could reply, she experienced the nudge and direction. "Want to ride up to the pier and marina?"

Betsy paused a tick, considering. "Since I'm working my way out of detention, I guess I'll agree to huff and puff myself there."

For the next fifteen minutes, Page cherished the silent

bike ride and allowed her focus to shift to the night's landscape. The waves' movement seemed angry, sending in white foam to dress the beach. And yet, the silvery stars twinkled, showing a cloudless sky vying for her attention and reflection. Returning her gaze to the ocean, Page wondered what unseen storm brewed that was causing the chop? She felt the nudge to hurry and subtly increased her pedaling, hoping Betsy wouldn't notice.

"Did we win?" asked a winded Betsy. She secured her bike in the corral by the marina.

"Win what?" Page joined Betsy and retied her ponytail.

"The marathon we just completed. Where's my prize?" Betsy looked around and pointed. "There it is. My frozen lemonade. You're buying."

Page laughed. "Right you are. Penance is paid, and reward awaits." She followed Betsy and her unwavering appetite to the young college girl dishing out the refreshment.

"I want the largest frozen lemonade you can scoop. Don't short me either, young lady. You're looking at one hot mama." Betsy snickered.

"Coming right up. And, what can I get for you?" asked the amused server.

"I want the same, but make mine small," Page said, elbowing Betsy.

"Ha. Some of us have bigger bones that weigh more." Betsy took the lemonade, wasting no time in spooning the flavored ice into her mouth. "What's next? Pole vaulting?"

"Betsy, no one provides comic relief better than you. Geez, pole vaulting. Bring your slurping sounds and walk with me to look at the boats." Page followed the inner tug.

"Haven't you had enough time with Dreamboat for one night?"

"Silly, I'm sure Steve's home with Barnacle, watching some sports nonsense on the screen. Let's go toward the—"

"Um, those look like charter boats. I don't care anything about visiting them. How about sailboats? I love their tinkling sounds." Betsy pivoted, only to have Page grab her arm.

"We need to go see the charters." Page's nudge got validated.

"You're so pushy," declared a confused Betsy.

"Shh, get behind this pole." Page turned sideways.

"Seriously, you think this body can hide behind—"

"Quiet. Look down that row," Page whispered.

"Is that Buck and Ralph talking to some other men? Yes, it is. Page Wright, you got a nudge tonight, and that's why we're hugging a pole."

Page gave a nod, not taking her eyes away from the group. "I've got to get closer and hear what they're saying."

"I don't approve of this plan. We need to leave." Betsy felt resistance. "Release my shirttail."

"Not until you promise to stay here while I go listen. Give me your scarf."

"Okay, okay, but you'd better not tangle with those two bad dudes." Betsy watched as Page transformed into a hippie-type. "How'd you do that?"

"Stay quiet and out of sight here. I'll be back soon enough, hopefully, a lot wiser." Page allowed the shadows to conceal her movement on the dock's walkway. She got as far as the restroom wall and hunkered down. Voices traveled on the water, which helped her cause, and a few peeps around the corner answered the question of what the men were about this night. What remained was to glean the roles Buck and Ralph played. She listened, recognizing Ralph's voice.

"Listen up, me and Buck came close to poaching the amount you wanted. Hell, we got both sand tigers and basking sharks on this last haul."

"Threatening us isn't wise," said an angry Ralph.

"I'm not threatening. I execute on what I say, so be warned. One more screw-up by you two will have you dining with Blackbeard, if you get my drift."

The man's evil laugh carried to Page, causing a shiver.

"Yeah, okay. We'll meet the quota next time," Buck assured.

"Are the fins ready for transfer? We need to wrap up. I don't want to court any curious types."

"Here are your fins. Now, we want our cash." Ralph put his hand out.

Page witnessed the transfer — time to go stealthy back to Betsy. Thanks to the nudge, she'd scored the motherlode. Page rose from her crouch and felt a hand touch her shoulder.

CHAPTER 9

"Goodness, you scared the puddin' out of me," Page whispered. She saw grey eyes that looked angrier than the seas of a nor'easter staring back.

"I'd like to scare more than pudding out of you, whatever that even means. Come with me where we can talk." Steve latched onto Page's arm, pulling her close.

"What are you doing?" she hissed.

"In case they're already watching us, we're an oblivious couple acting hot and bothered." Act your part. His lips found hers.

A shocked Page felt her body ignite as Steve kept the kiss alive, waltzing her toward Betsy. Her traitorous body had delivered hot and bothered with no effort. Sensing they'd escaped scrutiny, she pushed away. "I can't believe you—"

"You're still good at hot and bothered, Miss Drew." Steve stopped. "Once we're in the parking lot, you're going to experience my version of being bothered about your presence here tonight."

Betsy huffed, "I knew it. I knew it. You snookered me into another rendezvous. I saw you two locked up tighter than an oyster shell, and—thank you very much—that show woke my hot flashes. I'm leaving." Betsy fanned her annoyed face.

"See what you've done?" Page glared at Steve. "Betsy, you've got this all wrong, and I'll explain once we're home."

Steve hid his mirth by glancing back to where the exchange had happened and observed two boats pulling out of the end of the marina. "Listen up, you two snoops, the guys are leaving in the boats, so, fortunately, you're safe…this time. No more eavesdropping. It's late. Go home."

"Come on, Betsy. Let's get our bikes." Page turned away.

Betsy pondered her cousin's directive. "Hold up. I'm not in the mood to pedal anymore this night. I'm too hot, thanks to all this excitement." Betsy snapped her fingers to get Steve's attention on her. "Hello? Would you give me and my bike a lift home?"

"Happy to. That's one way to ensure you've cooperated with my…advice." Steve's eyebrow raised Page's way. "How about you? Want a lift?"

Weariness claimed Page. The day had exacted every ounce of adrenaline from her. "I accept your offer, but not the lecture," she replied.

Steve tied their bikes to the luggage carrier of his black SUV and hopped in the driver's side. Two silent women rode the short distance home with him.

"Hibiscus Cottage. All out," he said, trying to interject humor.

Page and Betsy exited and waited for Steve to handoff their bikes.

"Thanks again. Guess I'll head inside and let you two continue where you left off," teased Betsy.

Steve grinned at Page. "Hey, I'm willing if you're willing." He moved closer, threatening an encore.

"Don't be ridiculous." Page stomped up the sidewalk.

"Hey, Page?"

She turned back. "What now, Detective?"

"Tomorrow morning at my place, you and I are having a chat about your meddling in this investigation. I'm clear after tonight that you've got information, and those tinklings—"

"Inklings, Tanner, inklings. See you at ten." Page kept walking.

Betsy waited in the living room. "What? No more wanton, heavy-duty kissing tonight?"

"Funny, so funny, but I'd rather do heavy-duty suspect board updating before we call this night done. Where'd you hide the board?" Page looked in the hall closet.

"Do we have to?" Betsy pleaded. She watched Page venture out to the screen porch in search. "I guess we do. Look under your bed."

Page reappeared with the board and leaned it against a chair. "This won't take long. Aren't you curious about what I saw and heard a while ago?"

"Unlike you, I can control my curiosity," Betsy answered. Page scrunched her face.

"Fine. Get me up to speed." Betsy crossed her arms.

Page began writing on the board. "For starters, Ralph and Buck are involved in poaching and selling shark fins."

"Excuse my ignorance, but what's so great about shark fins?"

"They're a delicacy in some cultures," Page explained.

"Hmm, how have I missed that?" Betsy grabbed her phone.

"What are you doing? I'm trying to wrap this up before the birds start chirping." Page looked over Betsy's shoulder.

"I'm looking up shark fins."

Page snatched the phone and placed it on the end table. "Forget the fin education. Listen, if Jake suspected Ralph and Buck were involved in something illegal, he might have confronted them. Who knows, but it makes the whole limit fish catch angle seem a tepid motive by comparison."

Fully engaged, Betsy replied, "Double motives."

"Yep, and we've got to determine if they each had the means and opportunity." Page added that to the column of questions.

"I hate those guys. How are we going to find out?" Betsy squinted at the board.

Page hesitated. "Bets, I don't have that answer yet, but I trust we'll be shown."

Betsy nodded. "So, for giggles, confirm that you got a nudge to go to the marina and you weren't hoping to see Steve again."

"I got a nudge. Steve was an unwanted presence," Page replied. "Come on. Let's call this night done."

Betsy fluffed the sofa cushions back in place. "I second that. May Sunday reward us with a day under our blue-striped beach umbrella. I've neglected Dowager Gertrude too long." Betsy padded to her bedroom.

Closing the blinds, Page heard the black SUV's engine roar to life. Steve going out this time of night could mean one of their suspects was on the move. Tomorrow morning, she'd weasel that name from him…somehow. Wearing an elfin smile, Page went to bed.

CHAPTER 10

The sun's rays beaming through Page's window blessed the beach day. But first, she thought, she must navigate two daunting obstacles. No doubt, one of Betsy's three-alarm breakfasts awaited and the deserved dress-down meeting with Steve. Plastering a smile on her face, Page went to greet her cousin's culinary calamity.

"Top of the morning. You slept in, but I didn't. Nope, I've been creating another outstanding breakfast to fortify us to spend the day on the beach."

Page poured coffee. "You certainly seem in high spirits." She watched Betsy flip something foreign in the skillet. "What was that I caught a glimpse of?"

"This may be my best food combining yet. Instead of boring pancakes, we have fiesta cakes. I came up with that name. Catchy, huh?" Betsy sprinkled on more of her secret spices.

"Fiesta cakes sound —" Page swallowed.

"Amazing, right? What makes them a fiesta are the spices like red pepper flakes, cumin for the smoky flavor, chives, and I tossed in a couple of juniper berries. Bet you don't know about them." Betsy held up the bottle. "It's a purple berry that tastes like pine. Even though it's used primarily for game marinades, I took creative license."

"Wow, that sounds like a fiesta for the taste buds." Page needed an exit strategy. She looked at the clock and sighed. Too early to attend her dress-down meeting. Bested, she went to get plates and napkins and extra napkins for her. "What can I do to help?"

"Could you grab the bowl of fruit out of the fridge?" Betsy flipped another giant fiesta cake into the serving dish.

"A fruit bowl? How wonderful." Page released a happy sigh, seeing the bowl's contents of honeydew and cantaloupe. She'd devour the fruit and let her napkin have the fiesta.

"Here we are. Let's tuck in." Betsy forked the cake onto her plate and scooped fruit.

Page brought the smallest serving of the pancake to her plate, allowing the fruit to cover the rest.

Before her second bite, Betsy jumped up. "Hot flash. Keep eating while I find my fan."

"Yeah, get that fan." Page wrapped the fiesta cake in two napkins and managed to get to the garbage can before her cousin returned.

"These flashes try my good mood." Betsy fanned with one hand and ate with the other. "You're finished?"

"Yep, I had to hurry. Must go to Steve's now for what I assume is a lecture on interfering. You've been spared." Page ate the last bite of melon and put the plate in the dishwasher.

"I'm not a bit envious. Still, knowing you, I wager more information will come back here than goes there. Find me on the beach when you two finish." Betsy twisted to see Page had already gone.

~*~

Steve opened the door. "Come in and find a seat. You want something to drink?" He paused, taking in Page's expression, and grinned. "Let me grab you a fizzy drink. That should help. What did she serve for breakfast?"

"Fiesta cakes, and don't ask for a description." Page accepted the sparkling water. "Thanks. Will your pity lessen—"

"It will not." Steve joined her on the tan leather sofa just as his cell phone chimed. "Sorry, excuse me for a moment. Barnacle, come say hi to Page."

The dog came into the room, tail wagging, and plopped his head on Page's knee.

Page reached down to bestow a hug. "Hey, boy. Gotten into any trouble lately eating barnacles off Steve's dinghy?"

He gave a deep woof.

"Ah, guess that means you're still earning the name." Page scratched behind the spaniel's velvet ears.

"Thanks, Barn, for keeping our guest company. You can go outside, but remember the rules." Steve returned to the sofa, bringing a notepad and pen. "Let's talk, Miss Drew."

Page took a sip, gauging Steve's mood. She'd invoke humor to lighten things. "Great. I'll start. Miss Drew would very much like to learn where you went last night?"

"That's not how this goes. I'm the detective. I get to ask the questions, and you provide answers. "We'll backtrack since I've determined you know what Ralph and Buck were involved in last evening. Why don't you begin sharing what you have on each suspect so far?"

"What's in it for Betsy and me? It feels one-sided, and I thought we'd moved past me needing to prove myself worthy? I see this meeting more as collaborating, and that means working jointly on something."

Steve blew out a breath. "I know what collaborating means. How about this? You give me a piece of information, and I'll give you a piece."

"That works. You go first, and don't pull that I'm a gentleman, so you go first stunt. It didn't work before, and it won't work now. Impress me with your detecting." Page took a swallow of her beverage.

"I'm going to share the most important lead we have to date, which also answers where I went last night. That counts as two pieces of information."

Page laughed. "It might. Let's hear it, and I'll decide."

Steve's knee brushed her leg, waking up her hormones. She bit her cheek to regain control. "Well?"

"Jake kept a journal. The officers searching his residence found it last night. I went to retrieve it. After our amorous adventure, I needed a bedtime story. Your turn."

Ignoring the reference to their kissing, Page latched on to the news. "That's an awesome find. What all did Jake put in it because—"

Steve inched closer. "Maybe you didn't hear me say it was your turn? Lean in, and I'll say it once more in a different way." His eyes danced with hers.

Page scooted back. "I heard you fine, Tanner. Save your charms. I'll give you my first clue, but answer me this. Did your men find anything of interest at the scene?"

"Not that I heard. Why? What did you find?" Steve went to the kitchen and poured orange juice.

"A few yards from Jake, I saw a still smoldering cigarillo."

"So?" Steve returned, opting for a club chair.

"So, I don't think Jake smokes. That counts as two clues. I need an extra one from you. Your whereabouts doesn't count." Her control had returned, and if he'd stay seated in his chair, she'd go home the winner of this round.

Steve gave a lopsided grin. "You're playing me, Page Wright. In other circumstances, I'd enjoy it, but not when we're talking about a murder—enough of the tit for tat. I've got a surfboard waiting for me. Spill what you've got, and I promise to tell you a few things about Jake's journal that I know you'll appreciate."

Page hesitated, weighing her options. She felt anxious to get down to the beach, too.

"Don't you trust me?" Steve pretended hurt.

"Actually, I do. You know that." Page repositioned herself to face him. "We had two customers yesterday that brought me more clues. Buck and Ralph showed up wanting me to sign a petition to block Jake's proposal on catch limits and contests. They acted menacingly until Betsy's mouth came out and ran them off."

Steve chuckled. "She's a force, like I say."

"Yeah, well, I happened to notice Ralph's two fingers had tobacco stains, and the confirmation was he smelled like a cigar. Perhaps a cigarillo?"

"That's a piece of solid detecting, Miss Drew. Perhaps you've discovered who left that smoke near Jake."

Page watched Steve scribble something. "Must you keep calling me—"

"What's on your suspect board?" he asked, ignoring her last question.

"Not much." Page moved a sofa cushion.

"What not much?" Steve pressed.

Exasperated, Page ticked off each suspect and shared what she'd written on the board the night before. "There. You've got everything. Before you switch to lecture mode, I'm reminding you that my inklings and nudges serve the greater good. I'm not ignoring them. I can't ignore them. You know this. I promised you before that I'd not act stupid, and I won't. So, what's it going to be? A lecture rerun or collaborating to find Jake's killer so we can close the case? I've got a business to grow, and you've got...what have you got?" Page grabbed a breath after her rant, wondering how Steve might respond.

His expression softened. "Ah, Page Wright, I've never known any woman like you. Jake's journal had a few significant entries, but the man was frugal with words. We'll need to fit the pieces together. Here's the foundation of where we began. Jake used to work for the Defense Department as an investigator, so that meant—"

"He had keen observation skills and a respect for the law,"

Page finished.

"Yes. Anyway, here's a few clues I gleaned from reading. Buck and Ralph must have awakened Jake's suspicions because on the night he was murdered, he'd planned to go to the marina at two a.m. and again last night. I think Jake believed those two were into something. Maybe he knew. Maybe he didn't. Maybe he'd confronted them. Regardless, you and I know now the men have a motive. We don't yet know if they possessed the means, in this case, a gun or the opportunity. We're only beginning the investigation."

Page nodded. "That explains why you were at the marina last night. I wondered how you'd learned of the transfer of fins for cash."

"Listen, I want to get out on my board. I need a break from this case to clear my head. We're caught up on Ralph and Buck. What say we continue this Monday when we go for a sail? Maybe by then, I'll have deciphered more from Jake's journal. Besides, the culinary mastermind looks lonely under that umbrella." Steve turned from the window, wearing a smile.

"Your plan works for me." Page stood. "And, Steve?"

"Yeah?" He followed her to the door.

"Thanks for your trust and respect. On a personal note, I'm looking forward to our outing and picnic."

"Use me anytime to escape Betsy's—"

"Oh, I plan to. And you better know my calendar is ticking off the days until her bungalow's finished, and I can go back to enjoying my boring frozen entrees and morning bagel with cream cheese. Tell Barnacle to stop by later. I have a nice chew bone for him."

"What do you have for me?" Steve asked as he followed her.

Page halted at the door. Was he teasing? Of course, he was teasing her. She turned on her smile. "I'll save you a plate of tonight's dinner. I think I spied oxtails thawing in the sink."

"What the hell are oxtails?" Steve's muscular arm rested on the door frame, mere inches from Page. He cocked a grin. "I might have a better plan. Count on seeing me later, Miss Drew."

CHAPTER 11

Beach bag draped over her shoulder, and with a beach chair in hand, Page headed toward the blue-striped umbrella. She took a deep breath of the salt air and sighed. Despite having another confounding case, Page felt serenely happy. Passing the lifeguard, she gave a wave, careful to step around a sandcastle that two teenage girls had erected. Page gave them a thumbs up, understanding their ploy to hang near him. The lifeguard was plenty cute. Continuing, she found Betsy fully engrossed with the Dowager.

"Hello? I'm here. Where are you? London?" Page joked.

"Oh, we're enjoying afternoon tea in Devonshire. I'm positively brimming with recipe ideas, starting with making Devonshire cream."

"Now, that's a recipe I can get behind. We should top a wildflower honey cake with that cream," Page suggested.

"Great idea." Betsy laid the novel aside and studied Page's appearance. "You're wearing the magenta bathing suit, which tells me you brought a good mood to the beach. Things with the Dreamboat must have gone well."

"I'm still ignoring those taunts. Yes, things went well. As for your ability to read my mood based on my bathing suit, that's impressive. I do find myself feeling quite happy with my lot." Page applied sunscreen, unable to resist the urge to check out the surfers bobbing past the waves' break line. She watched one—a special one—ride a wave with mastery.

"Is he good at everything?" sighed Betsy. "I've been observing him giving tips to some of the novices out there.

Surfers must possess a strong camaraderie." Betsy lifted the lid on the cooler and peered inside. "Ah, perfect, a root beer. What can I hand you before I get the lowdown on your meeting?"

"Got a green tea?" Page dug into the cooler. "My word, Betsy, all I see are cans of root beer and cream soda."

"You didn't give me instructions on what to bring. What's wrong with those?" Betsy's expression showed hurt.

Realizing how inconsiderate her words sounded, Page's hand revisited the cooler. "You know what? I haven't enjoyed a cream soda in forever. My good mood craves a treat, and you chose one of my favorite sodas." Page popped the tab and saluted a pleased Betsy.

"See there? I know what's good for us. It's another one of my talents." Betsy yanked off her bonnet and turned it into a fan. "How come you're spared these flashes?"

Page quipped back. "We each have our crosses to bear." Hers was the never-ending plates of Betsy's food that even Barnacle wouldn't touch. "Now, for your briefing before I take a swim." Page stayed on topic, careful not to share any personal exchanges. Betsy didn't need more fodder for teasing.

"We three agree on Ralph and Buck sharing a similar, if not identical, motive for wanting Jake out of the way. Betcha that journal has more nuggets that Steve mines." Betsy adjusted her lounger.

"Agreed." Page felt the ocean call her. She craved time alone, a carryover from being an only child.

"Before you swim, I had a spark of brilliance to share," Betsy offered.

"I'm listening."

"What do you think about us paying a visit to Plant Hugger? I'd like to purchase a pot of Gerber daises for the porch dining table. I plan to serve dinner out there tonight. You know, mix things up and add spice to our dining atmosphere. Besides, maybe the doors of fate might open and—"

"I'm not sure we need any more spice, but I'm a fan of your idea to see what we can get from Bert and Rosa," said Page, pondering. "In fact, I love your spark."

Betsy gave a bow. "When should we go? Soon huh? Beat the detectives. I like it when we do that."

Page laughed. "Yes, we need to make that trip happen. Do me a favor. While I take a dip, find out what hours Plant Hugger is open."

"Will do." Betsy grabbed her cell phone from her tote.

"By the way, Bets, you're an awesome partner." Page tossed her cap in the chair and headed toward the water.

With the saltwater's help, floating on her back became effortless. Page gazed at the azure sky, focusing on one colossal cumulus cloud's shape, ever-evolving, much like her. Wasn't everything and everyone evolving? Yes, at varying degrees, she believed that to be so, but there existed two vital components in progressing…intention and attention. She considered that concept, applying it to various parts of her life. Of course, evolving took many directions, and not all of them were good. The law of duality played a significant role…right versus wrong, light versus dark. Page thought about the five suspects. Ralph and Buck acted from the dark side of their natures. What about the other three? In time, those answers would come. With eyes closed, her mind's chattering went silent.

"Woman, you're a human float. You and the ocean seem simpatico, and I thought I had an uncommon relationship with it."

Page squinted to see Steve straddling his board.

"That sounded like a rare compliment, which I'll accept. "What's up?"

"The surf?"

Page groaned.

"That bad, huh?" He swiped at the water droplets cascading into his eyes.

"Yep." Page flipped over to tread water and face the man who'd made her heart beat funny since the first day she'd met him. "Want to try again? What's up, Detective Tanner?"

"Not much since it's Sunday, and it's only been a short time since we met." Steve turned his board into the next wave. "No word from the tail I placed on Bert. For now, Eleanor and Rosa don't hold my interest. I guess that might qualify as newsy."

"I'd say so." Page splashed a piece of seaweed away.

"So, your turn. What's up with you and that redheaded cohort fanning herself? Plotting anything of interest?" Steve adjusted the strap on his sunglasses.

"Not much since it's Sunday, and it's only a short time since we met," parroted a grinning Page.

"Yo, Steve, can you show me again how to fine-tune my position on the crest?" hollered a nearby surfer.

"Later, Miss Drew." Steve paddled toward his student while Page swam toward the shore.

"Glad you decided to end the flirting and return before the sun went down." Betsy stuffed her empty snack bag into the tote.

"I wasn't flirting. I don't flirt," answered an affronted Page. "Do you think I flirt?" She grabbed the beach towel to dry off.

"You flirt. Enough said." Betsy folded her chair. "Hurry and pack up. We've got an errand to run."

Page shoved her towel into the bag. "What errand?" Her face brightened. "Oh, that errand. I'm right behind you."

~*~

"You drive in case we spy a nice plant for outside Hibiscus Cottage. My way of saying thank you for letting me stay here. Besides, your beloved British piece of kit has more room to stow stuff than my compact." Betsy handed the SUV's keys to Page.

"There's logic to your plan, and I like the gratis plant idea. How about another red hibiscus for the back planter?" Page locked the door. Glancing at Steve's bungalow, she saw Barnacle in the backyard chewing on the underbelly of the dinghy. It appeared Steve's refurbishing project would take longer. Page laughed, appreciating that Barnacle lived up to his name. The dog's escapades proved Steve's surfboard still had him captive on the water. She and Betsy could slip off without worrying he'd follow them.

"What's so funny?" asked Betsy, settling into the passenger seat.

"Oh, just Barnacle gnawing off crustaceans and probably some new wood on Steve's dinghy. Clearly, our neighbor's still hanging ten, and we—"

"Avoid him chasing after us. I hate it when he does that." Betsy removed a cloth from a plastic bag and blotted her red face.

"Is that a new flash attack strategy?"

"Yep. Stuck it in the freezer for an added chill. I'm going to win this battle yet."

Page grinned. "Hey, I don't recall seeing that muumuu before? The shade of yellow looks nice on you."

"Ya think? I ordered it online. Since you complimented me, I should buy one in every color," Betsy answered and smoothed the material. "I do that when I like something."

Page braked for a stop sign and tapped Betsy's forearm. "Just how many colors does your shift come in?"

"Seven, I think. One for every day of the week." Betsy's face lit. "Like those panties our mothers purchased for us back in the day. Remember?"

"Hard to forget those step-ins, as Tilly called panties. Monday was my favorite because it was pastel blue with the day embroidered in lilac." Page turned the corner.

"Saturday was my pick. Red and black. Sassy."

"Of course, you'd pick Saturday." Page shook her head. "Listen, on our way home, I need to stop by the market and get a few things for tomorrow's sailing picnic."

"Ah, yes, the boat ride. And, yet you tell me over and over, 'We're simply friends who share a love for sailing.'" Betsy held up her frozen cloth. "You need this more than me after last night's steamy kissing performance, which I was forced to witness."

"Keep your rag to yourself. I've got things under control." Page drove onto the nursery's gravel parking lot. "Good, they don't look busy." She grabbed the door handle.

"Hold up there, Sherlocka. What's the plan? We always have a plan." Betsy put her straw bonnet atop her head.

"Oh my gosh, you're right. We don't have a plan." Page paused; her mind scrambled for an idea. Instead, she got a nudge. "I think it's okay this time."

"Why is it okay? I prefer to know what I'm walking into with you. Maybe we should—"

"I got a nudge, Betsy. We'll be shown." Not waiting for a reply, Page exited the vehicle.

Betsy caught up to Page. "Why don't we amble over to the hibiscus bushes, and you can see if one calls your name?"

"Okay, as I recall, the flowering bushes live over in that far corner." Page moved in that direction.

"Afternoon ladies, how can we help you? Looking for some shrubs?" Bert asked.

Page ordered up her smile. "Afternoon, and yes, we're heading over to the hibiscus." She noted that Bert's dapper appearance didn't fit with the surroundings. Spotless khaki pants and green polo shirt testified to his hands-off approach to running the nursery. He presented the image of a successful businessman. Page felt relieved that he didn't connect her to Honey Bees and his last purchase.

Betsy bent down to check a price tag on a palm.

"That's a healthy tree. I can make you a deal on it." Bert pulled the pot away from the others.

"Oh, I'm window shopping until my bungalow renovation is completed, and then you can count on seeing me back with a list." Betsy dusted her hands.

Bert nodded. "We'll be here. Follow me over to the corner. Let's see what we can send you home with today," he said, directing his gaze to Page.

Betsy poked her cousin and mouthed, "Question him, already."

Nothing bubbled up for her to ask, which was uncommon. Page shrugged at Betsy.

Bert's cell phone rang, proving to Page her silence was golden.

"Excuse me for a minute." Bert stepped a few feet away. "Bert here." His face turned as red as the nearby display of begonias. "Why can't you read the will Monday? I don't care about some trial case you're handling. Listen up, Rosa and I are coming to your office tomorrow. I expect someone to read Jake's will and start disbursing funds my way." Bert clicked off and took a deep breath.

Page and Betsy exchanged smiles. It wasn't a big scoop, but it showed Bert's character and desire for fast money.

"Rosa," hollered Bert. "I need you now." Bert turned to Page and Betsy. "My daughter will help you find everything you need. I've other pressing matters." With that, Bert walked away.

"Guess Rosa's up next. Maybe you'll find the ability to ask questions?" Betsy joked.

"Focus on picking me a nice plant, and I'll take care of planting seeds to harvest," retorted Page.

A young woman in her early twenties with the same coloring as her father approached. Plaited blond hair hung down her back, but the flowers stuck in the braid were what fired Page with an idea. Rosa adjusted the strap on the denim overalls. "Hi. How can I help?"

"Hi, Rosa. I'm Page, and this is my cousin, Betsy. We're on a mission to buy a red hibiscus to go with the ones I purchased from Plant Huggers in the past. Plus, there's something else that we need your guidance on buying."

"Let's go choose the bush first," Rosa said with a bored tone.

Page stood to the side while Betsy fiddled with every hibiscus standing. An inkling rewarded her. Something significant would soon transpire.

"Page, how about this plant?" Betsy scooted the hibiscus away from the rest.

"Perfect." They all looked the same, but Betsy's eye saw differently. Page trusted her cousin in all growing things matters.

"Rosa lifted the plant. "I'll take this over to the register and come right back."

Betsy snagged her Gerber and handed it off to Rosa. Turning to Page, she asked, "What else do we need from Rosa besides answers to questions you've yet to ask? Come on. Let's get more from this visit than Bert wanting that will read pronto."

"Will you please show a little trust in me? I received an inkling," Page whispered, not wanting to risk being overheard.

"An inkling? In that case, I suspend further prodding. Here comes Rosa."

"Okay, what else do you need?" Rosa's eyes followed her father's leaving. "One moment." She turned away to send a text.

Page ambled over to the rows of annual flowers and signaled Betsy to join her. "Aren't the colors of pansies beautiful? I love their faces."

Betsy looked from the flowers to Page and back again. "Um, since when did you and pansies become fast friends? I've never once seen you own one."

"Since a few minutes ago, when the inkling visited." Page lifted a container of purple pansies. "Yep, I like them."

Betsy looked puzzled. "Never mind. Here comes Rosa back. Lights, camera, action."

CHAPTER 12

"What's next?" asked Rosa with a now impatient voice.

"Next, I'd like to tap into your knowledge of edible flowers." Page set the pansy down.

"Edible flowers?" Betsy screeched. "What in the world do you need with—"

Page shot a scowl toward her cousin and turned, smiling to Rosa. "Ignore her. She gets these lapses, probably hormonal. We're looking for edible flowers to decorate cakes and such. We've recently opened Honey Bees on Main Street."

Catching on, Betsy replied, "Yes, silly me and my lapses. We need direction on what flowers are safe to consume. Would you possess such knowledge, Rosa?"

"Wow, that's a super cool idea. Yes, I'm educated on edible flowers. It's a sort of fascination I've developed. So, you can definitely eat pansies." Rosa touched the purple flowers.

"Wonderful. I knew that I liked you." Page showed more of her friendly side. "What others can you recommend?"

"Let me grab a cart, and I'll point out the safe ones. You must choose carefully." Rosa walked off.

"Lapses. Now, I have lapses. Why is it always me with the issues?" Betsy lifted her palms skyward.

Page let a laugh escape. "Can I help it if you're slow on the uptake and provide me such great setups?"

"Slow on the uptake, am I? So, now I'm supposed to read your mind and know your scheme? From the ethers came edible flowers?" Betsy's smile broke through. "Though I confess, the idea is growing on me."

"Such a bad pun, but hey, good to have you back from the lapses." Page spun around, hearing the cart's squeaky wheels.

"Got the cart. How many pansies do you want today? They'll only live for a few weeks in these containers, but you must water them daily." Rosa grabbed one of each color.

"Yes, we definitely want one each of the different shades," agreed Page.

"Can you eat honeysuckles? That name pairs perfectly with our cakes," chimed in Betsy.

"Yes, honeysuckle flowers are edible, but the berries are poisonous, so best to avoid them." Rosa frowned. She took the plant from Betsy and put the plant back in the tray.

"Okay, no honeysuckles. What about marigolds? They're cheerful." Betsy held up a small container.

"Marigolds are fine. They have an interesting citrus flavor." Rosa took a whiff.

"No, kidding? This is fascinating." Page added six marigold plants to the cart.

Rosa nodded. "I think three types of flowers make a good start."

"Um, Rosa, another lapse must have befallen me, but I only count two here," Betsy frowned.

"Yeah, I was getting to that. Why don't you pick any hibiscus from your yard and use those? No upkeep and a steady supply of decoration." A distraction caught Rosa's attention. "Look, talk it over. I need to see someone for a couple of minutes."

Page watched Rosa approach a young man who looked as if he had stepped out of a sixties head shop in Haight Ashbury. "Bets, get a load of that one in the psychedelic shirt and body art." The nudge hit Page. "Keep fiddling with the flowers while I go eavesdrop."

"Fiddling, I'm good at doing. Be careful," instructed Betsy.

Rosa and the young man were engrossed in conversation,

making it easy for Page to slip behind a thick stand of palms.

"My uncle's finally kicked it, so Amalfi's on." Rosa's tone sounded elated.

"Like, why does him kicking off get you the bread for the trip?"

"Because I inherit, along with my dad. The guy was stoked with guap. Don't you see? I'll have enough for us to travel the world. Our plan can happen. I'm going to buy so much drip. Best of all, I cancel my dad, and we can quit peddling."

"Serious? Man, this is so extra. Wanna get lit tonight and celebrate?" The guy pretended to smoke.

"Yeah, I'll meet you after I get done cleaning my uncle's home."

"Why keep doing that if he's dead? That's dumb." He shook his head.

"You're dumb. One, I need to clean it so my dad can put the house on the market. Two, saying I need to clean the place might get me by the police. I left something there that I need back." Rosa stuffed a bag in her boyfriend's pocket and patted it. "Gotta bounce now. Make sure you show. You don't want me to feel mad again."

Page dashed back to Betsy's side moments before Rosa returned.

"Are we done? You're using hibiscus flowers, right?" Rosa rearranged the row of pansies to fill the gaps.

"Yes, we agree with your great idea, so I guess we're set to check out," Page answered and handed her credit card to Rosa.

"I'll go ring this up. Ray will load the plants in your vehicle."

"Thanks for your help," added Betsy.

Rosa shrugged and left them.

"That's a strange one," Betsy surmised.

Page motioned for Betsy to follow her.

~*~

Page pulled out of Plant Huggers and headed for the market, struggling to process what she'd overheard.

"I'll give you cash for the hibiscus you charged on your card. That's my gift to you," Betsy reminded.

No words came from Page.

"Knock, knock. Anyone home?" Betsy leaned over to see Page's face.

"I'm here. I'm here and wondering how I can interpret the millennial jargon I heard from Rosa and her boyfriend. Not only is she strange, but she speaks strange words." Page shook her head.

"I don't even understand what you said, but try me," Betsy encouraged.

"Okay, how about, Jake was stoked with guap."

Betsy looked perplexed.

"No? How about she's going to buy a lot of drip and cancel her dad?" Page supplied.

"This is what a nudge got you? Drip and guap? Are we still in America?"

Page chuckled. "I did glean some useful and understandable info. Rosa's feeling pretty happy about the coming life changes. Like getting out of her dad's house and not needing to pedal. No clue what that means."

"Maybe she's using an exercise bike. She is a bit chunky. Of course, lifting and toting plants all day should keep one fit and occupied and..." said Betsy, running out of steam.

"Continuing, Rosa declared her trip to the Amalfi Coast a go and plans lots more traveling with her boyfriend, all thanks to Uncle Jake. Get this. Rosa's been cleaning for Jake. I guess for extra money. Anyway, tonight she's going back to his house. There's something she's bent on retrieving. I assume the police have finished going through Jake's things, but who knows?"

Page gave a little shrug of her shoulders.

"Despite the language barrier, you managed to score a lot of drip and guap. What do we do with it?" Betsy asked.

"I'm not sure yet. Both Bert and Rosa hold big desires to collect on Jake's estate. Money acts as a strong motive for murder. For now, let's grocery shop and let things percolate."

Thirty minutes later, Page popped the gate on her SUV. "Hey, Betsy, what's missing?"

Before Betsy could reply, Page felt a strong inkling wash over.

Betsy held onto the grocery cart and peered inside. "Your hibiscus isn't in here. Ray didn't load it. We need to go back to Plant Hugger before they close."

"Let's stow the groceries and hurry." Page sensed a valuable clue waiting.

Parking the SUV in the nursery lot, Page turned to Betsy. "I'm leaving the engine running to keep the groceries cool while I grab the bush. Back in a few."

"Okay. I'll focus on munching this low-calorie tasteless apple."

Page went in search of Rosa or Bert. She got nudged in the direction of a shoddy-looking greenhouse located at the back of the property. Page let the open side door shield her presence to observe Bert and a shabbily dressed man in a discussion.

"Get these magics to the dock tomorrow night." Bert passed a garbage bag.

"Same boat as last month?" asked the man.

"Same boat. Once I get the word you've delivered, I'll leave your money —"

"I know, inside that disgusting toilet tank in the park. Can't you find a better place?"

Bert pulled the guy into his chest. "What better place to stash cash? Who cleans a tank? Quit your complaining, or I'll find someone more agreeable to handle my business."

"Tanks good, man. Let go of my shirt."

Page had heard enough and sensed they were wrapping things up. The hibiscus could wait. She jogged to her SUV and thanked her lucky feng shui star no one was around to see her.

"Where's the plant? Why are you panting? Let me guess. Dreamboat came to buy some grass seeds for where Barnacle dug up part of his yard," Betsy supplied.

"Are you done? Look behind and make sure you don't see anyone." Page turned onto the street and released a breath.

"Looks all clear. What happened?" Betsy offered Page the chilled cloth.

"No, thanks." Page glanced in the rearview mirror, relieved no one was back there. "What happened is I witnessed another deal going down. First, it was shark fins, and now something called magics. I think everyone at Plant Huggers speaks some altered dialect of English. For now, I say let them keep that hibiscus bush."

Betsy dabbed her forehead. "Great. Now we've got three suspects dealing. Hold on. Rosa isn't pedaling like a bike. She's peddling like—"

"You're brilliant, Betsy. Maybe those magics, assuming they're illegal, are what's being peddled? That makes four suspects in the trade, but how does that tie into Jake's death? Face it. We've quite a knack for discovering other crimes unrelated to murder." Page sighed.

"I do so love a good goose chase. And speaking of goose, I have another special dinner planned, but patience is required. I can't serve it until around eight," explained Betsy.

"Oh boy, I've something to look forward to, and eight p.m. gives me time to update the suspect board." *And, sneak a snack,* thought Page. The karmic cooking wheel wouldn't ease up even in the middle of a murder investigation. She'd probably cooked in an orphanage and fed the children gruel. In this lifetime, she was severely being paid back. Page glanced at Betsy scribbling. "What are you jotting?"

"Spices for the duck and oxtails. Don't ask more. Wait and see."

"Wait, I shall." She had bigger worries than Betsy's upcoming culinary debacle. Page knew the information she'd overheard at Plant Hugger belonged with Steve. How to share it without gaining his wrath from her eavesdropping left Page in a quandary.

CHAPTER 13

Page stood back, studying the updated suspect board. Some gaps were filled in, but she had more questions than answers. They'd identified motives for the five under investigation, yet no one person stood out as probable. Page felt confident that Steve possessed the information she needed. After the trip to Plant Hugger, she had bartering rights. Page sighed, thinking the next info exchange opportunity wouldn't happen until Monday. Hearing Betsy close the sliding door, Page frowned. The sound of pots and pans rattling sealed her fate.

"You left the Dowager?" Page parked on the kitchen island's stool to better monitor the meal fixings.

"Yes, I waited until Gertrude chose her gown for the Dimsford's gala. I think the chartreuse color will complement her coloring, especially in candlelight. She has her good eye on Sir Dimsford since he's a widower, so she must look her best." Betsy peeped at her watch.

"Well, I must say life for Dowager Gertrude looks rosy, which explains your good mood." Page couldn't fathom why she suddenly felt cheerful. "Can I help with dinner?"

"Maybe later. I've got time to grab a shower before preparing my Le Cordon Bleu worthy meal." Betsy went to the refrigerator and lifted the foil on a glass dish, and gave it a little shake.

"Very nice." She shut the door and smiled at Page. "The duck's having a nice marinade in pomegranate juice, Worcestershire, and my secret spices."

"Oh, happy bird," exclaimed Page, watching her cousin

head for the bath. She grabbed a bag of pretzels and moved toward the porch as the doorbell sounded. Upon opening the door, Page flushed with surprise.

"Howdy, neighbor. I told you that I had a better plan than oxtails for your dinner. I come bearing gifts." Steve grinned and held up some pizza boxes."

Without thinking, Page stood on tiptoes and bestowed a kiss on his cheek. She took in his scent of clean soap. Dismissing her mind's attempt to lead her astray, she tugged on Steve's arm. "Things have grown direr. Betsy's added duck to somehow go with the oxtails. Bring those boxes inside, you wonderful man."

"Hey, the invitation does include both Barnacle and me, right? We're two very hungry guys."

Barnacle didn't wait for his formal greeting but beelined to the basket holding his new chew bones.

Page and Steve exchanged smiles, watching him settle in Betsy's hammock with his bone.

"She'll have plenty to say about that. Speaking of the culinary genius, where is she?" Steve placed the pizza boxes on the kitchen counter.

"Having a shower. Hurry and help me set the table on the porch. Wait a sec, why are there four pizzas? Does Barn get a pizza, too?" Page asked, carrying them out.

Steve winked. "You'll see."

Betsy appeared on the porch. "What's all this?" She stopped and frowned. "Barnacle, get out of my hammock with that gross thing in your mouth."

"Steve surprised us with pizza. We've been waiting for you. Super nice of him, huh?"

Betsy pulled a face. "But I have the duck and oxtails—"

"We can eat them tomorrow." Page's spirits felt buoyed thanks to the dinner Fates intervening. "Come, join us. I'm excited to see what pizza Steve ordered us."

"Yeah, Betsy, sit yourself down. I put extra, extra thought into your pizza toppings." Steve gave Page another wink.

"Okay, since you went to this trouble and made mine extra, extra special." Betsy plopped into the chair. "Hand it over." She lifted the box lid.

Page bit her tongue to keep from laughing. Betsy's pie was covered in pineapple, anchovies, artichokes, and jalapenos — Betsy's intended pie. "Wow, is that ever original?" Page saw the amusement on Steve's face.

"I live for original. I am original. It's the perfect pizza for me. Steve, you feel free to bring an encore over any time." Betsy lifted a slice and took a generous bite. "So good."

"Really? You like —" asked a dumbfounded Steve. He glanced at Page and shrugged.

"So good," repeated Betsy, reaching for a second piece.

"Ladies, it looks like you have a sausage pizza for leftovers." Steve chuckled and opened his box.

~*~

Later, while Betsy loaded the dishwasher, Page chatted with Steve. "So, I'm ready to do more bartering of information. What about you?"

"Are you telling me you went sleuthing this afternoon?" Steve's voice sounded harsh.

"Hold on, mister. I see it more like being at the right place at the right time. Do you have anything to trade or not?" Page enjoyed her elevated bargaining position.

"As a matter of fact, Detective Koch blessed you and me working together again, but in a limited way. So, yes, I'm up for an exchange this evening."

"Excellent. We should wait for Betsy. She's part of our trio despite Koch seeing her as a nuisance. The guy's yet to recognize Betsy's value."

"My value?" Betsy returned to the porch with a tray

holding three dishes of ice cream with suspicious toppings.

"Yes, your value. Steve and I were discussing the important role you play in our crime-busting trio." Page accepted her bowl of ice cream and squinted at the concoction.

"How nice to hear you both discussing my contributions. Here you go, Steve." Betsy passed a bowl. "Tuck in all."

Steve's spoon stayed suspended in the air. "Say, Betsy, what's sprinkled on top of this strawberry ice cream? It is strawberry, right?"

Page grinned and swept her topping to the side. She'd learned when not to ask Betsy food identity questions.

"If you must know my secret, it's chopped mint, candied ginger, and a balsamic reduction. It's what I call elevated gourmet." Betsy shoved in a mouthful.

Steve glanced at Page's bowl and copied her actions. "Let's eat and talk. Time for Page's bartering exercise. Betsy, I'm sure you'll want to jump in and add to what your cousin deliberately leaves out."

"Nice ploy, Tanner, but it won't work. Tell him, Betsy." Page looked over at her cousin.

"Nope, it won't work as long as he doesn't bait me. I still struggle with my POR."

Steve's eyes mirrored a good mood. "There's that POR thing again. Forget it." He shrugged. "I expect the autopsy report tomorrow, and toxicology won't arrive for a few days, best case. I'm still struggling to interpret some of Jake's cryptic journal entries. It appears this guy gathered more dirt than a street sweeper."

Both women laughed at the reference.

Steve bowed. "Thank you. Thank you very much. Continuing with some good news, we did retrieve the cigarillo, and it's at the lab for analysis. So, Page, thanks again for noticing that piece of evidence. What else?"

"Alibis? What have you garnered there?" Page ate another spoonful of ice cream.

"Yeah, we like to gather those facts early on for our suspect board," added Betsy.

Steve released a laugh. "One day, I'm going to catch a glimpse of this infamous board of yours. Okay, alibis. Ralph attended the festivities with his wife, which she corroborated. She told me he left once, but only long enough to buy Bailey's barbeque ribs."

Page paused to ponder Steve's words. "Still, that could allow time for a quick Jake visit. That cigarillo might belong to Ralph."

Steve nodded. "True enough. Ralph has become a primary suspect with means, motive, and opportunity."

Betsy pushed her empty dish to the side. "Wow, Ralph, rings my bell as the one who done it. Page, want me to make notes? We can fill that in—"

Page nodded absently. "What about Bert?"

Koch questioned Bert and Rosa together. Bert was at the park July Fourth, and I quote, 'mingling around' that night. He claims not to have seen his brother, though he had plenty of opportunities to do so. Rosa told Koch on the side that she saw her father disappear behind the vendor trailers but didn't know why."

"Family loyalty seems in short supply," interjected Page.

Betsy leaned in. "Don't I know it? My second husband's sister tried to claim more than fifty percent of their parent's estate because she'd done so much—"

"Not relevant, Betsy." Page's eyes glinted at Steve.

Betsy snagged the spoon from Page. "Listen to me. It sort of is relevant. You see, my point is that Rosa wants to cancel. Is that the word she used, Page?"

"Not our turn, Betsy. Stifle." Page reached for her spoon.

"POR."

"Right, not our turn. POR," murmured Betsy, scooting down in her chair.

"May I continue if you two are finished speaking your secret lingo?" asked an amused Steve. "Rosa joined her friends for the fireworks. Other than making a trip to her vehicle for bottled water, she was present. We verified this with her group."

Page saw a pattern. "I'm going to say again that the three of them were missing for a short time. Can we agree that walking to the point where Jake was to fire the cannon didn't take but a few minutes? Thus, we add two more suspects with the means and opportunity. But let's review the motives."

Betsy lifted her hand to speak. "You did hear Bert and Jake arguing and threatening to spill some dirt on each other. Plus, Steve just told us Jake excelled at sweeping. No, that's not what you said, but I remember it was funny. What was it again?"

Steve chuckled. "I said Jake could gather more dirt than a street sweeper. I agree, Betsy. Whatever Jake knew or thought he knew could act as a strong motivator for Bert. He checks our three boxes, but Rosa doesn't. Jake refusing to give her money for a trip doesn't strike me as a powerful enough motive to kill her uncle."

Page shook her head. "I don't know. Money travels with a lot of murders, though I get your point. She's young and self-absorbed —"

Betsy threw her arm up. "Hold the fort. I heard about this sixteen-year-old boy who wanted a bass guitar, and his dad refused to give him money for it. He grabbed his dad's gun, shot him in the you know what, and stole his wallet. They found the kid playing with a band outside of town."

Page and Steve stared, trying to take in Betsy's latest side trip.

"You two are slow on the uptake." Betsy released a heavy

sigh. "My point is that Rosa may be young, but if she's determined to travel, she possesses the motive which fits her age. Now, this is the place where you say: Why, Betsy, your input and stories are so valuable to this conversation."

Steve smiled at Page. "On the count of three. One. Two. Three."

"Why, Betsy, your input is so valuable to this conversation," chorused Steve and Page.

"That's much better. Now move along, my chickadees. We've got Eleanor and Buck left." Betsy's hand made a forward motion.

Steve opened the screen door to let Barnacle out and returned to his chair. "Next up is Buck Lester. Good ol' Buck has an airtight alibi, corroborated by the guy working at the Bait Shak. He's the one who allows people access to the charter boat dock. According to him, Buck spent the evening working on his boat engine. He had a charter fishing group scheduled for the next day and needed to install a couple of motor parts. The bait guy said Buck stayed at the marina until eleven, which is when the Bait Shak closed."

"So, this bait guy would see anyone who came or went while he was open. What about after hours?" Page thought Buck was an unlikely suspect based on what she was hearing.

"Any owner wanting to enter that dock after-hours must use their card on the electric entry gate. There's a record of who accesses the gate. Buck's alibi is about as clean as they come. So, he lacked opportunity and means, but motive Buck still possesses."

"What do you see as his main motive? Did you bust him on the poaching? You told me Jake's journal indicated he was suspicious of Buck and Ralph's doings." Page's interest piqued.

"I see two motives. The first was to put an end to the limit on fishing. That's bothered both men enough to circulate that petition. Obviously, if they knew Jake was suspicious of their side work, that makes a second even stronger motive. Poaching is a serious offense that can get them a long vacation at the correctional facility. However, Buck moves low on the list because he was on the boat tinkering with the engine. He couldn't have been with Ralph."

Betsy's head bobbed. "We can't ignore logic, Page. I guess we leave Buck alone. I want to hear about that snooty Eleanor. Hold up. I'm thirsty from that pizza. Anyone want a soda?"

"I'll take one," replied Steve.

"You might want to be specific about what kind," warned Page. "Make mine sparkling water without any embellishments."

"And, you detective? Be specific," Betsy taunted.

"I'll take a plain cola. Plain," said Steve, emphasizing the word.

"Got it. Back in a sec." Betsy scurried inside.

Steve turned to Page. "Promise me you won't let her get near our picnic lunch."

"I can't believe you'd ask. Hush, here she comes."

"Get your sips in. I want to hear more." Betsy placed three glasses down. "What did you dig up on Miss Hoity Toity?"

Steve took a gulp. "Not much at all. Eleanor didn't make Jake's journal. At least I haven't found her in it. Of course, she attended the celebration and made herself visible to anyone with a beating heart. I only interviewed her husband at this point and kept things general."

Page nodded. "Good move there. What did the mayor say?"

"I think it's common knowledge our mayor's totally into his political aspirations, and Eleanor's the window dressing. I believe they each have their own agendas." Steve's expression showed his dislike.

Betsy and Page voiced agreement.

Steve continued, "Anyway, the mayor had no problem

volunteering that Eleanor was missing for twenty minutes or so when he needed her to introduce the high school band. Again, I come back to having little to no reason to suspect her in Jake's death. I'd appreciate hearing what you two have on her." Steve lifted his soda glass. "Good plain cola, Bets."

"You're hilarious, Tanner," Betsy's tone dripped sarcasm. "You are missing out on the spice of life—correction—spices of life. Is it our turn to enlighten?"

Steve nodded. "Go ahead and add some spice to my investigation."

Page shared the details of their two visits to Plant Hugger and was surprised when Steve refrained from chastising them for eavesdropping. She had to pause recounting while Steve called the officers at Jake's house and verified that they'd denied Rosa access. Last, she filled in the blanks for why Eleanor made the suspect board by revealing the conversation between Jake and Eleanor at City Hall.

"So, you think Jake may have something in his journal about Eleanor?" Steve rubbed his chin, pondering the notion.

"I think it's a possibility. Eleanor is or was doing something that Jake felt warranted a smackdown. I trust guidance will come to me if she's involved in Jake's death."

"Cousin, you'll be led even if Eleanor didn't kill Jake but did something else of consequence," smiled Betsy. "We are the most ambidextrous of sleuths."

Page's eyes crinkled at the corners in amusement. "Now, that's a description of us that I've never heard out of you. Ambidextrous sleuths."

Steve joined in, laughing, "Hey, it's true, but damn impossible to say fast three times. Listen up, you two snoops, I'm going to cut out. Thanks for letting Barnacle and me dine with you tonight." He stood.

"Thanks for bringing dinner." Page wrinkled her nose.

"Oh, I forgot to ask. Did you happen to check on your dinghy's—"

"Yes, your dinghy's transformation," supplied a teasing Betsy. She cocked her head toward Barnacle, looking pitiful through the screen door.

"Him? What did he do to my dinghy? Not more chewing." Steve's eyebrow shot up. He glanced at his dog.

Page opened the door as Steve shot out.

"Not going to be a good night for Barnacle. Let's go to bed. I've got bowling with The Mermaids tomorrow, and you've got a sailing date with Dream—"

"Good night, Mermaid," interrupted Page.

"Dreamboat!" Betsy hollered and closed her bedroom door.

Noticing the porch light bulb was burned out, Page went outside to replace it.

A man's voice startled her. "Lady, consider this a friendly warning. I don't want to see you anywhere near my charter boat again." Ralph stepped out of the shadows and then disappeared down the beach access walkway.

CHAPTER 14

"I had a visitor after you went to bed." Page pushed the button on the espresso machine and watched Betsy devour a bowl of cereal any child would covet. "Are those marshmallows and chocolate chunks? I suppose you're getting sugared up for bowling."

"Yeah, my secret weapon—a bowl of energy. Who came calling?" Betsy looked up, mildly interested.

"Ralph Owen."

"Holy cow and calf." Betsy jumped up, heading for the front door.

"Where are you going?" Page followed behind.

"To Steve's. Where else? He needs to know who showed up here."

Page reached to grab her cousin's arm. "Wait. First, I need you to stand still and listen to me."

"No way. Not on your life, kiddo." Betsy tried to break away.

"Give me five minutes, and then if you want to go blab, I won't stop you. Five minutes? Come finish your cereal." Page begged and returned to the kitchen. She waved the bowl to chum Betsy.

"Put my breakfast down. I'm listening." Betsy claimed her spoon and began munching.

"I went outside last night to change a lightbulb, and Ralph was standing on the side by the beach access, watching me. His exact words were, 'Lady, consider this a friendly warning. I don't want to see you anywhere near my charter boat again.'"

"That was supposed to sound friendly? We already know

he's a bad hombre, which means we're staying far away from those two. Let them move their shark fins around Mother Earth. We don't care. Do we?" Betsy studied a silent Page. "That's it. I'm going over to Dreamboat's."

"Go ahead, but all you'll find is a tethered Barnacle. Steve's SUV left earlier."

"Fine, I'll call Steve's cell phone. What's the number?" Betsy grabbed her phone.

"Relax. I left him a message. Besides, he's picking me up at noon. This tidbit can wait." Page made a second espresso.

Betsy returned to crunching her cereal. "Are we safe here? How I wish my bungalow was finished. We could go there." She took another bite and choked. "Hold the fort. How did Ralph find out where you lived?"

"There are all kinds of ways. Shell's a small town. Register of Deeds or asking around are ways that come to mind. As for the questions about our safety, I honestly don't know, but Steve will make sure we're protected."

"I thought Ralph and Buck didn't see you on the pier?" Betsy exhaled loudly.

"Well, I guess Ralph saw me with Steve. Maybe he didn't recognize that it was Steve, or I lay you odds that he'd never shown up here. Who knows. Let's not worry yet."

"I'm glad Ina and the other two Mermaids offered me a lift. I'm going to swim with them until you come home from sailing." Betsy looked out the kitchen window as she rinsed her bowl.

"You're going swimming? I thought you were bowling —"

"Figure of speech. Mermaids. Swimming. Get it? I needed a dose of humor to counteract the raging fear inside of me." Betsy gave a little shiver.

"Go spend the rest of the morning in the hammock with Dowager Gertrude," Page encouraged.

Betsy moved to the end table, where her book waited. "What are you going to do?"

"Listen," Page said cryptically.

Page settled into her comfy upholstered den chair. The fabric's muted colors of a sunrise always lifted her spirit. Outside, the ocean's sounds played in the background as she closed her eyes. She needed direction to uncover Jake's murderer. Page mused that the inklings and nudges were active, but the necessary insights seemed MIA. It was time to quiet her mind's constant chatter and listen. Time slipped away, no longer mattering. Only then did Page get her answers.

~*~

"I've got thirty minutes to prepare the picnic lunch and dress," Page announced to Betsy, entering the kitchen. "I lost track of time." In a frenzy, she grabbed the bread and sandwich bags from the counter.

Wearing her Mermaid shirt, Betsy sat munching a sandwich with enough ham to feed a family of four. "You'll make it. Slide me that jar of pickles."

Page set the jar down and took a second glance at Betsy's sandwich. "Oh my gosh, what are you eating? Is that my ham?" Page opened the refrigerator and didn't see the deli bag.

"Of course, it's ham. I thought it was our ham. Uh oh, I messed up." Betsy scooted the deli bag toward Page. "There's enough left—"

"For half a sandwich," replied an exasperated Page. "Great. I need a plan B. Any fast ideas you lunch meat moocher? No, don't answer. Just eat your humongous ham hoagie." Page opened the freezer. Nothing picnic-worthy stared back.

"I know. Take the cold sausage pizza," suggested helpful Betsy.

Page opened the pantry door. "You want me to feed Steve what he brought to us? Brilliant. Why didn't I think of that?"

"See? And you didn't want me to talk. You're all set."
Betsy plopped a dill pickle in her mouth.

Page looked heavenward. "I'm going to dress. Maybe an
idea of something to go with chips and pickles will come to me.
Pickles?" Page looked closer at the near-empty jar. "Geez, Betsy,
I'm down to a half bag of chips and brownies. You haven't eaten
the brownies yet, by any chance?"

Betsy's face reddened. "Only two. You're still good with
dessert. I'll make this up to you. Tonight, I'm delivering on
the duck and oxtails. We're having a green salad and roasted
rosemary potatoes…" Betsy noticed she was alone. She shrugged
and ate another pickle.

Dressed casually in jeans and a blue surfer's t-shirt with
the words, *Hang Ten*, Steve rang the doorbell.

"Come in." Betsy laid her bowling bag on the foyer's
bench.

"Nice Mermaid shirt." Steve grinned and walked toward
the living room. "Where's Page?"

"In her room, recovering from a meltdown. I ate your
picnic." Betsy hung her head.

"You ate our picnic? How did you manage—?"

"I'm a big eater, but there's something more worrying than
your lack of food. We've got Ralph threatening us. Page called
you. I'm jumpy as a Mexican jumping bean. This guy is bad to the
bone." Betsy came closer to thump Steve's chest. "Furthermore,
Mister Detective, I'm afraid to go bowl if this guy—"

Steve stepped back. "Stop the finger-pounding on your
neighbor. I know all about Ralph's visit. I left Page a message
this morning. Didn't she get it? Page? Can you please come out
here?" Steve hollered down the hallway.

Page wandered out, unable to hide her puffy eyes. Her
open floral cover-up showed a figure-flattering lavender bathing
suit underneath. Gold hoop earrings and deck shoes completed

the look. A smile was absent from Page's face. She stared at Steve and Betsy.

"What's with the red eyes?" asked a concerned Steve.

"I told you already. She had a meltdown. Plus, we suffer from hormones," Betsy explained, taking her plate to the sink.

"Okay. Both of you park it. Let's clear up some things." Steve waited for the women to grab a stool. "Let's start with ol' Ralph. Page, didn't you listen to my message?"

"No." Page's expression changed. "Oh my gosh, I turned my phone off this morning to have quiet time. What was your message?"

"I told you that I'd nabbed Ralph last night and not to worry. I saw him talking to you. When I pressed him — and I use that word loosely — he confessed to warning you. I'd planned to arrest him and Buck this morning for the shark poaching. However, his showing up at your house forced me to activate their room reservations at the police department earlier than I wanted. I woke up a grouchy Koch last night to apprehend Buck. Even if Buck and Ralph get out on bail, they won't bother you. They're in enough trouble and won't be looking for more. These types I know well."

Betsy's expression relaxed. "That's a huge relief. I hear Ina's car outside. This Mermaid has to dash. You two enjoy your sailing day." Betsy flew out the door.

"Page?" Steve moved closer. His hand tilted her chin to meet his eyes.

"Yeah?" Page sniffed. Maybe Betsy was right about hormones messing with her normally even-keeled personality. She stole a glance at Steve.

"Are you feeling better about Ralph? I promise that I won't let anything happen to you or Betsy." He released his hand and stood back, and waited.

"Yeah, I'm fine about Ralph. I'd been given the awareness

earlier that he wouldn't pose any real problem." Tears pooled in Page's eyes.

"I don't understand then. Why the tears?" Steve handed her a napkin.

Page hiccupped. "Betsy ate our picnic. All of it, except for the brownies and a half bag of chips. I don't know. Maybe there are some dill pickles left."

Steve broke into laughter. "I already heard about the picnic fixings. Betsy confessed to me right off. It's okay."

"No. It's not okay. I was supposed to make us a lovely picnic lunch, and all I can offer you is a cold pizza...that you brought." Page allowed him to dab away the tears. Why did he have to smell all manly? She finally understood what that meant.

He tossed the napkin in the trash. "Get your beach bag. We're going to stop at the Crab Shak. Velma will make us two oyster Po' Boys with all the trimmings. Bring those brownies. We've got fun to be had. It's time to *Carpe Diem*." Steve grinned and held open the door.

~*~

Onboard and feeling herself again, Page stowed their lunch and her belongings in the cabin. She adored sailing with Steve. He and *Carpe Diem* became one as soon as the sails unfurled and the wind grabbed them. Tying her hair back, she hurried to assume first-mate status.

"Just in time to take the wheel." Steve waved to a passing boat full of teenagers.

Page assumed her place. "I've got it. Ready those sails, 'O Captain! My Captain!'" she said, drawing from the famous poem by Walt Whitman.

Steve returned a smart salute and went to work.

Adjusting her sunglasses and baseball cap, Page focused on navigating while Steve secured loose rigging and readied the sails for when they entered open water. Two of the main allures for her to make Shell Isle a permanent home were the call of the ocean and her love for sailing. Once Honey Bees was buzzing with steady business, she'd entertain the idea of buying a small sailboat. "Ahoy, where we headed this afternoon?"

"To our favorite island, of course."

"Aye, aye. Calypso, the bewitching island." Page grinned, recalling her Greek mythology. With any luck, maybe she'd succeed at cajoling the medical examiner's report out of her Odysseus.

CHAPTER 15

"Hey, Page, I've got the food and drinks if you'll bring the towels and blanket." Steve stepped into the shallow water and noticed the small fish swimming around his ankles.

"Got them. Anything down there I don't want to encounter?" Page peered over the side. "You know I hate stingrays." She noticed that the water appeared the most beautiful iridescent aqua.

"Only a few small baitfish. Climb over. I'm starving." Steve reached for Page's hand to steady her. "Good?"

"Yep. You go ahead, just in case." Page stepped gingerly, watching for sand holes.

Calypso Island was tiny and uninhabited, which appealed to Steve and Page. One side had an impressive grouping of mangroves, whose roots entangled to resemble living sculptures. They always made time to admire them. Craving nature's company, they'd sit for an age in comfortable silence. Logging time together, sailing had drawn them closer over the past year. They moved carefully, navigating their relationship's waters, striving to keep things light and fun.

Now reclined on the blanket, Steve turned on his side to face Page. "Question for the mythology maven. Didn't Calypso keep poor Odysseus on the island for like seven years, promising him immortality?"

Page's eyes sparkled, matching the water droplets on her cheeks. "Yes, Calypso detained him. Don't you men know that you have to watch out for those nymph-types?" Page placed their empty lunch containers in a garbage sack and stretched out next to him.

"Oh, believe me, I am trying," answered Steve, with a wide grin.

"Very funny. Can we interrupt the Greek mythology chat for a murder solving chat?" Page turned on her stomach and absently sifted the white sand through her fingers.

Steve groaned. "You want to talk about murder here, around all this beauty?"

"Come on. Give your helpful and intuitive sleuth five minutes. What's your latest scoop? I know you arrested Buck and Ralph and expect them to get out on bail pretty quickly. Give me some little something to take home." Page batted her eyelashes for effect.

Steve's eyes took in Page's figure. "I'm lying next to a nymph."

"If you say so." Page sucked in a breath and dusted the sand off Steve's cheek.

"You're killing me. Don't do that again or…" Steve reached for Page.

"Behave yourself." Page pushed him back playfully, breaking the spell.

Steve sat up in a crossed-leg position. "Okay, I'm behaving, but not happy about it. Give me a moment to cool off." He stared at a seagull looking for a handout.

Page gave a coy nod and waited. She could use a moment to compose herself, too. She admonished herself for flirting with Steve. The whole playing with fire thing fit her actions. Getting burned at her age wasn't something Page wanted to court. She made eye contact with Steve and smiled. "Ready to proceed, Detective Tanner?"

Steve's expression changed to somber, and he nodded. "The report confirmed the obvious. Jake died by a nine-millimeter bullet piercing his heart's right ventricle. We've yet to identify the gun's owner or whereabouts. Here's where things get interesting. According to the forensic pathologist, Jake had advanced heart disease and could have died at any moment. The doctor told me this morning that it was a race to the finish line between the bullet and the disease, and the bullet won. Poor guy wasn't going to be around much longer."

"Yeah, poor guy, for sure. He's the kind of man everyone misses for a long time, too." Page paused and reflected on her words before continuing. "You've got more."

"Really? You want more info?" grinned Steve. "Bat those lashes again, nymph."

Page batted her lashes as fast as hummingbird wings.

"Stop. Stop. I'm putty." Steve reached into the cooler for a bottle of juice. "So, I researched those magic mushrooms from your Plant Hugger eavesdropping."

"Great. I forgot to do that. What did you discover?"

"They're psychedelic mushrooms and quite trendy to trip with, I hear. And, here I thought those colorful days of the sixties were behind us. Koch and I discussed doing a bust at Plant Hugger, but we need solid evidence."

"Which you don't have yet," Page affirmed. A gentle inkling rewarded her.

"Plus, Bert and Rosa are still murder suspects, and that crime carries more weight with us at the moment. Bert's possible side hustle can wait a few days."

"I say again. There's too much dirty dealing happening at Shell Isle. These folks don't fit the template of ideal residents." Page watched a nearby pelican snag a fish.

Steve's eyes followed hers. "That's his fourth score. The bird's got a monopoly on this fishing locale. And, yes, I agree about these lowlifes needing to relocate. I think we're going to help them do that soon." Steve's face wore a smirk.

"Anything on the cigarillo?" prodded Page. That remained

a critical piece of information to be gleaned.

"Not yet, which brings me my last bit of evidence. You'll like this." Steve paused.

Page's curiosity built. She reached over and slapped him on the shoulder. "Stop tormenting me. Tell me what I'll like, Detective."

"Besides me, you'll like my invitation to observe our interrogation of Ralph and Buck tonight. We'd appreciate knowing if you pick up on anything or get one of your tink— inklings. No doubt, Betsy's must come along, too."

"Yes, and, of course, we'll attend," exclaimed Page. She got on her knees and leaned over, hugging a surprised Steve.

"Whoa. I didn't see that coming. So, if I repeat the invitation, can I get a kiss?"

"Absolutely not. You got your thank you. To get a kiss, you'd need to deliver something pretty extraordinary," Page teased.

"Then, I'll make that my mission. How about a walk to explore Calypso's charms? We've got another thirty minutes before we should head back." Steve hopped up and extended his hand to Page. "Ma'am?"

Page allowed him to pull her up. "Exploring is my most favorite activity on the island." That was just a tiny white lie. It was her second-most favorite activity. Hugging Steve had become her new favorite. How old was she again? Sixteen going on fifty-two with raging hormones.

~*~

Steve hauled in the anchor, making ready to sail. He glanced at his diver's watch and then the weather radar. "Hey, you over there, untying the jib. Want me to take the long way back to the marina?"

Realizing she'd been focused on Steve's muscular biceps as he lifted the anchor, Page's face colored. "I...I would like...

yes," she sputtered out.

A knowing smile found Steve's mouth. "Want me to put my shirt on?"

"Suit yourself, Tanner." Page hid her embarrassment with the snippy reply. Why must she feel an attraction to a detective who missed nothing? She blamed it on her dumb kismet.

Within minutes, Steve had both sails billowing in the wind. Carpe Diem skipped across the white-capped waves like a young girl playing hopscotch. Page and Steve's exhilaration built with each breath as the sailboat gathered speed.

"So much for us taking the long way back," Page hollered.

Steve's leg wedged against the wheel while he tugged a line. "Yeah, Poseidon must want us home."

Sitting at the bow, Page draped her arms around the railing and tossed her head back. She licked the salt spray from her lips and acknowledged that sailing awakened her inner passion. Page's appreciation to Steve for giving her this day needed sharing. "You, at the helm, thank you for this…all of this." Page waved her arms in a wide arc, expressing joy. "Can we stay out here forever?"

Steve laughed. "My pleasure. How about I promise a sailing encore once we wrap this case?"

"You've incentivized me to solve this whodunit," Page answered.

"Now, those words I didn't need to hear. Want another lecture, Miss Drew?"

"Sure don't, Detective Tanner. Keep us on course."

"Oh, I plan to do that. Have no doubts there." Steve's wink signaled to Page that there was more to his reply.

~*~

Steve parked the SUV in his driveway and accompanied Page to Hibiscus and a waiting Betsy.

Page entered the cottage with Steve on her heels. "Hi,

Betsy. We're back from a fun—"

Betsy appeared. "Boy, am I ever glad you two decided to return to dry land. You're never going to believe what these heard." Betsy touched each ear.

"Try us, Mermaid," Steve answered. "By the way, did you all win?"

"Of course, we won. Mermaids possess enchantments." Betsy followed Page and Steve to the kitchen. Would you please stand in one place and listen? I've got a scoop."

Page poured three glasses of iced tea for them. "We're listening."

Betsy sucked in a breath. "For starters, you'll never guess who bowled next to us?"

"Nope, we won't because you're going to tell us." Steve took a sip of his drink.

"Rosa and friends, that's who." Betsy tipped her tea glass and swallowed.

"Small town. Small world," added Page. "And?"

"And, it seems Jake's will reading happened this morning. Our Rosa was treating everyone to beers and celebrating. She and her dad are sole heirs to Jake's estate."

Steve's face grew thoughtful. "Sounds like Bert and Rosa have what they each want now. Bert's debt is wiped out, and whatever dirt Jake had on him went to his grave. I'm still feeling confident it had to do with Bert's drug dealing. As for Rosa, her wants center around immature, immediate gratification and not much else. Do I hear agreement?"

"I agree," voiced Page. "Maybe you'll gain more insight from reading Jake's journal. If nothing else, it might confirm Bert's magic mushroom business."

Betsy chimed in. "Don't forget that journal led you to Buck and Ralph's shindig and hot kissing Page on the dock."

Page smacked Betsy's arm. "Enough with the hot kissing

remarks."

"I don't think it's enough," teased Steve. "I like the reminder."

Betsy laughed. "See Page? I told you I know my men."

Page threw her hands up in the air. "That's it. I'm going to take a shower. Thanks for the sailing fun. See you later, Detective."

"Make it a cold one." Betsy hollered to Page's back.

Steve placed his empty glass in the sink. "We may have pushed that teasing envelope too —"

Betsy shook her head. "Nah, she's good. My dinner will gain forgiveness."

"If you say so. Do you have anything else for me? Otherwise, I'm going to cut out?"

"I did hear Rosa tell her boyfriend that Bert was making some secretive plans. There's something kooky acting with that girl." Betsy shrugged. "Anyway, they finished their game shortly after we arrived."

"Good job gaining more information, Mermaid. Be sure to ask Page about my evening's invitation for you two. It should prove interesting. See you later." Steve disappeared outside.

CHAPTER 16

Page and Betsy arrived at the police station, brimming with eagerness to watch Buck and Ralph's interrogation. The unimpressive one-story red brick structure didn't reflect the capable people who worked inside. It was known around Shell Isle that Detectives Koch and Tanner proved a daunting team against any sap who had the misfortune to occupy their grilling hot seat.

An officer escorted Page and Betsy into a small room with a two-way mirror. The walls, painted a depressing gray, were meant to encourage a short visit. Four uncomfortable metal chairs circled a wood table that had seen its share of anger nicks. In a corner, a coat rack held a faded Yankees baseball cap. The single fluorescent light fixture cast an unflattering pallor to all occupants and set the mood.

Betsy looked around the room. "I still don't like the juju here. Someone needs to smudge it with sage."

"I know." Page's expression pretended to care. "Why don't you suggest smudging to Koch? I hear him talking in the hall."

The door opened, showing Koch's face. "Evening, my favorite busybodies. Happy to see you settled in the observation room. Do you need anything before the show begins?"

Betsy chose to ignore the unflattering nickname. "As a matter of fact, yes. This place has exceptionally bad juju. It needs a sage smudging stick to clear the negative energy. Can one of the officers see if The Stick Emporium is open? If you bring me—"

Page's hands covered her face. She wasn't sure whether

she felt more embarrassed or amused.

"Ms. Ross, I haven't understood a word you said, and that's probably a good thing. I'll check in again later. Maybe the ability to speak your native tongue will return. Evening, Ms. Wright." Koch closed the door with a chuckle.

Moments later, Steve poked his head inside the room. "Practicing witchcraft, I hear, Betsy? If you brought any abracadabra, send it to Ralph and Buck for truthful answers."

Betsy gave a huff.

"Good luck," Page tossed out. "Fingers crossed, we'll have some valuable insights to offer if Betsy's wand fails to deliver."

Steve flashed a quick grin and closed the door.

Betsy turned toward Page. "I swear. No one appreciates my many, many talents. If not for my cooking and recent baking genius, I'd never hear a compliment."

Page forced her expression to go sober. "Ah, Betsy, I pledge to deliver you more compliments starting right now. Ralph and Buck have entered the interrogation room. Time to dazzle me with your keen observation skills."

Betsy nodded and shifted her chair to watch.

Koch and Steve joined the two prisoners. Steve placed two files on a table and adjusted his belt badge. Koch chose to lean against the door, affording him a view of the hallway and, more critical, blocking the exit.

"Let's begin. I've turned on the recorder. The time is six-forty on July seventh. Present are Detective Steve Tanner, Detective Randall Koch, and two suspects, Buck Lester and Ralph Owen." Koch nodded to Steve.

"We've charged you with shark poaching. Listed here are various other laws you broke, and the Feds will deal with those charges at the appropriate time. For now, maybe we can elevate your criminal reputations and push you into the big time. You've been Mirandized regarding Jake's murder case, and you've waived having an attorney present. Is this correct?"

"We don't need an attorney. We know our rights and what we should and shouldn't say. This is all bogus anyway." Ralph's red face testified to an elevated blood pressure.

Steve nodded. "Duly recorded. Ralph. I understand you've made bail and plan to forfeit your cell reservation tonight. Is that correct?"

"Yeah, I'm outta here once we get done with this nonsense." Ralph didn't bother to hide his condescending tone.

Page tapped her cousin's hand. "First mistake by Ralph."

"Pardon me? Did I understand you to say nonsense?" Steve's voice went icy.

"Yeah, he said it. I heard him," Buck replied, with a sneer.

Koch abandoned his corner. He bent down inches from Buck's face. "Get this, wise guy. Your mouth only opens to answer a question directed at you. Remember, you're a guest with us, and I get to choose who you bunk with tonight since your boyfriend here is abandoning you. And, right now, I think you and Diesel will hit it off."

Buck stared at the mirror. "Who's Diesel?"

Koch laughed. "Wait and see. He's going to take to you. Steve, sorry for the interruption."

Steve slid a chair to face Ralph and sat. "Let's get to it. Do you smoke?"

"Why do you ask if I smoke?" Ralph fidgeted in his chair.

"Listen up. I get to ask the questions. If you've got any functioning brain cells, you'll answer my questions starting *now*," shouted Steve.

Betsy sighed. "That Steve's such a hottie. Lucky you."

"Shush." Page secretly agreed with her cousin, noticing Steve's broad shoulders. Then, an almost imperceptible inkling interrupted.

"Okay, I smoke sometimes. So what?" Ralph's fingers

tapped on the table.

"Koch, did he volley another question to me?"

"Depends on the inflection. Might have been a statement. Ralph?" asked Koch.

Ralph exhaled loudly. "Statement. It was a statement."

Steve reached for a file and opened it. "What do you smoke? Cigarettes, cigars, a pipe?"

"Yes." Ralph sent a threatening glower to Buck.

Steve took a few steps back as anger bubbled inside him. "This is your last chance to cooperate and answer my questions fully. You've managed to awaken my last nerve, and that's never a good thing."

Koch poured a cup of water and handed it to Ralph. "It's never a good thing. Here. Wet your whistle and answer the detective what you like to smoke."

Ralph drained the contents while staring at the mirror. He handed the cup to Koch, who disappeared out the door.

"I hate it when the bad guys look in that mirror. Creeps me out." Betsy scooted her chair further away.

"Yeah, it can feel unsettling, but we're protected. Listen, Ralph's talking."

"I don't feel inclined to answer that particular question. Do you have another?" Ralph glanced at the clock.

"We're done. That's strike three. I count your 'so what' as strike two. Excuse me for a minute while I decide if I'm charging you tonight." Steve walked out.

Koch came toward Steve. "The cup is on the way to the lab. What's next?"

Steve rubbed his neck. "Since I can't rough him up, should we book Ralph on something or let him go? You make the call, Koch."

"I say, let him go. Maybe he'll mess up and give us a solid lead or a reason to charge him with Jake's murder," Koch answered.

"I concur. He didn't take his cooperative pills. And, right now, I'm not in the mood to play in his head. Before you tell him, give me a moment with Page."

Steve entered the room where the women waited. "Have any ideas for me?"

Page nodded. "I did get an inkling, but it's not tied to Ralph's smoking habits. Besides, you scored the cup for DNA tests. I sense it's smart to wait until you get that piece of information and deal from a place of strength with the jerk."

"Hello? I agree if anyone cares."

Steve chuckled. "Betsy, thanks for the comic retort. To show my appreciation, I'm treating you and Page to banana splits later."

Betsy's face lit. "Hear that, Page? Splits. Can I have them put—"

"Yes," Steve answered. "Page? Anything else before I work Buck over?"

"My inkling is that Buck wants to talk about Ralph." Page's expression grew thoughtful. "He's already signaled you by trying to answer Ralph's question. Go open that door wide and see what information walks through. He's carrying a burdening load."

Steve saluted her and left.

"I still hate those annoying smart salutes of his," Page said to Betsy.

"He's an ex-Seal. I think they're sexy." Betsy set her fan in motion. "If you hadn't declared me on a man-free sabbatical, I'd ask Steve to introduce me to one of his friends."

"You need that sabbatical and a break from dating. Your track record is lousy. Besides, I'm not convinced you and Mickey aren't dallying," responded Page. "Mickey's everywhere. Let me count the places. We get honey from him. He works at our favorite coffee house, not to mention he's part-time at the bowling alley. I see lots of opportunities for dallying, Betsy Ross, lover of all men."

"Point made, but you've got me all wrong. Mickey's not my type." Betsy wrinkled her nose. "Look, Steve's back in the room."

"He's going to score off Buck. Here we go." Page turned to the glass.

Koch started the recorder and introduced the interrogation.

Steve pulled up a chair. "Okay, Buck, maybe you know how to give straight answers to questions. Let's find out. Do you smoke? And, if yes, what?"

Buck cleared his throat and assumed a relaxed posture. "I don't smoke, but I confess that I drink too much beer."

Steve gave a curt nod. "Do you own a gun?"

"Yes, I'm a big believer in the Second Amendment. The world's crazy." Buck shifted in the chair, causing the metal to pop from his large frame.

"What caliber bullets do you shoot?" asked Steve, making notes.

Buck took a deep breath and puffed his pigeon chest. "Nine millimeters."

"Now, that's interesting to me. Want to know why?" Steve put his pen down and made eye contact with Buck.

"Sure, if you want to tell me." The edginess to Buck's tone appeared.

"That's the size bullet our examiner pulled out of Jake West. We're going to need your weapon. Where is it?" Steve motioned to Koch.

"It's home." Buck wiped the perspiration from his upper lip.

Steve's tone grew forceful. "Good answer. We've got your keys and a warrant. Tell me where the gun is so my officer can retrieve it?"

"Nightstand drawer, but listen, I fired it recently. Ralph and I went target shooting."

"How convenient. Don't you agree, Koch?" Steve glanced over at the other detective, wearing a somber expression.

"I agree. As a matter of fact, it kind of gets my hackles up." Koch gulped his coffee, staring Buck down.

"Look, guys, I see where this is going, but I didn't kill Jake. You forget I was on my boat that night working on the damn engine. I let Ralph convince me to buy that piece of —"

Steve stood. "Let's get back on track. You've got a good alibi, but that doesn't mean you aren't involved somehow. You and Ralph are joined at the hip. Koch, perhaps we should afford Buck the opportunity to help us."

"Good idea if you think he's got anything of value. We might put in a good word with the prosecutor when the time comes."

"What do you say, Buck? Tell us what you know about Jake and who wanted him out of the way, and we'll help you."

"Say, maybe I know some things. Will you protect me? How can I trust you to make things go easier? Make it worth my while to cooperate, and I might —"

Steve's expression shifted to anger. "Pay close attention to me. You have zero bargaining power. Zero. You're going down for the shark poaching. How far down depends if you're involved with Jake's death."

"I'm telling you, I've got nothing to do with Jake's killing. I liked him. He helped me out a time or two." Buck pulled out a handkerchief and wiped his forehead. "Did you guys turn up the AC thermostat?"

"No, but I like the idea," Koch replied with a scoff. "Seems to be working on you."

Steve stared at Buck, allowing the silence to worry the

charter boat captain.

"Will you protect me and tell the DA I cooperated in another case? I got the information you need."

Steve nodded and sat back down. "I will if it's something we don't already know. Let's hear it, and then we'll decide."

Buck sucked in a breath. "Okay, okay. Ralph smokes cigarillos."

"Go on," said Steve.

"He shoots nine-millimeter bullets, too, but his gun isn't registered. Ralph wouldn't get approved to own a gun," supplied Buck.

"Why is that?" Steve's eyebrow raised with interest.

"For starters, Ralph Owen isn't his real name. You dig deep enough, and I bet you'll find that out. He's one bad hombre from Central America."

Koch nodded to Steve. "Well, that explains the abbreviated background report on Owen."

Buck's demeanor shifted to confidence. "See? That's solid proof that I'm a straight shooter."

"You might want to rephrase that declaration, seeing how we're talking to you about Jake being shot," suggested Koch.

"Man, don't take things so literally." Buck eyed Koch, unsnapping his holster.

Steve sat down next to Buck. "Keep talking."

"Yeah, well, I only got involved with Ralph because of some poker debts I'd managed to rack up. Ralph told me if I'd fish some sharks a few nights, my money worries would end. I held that back when you arrested me because I knew if Ralph got wind of me talking, he or the goons he's working for would find a way to take me out."

Steve leaned forward in his chair. "You know what, Buck? I believe you about Ralph and his friends. You've tangled with a group that sees killing as a sport. What else?"

Buck coughed, looked around the room, and dropped his voice. "About a week before Jake got snuffed, Ralph and I were at the dock when Jake visited us. Jake suspected we were doing something illegal, and he swore he'd figure it out soon enough if we didn't stop. He lectured us on how our types ruined the good reputation of other charter captains. Even though he acted all mighty, I knew he was right." Buck rubbed his face. "Can I have something to drink?"

"I'll go," offered Koch.

"So, what did you say to Jake when he accused you?" Steve picked up his pen and wrote.

"I told Jake that he should stay out of our business. I mean, I didn't want the guy hurt. As I said, I liked him." Buck leaned back in his chair.

"Point made. What did Ralph tell Jake?" Steve glanced at his file.

Buck shut his eyes. "That's where things turned south. Ralph got hot. He warned Jake to quit sniffing around, or a bullet would find him. He got in Jake's face and said he'd killed before for less reasons. Jake backed down that night, but I guess he'd said too much to Ralph."

Detective Koch returned and handed Buck a cola.

Betsy's hand fan was going at high speed. "I could use one of those refreshing drinks. That Buck is one rotund, loud canary."

Page nodded. "Keep thinking about the delicious banana split waiting. I think Buck's about done singing."

Steve waited for Buck to put the can down. "So, I want to make sure I've got things straight. Ralph, or whatever his real name is, enjoys cigarillos. He owns an unregistered gun that shoots nine-millimeter shells, and he threatened to kill or have Jake killed if he didn't stop nosing around. Is that correct, Buck?"

"That's right." Buck hesitated. "I've got a piece of advice if you want it?" Buck downed the rest of the can's contents, waiting for Steve's reply.

"I'll bite. What's that?"

Buck leaned in toward Steve. "Now that Ralph's out on bail, he's going to bolt. You want him. You better grab him because you'll never see his face in court. I lay odds he's out of the country by tomorrow night. But listen, man, I still need protection from that gang left behind."

Steve signaled Koch. "We'll see if we can't activate Ralph a new reservation with us. That's helpful information. Are we done?"

"Yeah, that's everything. Are you going to protect me?" Buck's voice cracked.

"If we see evidence that you need protection, you'll have it. Are you agreeable to testifying to what you told us?" Steve closed the file.

Koch interrupted Buck's reply. "I bring happy news to Mr. Lester. Someone has posted your bail. Unless Steve wants to charge you, I guess we'll do the paperwork and release you."

"Well, Buck Lester, it seems like this is your lucky day." Steve's smile didn't reach his eyes.

"More like my unlucky day," replied a worried Buck.

"Koch, get him out of here." Steve walked toward the door and pivoted. "Buck, make sure you don't bolt with Ralph. The consequences won't be pretty."

"What about my safety?" asked Buck, his voice still shaky.

"Find yourself a nice hidey-hole to crawl in. Koch will assign an officer to keep a check on you. Make sure you give him that weapon." Steve shut the door.

"Guess it's a wrap." Page massaged her temples.

"Oh, goody, banana split time." Betsy grabbed her tote bag. "Let's get out of this claustrophobic room. We can meet Steve in the waiting area."

"Okay, let's go." Page's eyes widened with concern, seeing

a familiar face in the lobby. A face she'd hoped never to see again.

CHAPTER 17

"Betsy, follow me outside." Page hurried through the door.

"Why out here? It's hot. It's muggy. And I'm flashing." Betsy looked around. "What'd I miss now?"

"I couldn't risk that man in the waiting area seeing me."

"What, man? Why is that a problem?" Betsy looked confused.

"Because he was the third guy involved in the fin rustling with Ralph and Buck. Don't forget that we know that Ralph saw me snooping on them because he showed up at Hibiscus. Maybe this guy noticed me, too."

"Uh-oh." Betsy stole a glance at the police entrance. "That's not good."

"What's not good?" Page moved further into the planter and immediately felt something crawling up her leg.

"Your man stepped out for a smoke," Betsy whispered. "I hope he doesn't see us."

"Geez, where's Steve? We need to leave." Page slapped her leg.

"I'm right here. Do I want to know why you are standing in the shrub planter stomping one foot?" Steve looked on, amused.

Betsy bobbed her head like a cork. "Tell him, Page, so that we can go to the dairy bar. I'm hot enough to combust." Betsy began walking toward the parking lot.

Page stumbled behind Steve, smacking at her leg. "The third fin pilfering Musketeer was in your building, and I didn't want to risk him recognizing me."

Steve opened the door for Page. "Glad you caught sight

of him. I'll find out why he was there. And the hopping and slapping?" he asked, grinning.

"Something was crawling up my leg. It probably lived in those bushes." Page caught his expression. "Just drive."

"I second that," said Betsy from the backseat. "That is if anyone cares to hear what I think."

"We care," said Page and Steve in unison.

~*~

Steve carried a tray of three banana splits to where Page and Betsy were sitting. "Here you go, ladies."

"Yum," said Page, scooping in her first bite. "Finally, something good tonight," she mumbled to herself.

"Perfection," echoed Betsy, rearranging her toppings.

"Um, Betsy, heads up; the manager is coming over to meet you." Steve flashed a grin to Page.

"Why is the manager — hello there." Betsy looked up at the man wearing an apron.

"Hello. Excuse me, but I had to meet the woman who ordered a banana split with — "

"So much creativity?" supplied Betsy.

"That wasn't my word, but it'll do." The owner nodded at Steve. "So, is your split to your liking?"

"Since you asked, it could use a few more dollops of strawberry sauce and coffee crumbles."

"I'll send out those dollops post haste. Enjoy your ice cream, folks, and stop in again."

"Wasn't he nice? Next visit, maybe I could offer some sundae topping combinations for his menu? You know, spice things up?" Betsy swirled the walnut syrup around in her dish.

Page and Steve exchanged amused looks.

"I know. You want to discuss the case. Go ahead," sighed Betsy. "Ruin a perfectly good dessert."

"There are two questions that keep nagging me," stated

Page. "Who's worried enough to bail out Buck? And why?"

Betsy grew animated. "I can answer the last one. I'm guessing they don't want him talking. I wonder what made me say they?"

Steve jumped in. "I'll take this. You're correct in saying 'they.' I'm betting Ralph and company see Buck as a problem to remedy, and the sooner, the better. That's why I assigned a plainclothes officer to watch Buck. We're looking for Ralph right now. I'm concerned he's hiding or worse, preparing to flee. Right now, Koch and I believe him to be the number one murder suspect. Would you agree, Page?"

"I agree that Ralph has the means, motive, and opportunity. The lab report on his DNA and cigarillo carries weight, but so does finding the gun matching the bullet fired."

Betsy shoved her empty dish to the side and rejoined the conversation. "You'll have Buck's weapon soon enough to check, but that's going to prove a dead end. He's got an alibi. If you want to know what I think—"

Page laughed. "We do. Tell us more, Betsy."

"Thank you. I believe Buck got in over his head and realized too late that Ralph wasn't the answer to his troubles, but ultimately the cause of them." Betsy's self-assurance was mirrored on her face. "Look, chickadees. His gambling debt seems minor in comparison to what and who Buck's entangled with now. He's nothing but a blusterer and doesn't have the mettle to cope." Betsy sat back in her seat, looking satisfied.

Steve engaged. "You made some valid points, Ms. Ross. Also, the Buck that we interviewed tonight acted cooperative and scared for his well-being. He exhibited zero nervousness being questioned over Jake's murder."

Betsy nodded her agreement. "That's my view, too. Buck's not worried about a murder charge since he worked on his boat that night. So that still leaves—"

"Ralph, of course, as a primary suspect, and Bert, Rosa, and Eleanor are tied," finished Page. "Currently, we're nowhere there unless you want to count the possibility of selling magic mushrooms for a murder motive. That gives us Bert as a strong contender, but I remain cloudy over Rosa." Page chose not to share her afternoon inkling about returning to Plant Hugger. "Somehow, we need to discover if Jake had something of consequence on Eleanor."

"You're right," said Steve. "In fact, both of you bring fresh insights into this case, which I appreciate."

"Yeah, we're mega-talented at sleuthing." Betsy fluffed her hair. "We carry clout."

Steve chuckled. "Come on, you gifted ones. I know what the next couple of hours are asking of me."

"What does that even mean?" asked Betsy. She waved goodbye to the manager.

"It means I need to get back into Jake's journal. With any luck, that information holds the motives for our motley bunch," answered Steve.

~*~

Aunt Tilly's cuckoo clock greeted Page and Betsy inside Hibiscus.

Betsy counted the bird's appearances out his little door. "Nine cuckoos. I thought you were getting rid of that annoying bird and his home?"

Page chuckled. "Oh, I tried. I couldn't get the thing to release from the wall. I swear Aunt Tilly's protecting him. For now, the clock lives to cuckoo another day."

"Stupid clock." Betsy sauntered down the hall. "I'm going to enjoy a nice soak, which will help me unwind. Our day off felt like anything but, and tomorrow, I'll welcome our time at Honey Bees, where life is sweet. Get it? I'm talented at—"

"I get it, and yes, your talents are boundless. I'm quite in awe." Page answered.

"Humph. I'm not sure if you're sincere or teasing. No matter. I know what I know. I'm a woman of many talents." Betsy began humming a song only she would recognize.

Page sat reflecting on her gift of intuition. Helping to make things right for someone wronged had blossomed within her as a teenager. The inklings and nudges served as her guidance. She'd tried early on to ignore the sensations, only to find they increased. A wiser Page had learned to acknowledge and act at the appropriate time. She expected the nudge would come soon enough to visit Plant Hugger, but for the next couple of waking hours, she'd claim the solitude of her bedroom. She flicked off the living room lamp.

A rapid sounding knock came from her front door. Through the glass, Page saw Steve's face. "You again and so soon. It's enough to make a girl's head swoon—"

"Hurry. Get your handbag and tell Betsy you're leaving with me. I need your tinklings to start working fast," instructed a breathless Steve.

"Okay, give me thirty seconds. You can use that time to practice saying, "Page gets inklings." She scribbled a note to Betsy and left it taped to her bedroom door. There wasn't time for questions or a fresh lipstick application.

~*~

Steve drove his SUV at Mach speed toward a destination. His weary face gave nothing away, but his words told the story. "Koch, I've got Page next to me and able to hear our exchange. What's their last location?"

"Hello, Page. We're hoping you can help us out here," Koch said.

"I'll sure try once I know why I'm on this goose chase." Page grabbed the armrest as Steve took a hard left.

"Koch, I need that location."

"Right. It's a black van traveling north on Ocean View. I've dispatched two nearby patrol cars. Get back to me if you're able to have eyes on the van. Stay in stealth."

"Roger. I'm a couple of miles from Ocean. The officers will beat me there." Steve disconnected the call. "Okay, Miss Drew, our plainclothes cop watching Ralph called into Koch. He said Ralph and three goons were heading out of town, but that one stayed behind. The officer had to choose who to tail, and he correctly picked Ralph."

Page frowned, taking in the latest news. "What do you need from me?"

"Hang on. I have to check something out." Steve pulled the vehicle over and grabbed his cell phone.

Page closed her eyes, hoping to gain any insight. Within seconds, she experienced a rare occurrence. Two nudges came back to back. Page gulped air as the sensations eased her toward the intuiting piece. Now, she was ready to help. "Um, Steve, I may have something for you."

"Great. One sec." He finished typing and turned in the seat to face her. "Talk to me."

"Call the officer watching Buck. It's time to get him someplace safe. The man who stayed behind drew the short straw. He's coming for Buck and soon." Page released a breath and touched her temple. She felt the first migraine pang, as Steve called Koch.

"Listen, Page says we've got to get Buck out of his apartment yesterday. The guy who stayed behind is going to take out our star witness."

"I'm on it," Koch said and disconnected the call.

Steve turned back to Page. "Have I told you lately how incredible you are?" His eyes admired the woman who sat next to him.

"Define lately." Her heart felt all fluttery.

Steve's cell phone chimed and broke the moment. "I'm here."

"I thought you'd like to know that the officer already hustled Buck away. He'd noticed a black van earlier parked outside. That sighting got Buck jumpy."

"Give that plainclothes cop a fat raise. Got more for me?" Steve passed a couple enjoying a late evening ride in their convertible.

"Yeah, Buck insists he'll be safe on his boat. I told the officer to stay close to him tonight."

"Good. Anything else?" Steve held out a couple of their favorite mints and offered one to Page.

"Yes, with all this drama unfolding, I forgot to tell you it was one of the goons who paid Buck's bail. That proves they wanted him. For now, we're left with the quartet on the move."

"Roger, Koch. I've pulled over. Depending on what Page tells me, I'm probably traveling their way again. I'll let you know. Keeping her safe tops my list. Out."

"So, Miss Drew, what's next? I'm at your beck and call, which is a place I seldom reside with any woman." Steve grinned.

Page returned the grin. "Is that a fact? Let me savor my lofty position for a few seconds, Detective Tanner." Page touched a button and adjusted her seat higher. "Wow, lofty is good, but alas, time for us to mosey."

Steve put the vehicle in drive. "Are we trying to catch up with our bandits on Ocean View?"

"Nope, you're dropping me at Hibiscus. My work is done for this night."

"Got it. That's a relief." Steve turned the vehicle around. "Then what?"

"Then you're going to the airport. Ralph's become a special delivery to the bad guys in another country," Page replied.

"Do tell. It couldn't happen to a nicer guy. He's a real

prince, that one." Steve's words were laced with sarcasm.

"Let's just say our Ralph isn't going on this trip willingly. He knows what fate awaits him down in Central America. Oh, and you'll need backup."

"Yes, ma'am." Steve gave a salute. "That was my next move." Steve touched Page's hand. "Have I told you lately how —"

"As a matter of fact, that's a resounding no, but I'm giving you a raincheck to expound under better circumstances. Call Koch." Page looked out the window at the night sky. Dark clouds were gathering.

CHAPTER 18

The early morning rain kept a steady beat on the cottage's metal roof. Page stretched and stared at the ceiling. Hearing Betsy rattling around in her bedroom reminded her of two things. First, she owed Betsy an account of last night's outing. Second, Honey Bees' display window awaited baked delectables. Page thought about their quaint shop and what it offered, and despite feeling sleep-deprived, happiness wrapped around her. She dressed quickly and went to find Betsy.

"Whatcha doing on the porch and not in the kitchen?" Page teased.

"I've had my time in the kitchen. You missed out," Betsy put down a cooking magazine.

Dodging a Betsy breakfast meant the day held promise, thought Page. "I'm grabbing a yogurt and will sit with you. Before we leave for Honey Bees, I need to catch you up on my—"

"On your late date with Dreamboat. Spare me the details." Betsy watched Barnacle chase a bird in his backyard.

"It wasn't that kind of date," said a returning Page. She filled Betsy in on the particulars, eliminating the inkling that she needed to return to Plant Huggers. "So, that's your morning briefing. I guess we should leave a bit early for the shop. Remember, Ina isn't coming in until after lunch, which means you and the mixing bowls—"

Betsy popped up like a jack-in-the-box. "Oh my gosh, Ina's bridge club meets this morning, and Daisy can't work because of some workshop she's attending. It completely slipped my mind that we fly solo. We'd better hurry." Betsy grabbed her keys. "It's my day to drive."

~*~

The two cousins entered Honey Bees and busily set about their list of tasks. Page focused on enhancing the cheerful vibe out front, while baker Betsy woke up the mixer and her creativity. In the short time since opening the shop, both women had discovered their niche. What mattered most was that Honey Bees provided a kind of sweet essence to every customer who made a purchase.

Page felt growing anticipation, thinking of upcoming holidays and how Honey Bees could meet their customers' needs. She smiled and jotted some inspirational ideas into a notebook hidden in a drawer.

"Page? I need your hands, now," hollered Betsy.

"I'm here." Page took stock of the kitchen. Ceramic bowls full of batter lined up like sentinels awaited their mission. Two timers chattered while cooling muffins on racks welcomed a drizzle. "How can I help?"

"Squeeze the orange blossom honey icing on the scones and then—" Betsy's eyes scanned the room. "Oh, no. I forgot the fresh flowers to decorate. I left them on the porch."

Page dribbled the icing along the scone tops, creating a free-form floral design. "Don't worry. You can bring the flowers tomorrow. How's this look to your discerning eye?"

Betsy came over. "Wow, that design looks amazing. You created petals." Betsy studied her cousin's face. "You've discovered another gift. With my charmed honey recipes and your artistic divining, Honey Bees will soon be all the buzz."

Page laughed. "I admit your puns are improving, and thanks for the compliment. Right back at ya, baker of enchantments."

"Still, I wanted to make use of my flowers today." Betsy's lower lip made a pout. "Oh well, time to open for business. Here, take these trays of Ina's defrosted goodies. I'll bring the warm muffins and scones."

Having finished arranging the morning's pastries and cakes, Page heard the bell jingle. Surprise flickered in her eyes as she watched the young woman approach. The powers that be were orchestrating this encounter.

"So, this is your place." Rosa's eyes scanned the shop before returning to Page. "Here are some fresh blooms for today's decorating." Rosa placed a container on the counter and lifted the lid for Page to see.

"What a pleasant surprise to see you again, and thank you for the petals." Page glanced at the contents. "Oh, they're lovely. Betsy will be ecstatic because she left home without her flowers this morning."

"Yes, you have violets and bee balm." Rosa's expression softened as she stroked the blooms.

"Bee balm. That's fitting for Honey Bees. I've never seen that shade of red in a flower. Please, you must pick something from the baked goods display as our thank you. Choose anything at all."

"Okay, let me see..." Rosa bent over and peered into the glass. "Hmm, I want one of your scones with the orange blossom honey."

"Excellent choice. They just came from the oven. I'm putting two in the bag." Page smiled. "Here you go, Rosa. Enjoy."

"Thanks." Rosa hesitated. "Do you plan to get the hibiscus bush that dimwitted Ray forgot to load? You should, you know."

"Funny, you should ask. I planned to stop by Plant Hugger after we close at four. Will you be working? I'd love to hear what you think about Betsy's latest scone recipe." Page waved to a new customer.

"Yeah, come find me in the annuals greenhouse. I'm trying to get the plants ready for customers' gardens before I cut out of

Shell." Rosa moved to a display of honey almonds and touched the jars.

Page played dumb. "Cut out of Shell Isle? Do you have something wonderful planned?"

The customer approached Page. "I've decided on my order."

Rosa slipped out the door, leaving Page's question unanswered.

Thirty minutes ticked by before Page got a break from customers. She hurried to the kitchen. "Betsy, guess what the plant fairy brought you?"

"Some help?"

"No, silly, petals for decorating." Page waved the container in the air. "Come see."

Betsy ambled over and lifted the lid. "Are these violets? Can you eat violets? Who knew?"

"The other flowers are called bee balm. Cool name, huh?" Page laid some of the blossoms on a dishtowel.

"Yes, cool, but who's my plant fairy?" asked a curious Betsy.

Page went shoulder to shoulder to Betsy and leaned in. "None other than Rosa."

"She came to Honey Bees?" Betsy's expression mirrored surprise.

"She did and left with two of your orange blossom scones as a thank you. Happy decorating." Page scurried away.

~*~

At high noon, Ina breezed into Honey Bees with an air of gossip following her to the kitchen. "Come hither, my Bees. Gather around the marble pastry counter. I bring fascinating tidings from my bridge club meeting." Ina's brown eyes danced with delight as she motioned Betsy and Page to join her.

Page stole a glance out front. "No customers at the moment,

so hurry and spill these tidings."

Betsy slid Ina a glass of tea. "Thank the baking gods you're here. It's been crazy. My rolling pin arm is screaming."

"Ah, Mermaid, I'm sorry—"

Page shook her head at her cousin's flair for drama. "Ignore her. She's fine. Bring forth the tidings."

Ina took a sip of her tea and perched on the metal stool. "So, you know Eleanor is in my bridge club, but she doesn't always attend because of her many mayor's wife duties." Ina placed her hand across her forehead. "As mystery-solving karma would have it, today she shows up at my house, full of herself as always. Such a klafte, that one. Oy."

"What's a klafte?" asked Betsy.

"Sorry, in Hebrew, it means naughty one or bitch. You choose," clucked Ina. "Anyway, I'd dashed out to my herb garden to pick mint for the lemonade. I find Eleanor tucked behind my trellis, talking on her cell phone with the speaker turned up. She's got her own brand of honey, and it's male."

"No, kidding?" Betsy's eyes grew as large as the pie tin she was drying. "She's got a side of honey. My gossip gene is awakened. What else?"

Ina laughed. "Let me tell you. It sounded like they were plotting some getaway because she kept asking how much money he planned to bring. His answer must have thrilled her. She agreed to rendezvous at the airport Thursday night. Good stuff, huh? What do you think about my scoop, Bees?"

"You sure got the lowdown on that klaf—" Betsy faltered.

"Klafte," supplied Ina.

Page nodded. She wondered if Jake's talk with Eleanor had to do with this dalliance. It had to. The mayor's wife must have caught a bigger money fish.

Ina clapped her hands. "I'm not done. Listen up. There's more. I, Ina Funk, scored the name of the man Eleanor's *in flagrante delicto* with."

Betsy's mouth dropped open. "Tell us."

"Get out your fan, Betsy. You're going to need it. I'll give you a hint. He's tall, blond, blue-eyed, and a bad boy to all women." Ina paused. "It's Bert West."

"Bert West? The Plant Hugger's owner, Bert West?" repeated Page.

"Bad boy Bert, huh? I didn't know he had that kind of reputation. How did I not know this?" exclaimed Betsy.

"Because you're on hiatus from men." Page shook her head.

"I hate, hate, hate this hiatus." Betsy activated her fan.

"Ina, you brought home the gold. This information has real value to our case." Page hugged their friend. She'd have to process this revelation later. "There goes the bell. Have Betsy show you our latest decorating inspiration."

~*~

While Ina and Betsy baked and laughed in the kitchen, Page allowed her creative side full reign in the shop. She had an objective that perhaps could tap into Daisy's interests and abilities. In the storage room, Page was engaged in a battle of strength with an antique solid walnut bookcase that refused to budge. "You're not going to win this round," she said to the piece of furniture.

"I'm not so sure about that," came a familiar male voice from behind. "Where do you want it?"

"Hi there, Detective. Your timing is perfect." Page grinned. "I want the shelf unit out front, but it's super heavy. Do you think? Why, yes, you can. Now, that's clever." Page watched Steve shove heavy cardboard under the four legs. "I'll get the door." Page watched Steve slide the unit into the retail area.

"This sucker weighs six tons. Where's it going?" Steve halted and took a breath.

"Over in the far corner, against the brick wall." Page bustled ahead and pointed.

"Okay. Done." Steve stepped back, admiring the wood. "You don't see this quality of walnut anymore. Nice piece of furniture."

"I agree." Page touched the wood. "We discovered it hidden behind a ton of old throw-away boxes and a jumble of gardening relics. Now I know the role it plays at Honey Bees."

Steve leaned against the counter, taking in the shop. "Shell Isle is fortunate to have Honey Bees and its two owners. This place looks even more incredible since I last visited. It actually feels homey in here, if that makes sense coming from a cop?"

"Hey, that's nice to hear. Thank you." Page noted Steve's casual dress of jeans and a white knit shirt, which mirrored his light-hearted mood. But it was his dimples, whenever he smiled, that melted her…every time. She did a quick mental scolding and lifted the dome from the cookie tray. "How about a honey oatmeal cookie as a reward for helping?"

"Maybe. Who made them?" Steve walked toward the platter.

Page put one on a napkin and passed it. "Ina," she answered with a grin.

Taking an impressive bite, he added an affirmative nod. "Which ones are Betsy's?" Steve tapped on the glass.

"The honey molasses and honey sugar cookies are her recipes. Why?" Page was curious about his question.

"Why? It's time Betsy gets an ego boost without having to beg for one. Bag me up a half dozen of each. Is she in the kitchen?" Steve moved toward the back.

"She is. Be warned. She'll show up at the bungalow with a batch of cookies every day if you fawn too much. That's how I ended up in my Betsy-making meals predicament."

Steve winked. "It's a risk I'm willing to take. Wait." He

returned to Page. "I'd better have one of those molasses jobs in my hand."

Page passed him the cookie. "You're a good egg, Steve Tanner. A real good egg."

Steve saluted and headed for the kitchen.

Studying the bookshelf, Page sketched her ideas for adding potions to the inventory. She wondered if their honey supplier, Mickey, could guide them toward someone who bottled body products. She and Betsy were overdue to enjoy iced coffees at The Perk, where Mickey worked part-time. Tomorrow morning, they'd stop by. Page heard Steve's baritone voice saying goodbye to the bakers. She glanced at her watch—fifteen minutes until closing.

Steve approached and lifted her sketch to peruse. "Ah, a new direction, I see. What is it they say? You're aiming to appeal to the body, mind, and spirit?"

"Now, in what alternate reality did a strapping detective pull those three words from?"

"Hey, I'm a Renaissance type of guy."

"A Renaissance type of guy? Really?" Page threw her head back and laughed. "I bet you can't even name me one quality of a Renaissance man. One." She raised her index finger.

Steve rubbed his chin. "What do I win?"

Page pondered. "I'll treat you to dinner at the Crab Shak. You pick the night."

"Miss Drew, I'd classify that as a win for you and not me. You escape one of Betsy's dinners. Do better."

The corners of Page's mouth lifted. "Yeah, I guess you're right. Let me think." She stared out the window. Her face brightened. "I know. We'll go to the new miniature golf course where you can slay dragons and dodge the giant waterfall. That plays off your competitive spirit. Afterward, we can eat pretzels with mustard from the nearby food truck."

"Okay, here's the deal. Yes, to the golf, but I'd like to exchange the pretzels for a caramel apple from said truck. Now, it's my turn. If you win, I'll take you on a moonlight sail and provide a fantastic dinner guaranteed to earn me…something."

"I gotta win that prize." Page put her hand out. "Shake."

Steve grabbed her hand, pulling her close, and whispered, "A Renaissance man has a curious and creative nature. He craves a challenge and is proficient in a wide range of fields. He defines a Navy Seal. That's four qualities if you're counting."

Page stepped back in awe. She was staring at a modern-day version of a Renaissance man. "What night do you want to golf?"

"Tonight."

CHAPTER 19

Betsy found Page standing statue-still and staring out the shop's entrance with her mouth agape. "UFO sighting?" Betsy waved her hand in front of Page's face. "Hmm, no reaction. Let's go home."

"He's a Renaissance man." Page turned toward Betsy.

"Who's a Renaissance man? You're going to need to catch me up on what I obviously missed while in the kitchen baking these fingers to—"

"Steve. He declared himself one. I made a bet that he couldn't even define the qualities of a Renaissance man. I lost."

"I swear the two of you keep my fan moving. Do I want to know what Dreamboat won?"

Page grabbed her handbag and followed Betsy out. "I'm treating him to a game of miniature golf and a caramel apple, tonight."

Betsy howled. "After all these years, you've met your match, Page Wright. I love it."

"Ha. Ha. Just so you know, I plan to win something too." Page adjusted her sunglasses.

"Oh yeah? What's that?" Betsy opened the driver's door.

"More information on Jake's case. Our suspect board comes out when I get home," replied Page. She felt confident that Steve had garnered more evidence since last night—evidence her board needed. A sheepish grin found her face. She vowed to gain added facts before the north star appeared in the heavens. Betsy's typical heavy foot braking at a red light brought Page back to the present.

"Why do I always catch every light?" Betsy complained. She adjusted the air conditioning vent toward her face.

"You do seem to attract them. Listen, I forgot to tell you that we need to stop by Plant Hugger and grab that bush. I told Rosa to expect us after four." Saying *Plant Hugger*, Page felt the inkling return.

"No problem. That means I need to turn right instead of staying straight. In that case, the red light wasn't an annoyance but a help." Betsy tapped the gas pedal, causing the vehicle to lurch.

Page rubbed her neck. Cooking and driving were Betsy's nemeses and Page's crosses to bear. "So, Ina seemed enthusiastic about using the flowers for garnishing."

"Yes, she suggested we might want to consider taking small catering jobs by and by. We could offer specific items and not get into much customizing. What do you think?"

"I think it's a wonderful idea." Page's mind took off with ideas. "To build on that theme, I'd like to propose we explore adding honeyed body products to our inventory. I sketched some display ideas that I'll leave for you to study tonight. How do you feel about involving Daisy with that project?"

"To parrot you, I think it's a wonderful idea. Isn't this business adventure so exciting?" Betsy pumped the gas pedal.

"Yep, I'm feeling pretty jazzed." Page wanted to say *queasy* but instead popped a tummy-settling peppermint into her mouth. How could one get car sick going thirty miles an hour? Thankfully, the nursery appeared ahead.

Betsy continued, "Eventually, I foresee us having employees work the retail part of the business while we concentrate on what we relish most. Me baking, and you, merchandising and marketing. We must hold to our pledge of enjoying free time, too. Right?"

"Right," agreed Page. "The balance of work and play

ensures that Honey Bees enjoys a long run. Before I forget, should we visit Mickey tomorrow morning and see if he can offer some input on getting potions made?"

"Great idea, and I'll order me a large iced hazelnut latte with extra whipped cream." Betsy smacked her lips. "We've arrived at our destination. You know that whenever we're working a case, I ask if an inkling is involved with a side trip?" Betsy lifted Page's sunglasses and studied her face. She dropped the glasses in place. "What's my role?"

Page laughed. "Your ability to read me is worrisome. As for your role, I haven't a clue. All I know is we're about to find out...something. With me?"

"Always. Lead the way." Betsy grabbed her straw hat and followed Page toward the greenhouses.

Customers wandered around the rows of plants, choosing what to place in their carts. Three college-aged guys were busy answering questions and setting the heavier pots onto wagons. A bored delivery truck driver waited while Ray unloaded an order of palm trees. To the casual observer, Plant Hugger's business seemed thriving.

Yet, Page was puzzled as to why Bert chose to walk away from everything he'd built. Whose idea was it to fly the coop Thursday night, Bert's or Eleanor's? Moreover, why the rush? Unless they were somehow involved in Jake's murder. Steve said the police weren't yet pursuing the magic mushrooms in the investigation, so that couldn't account for Bert and Eleanor's fast escape from Shell Isle. Page allowed that these questions indicated some degree of progress. She stopped walking, realizing Betsy wasn't behind her, but bent over, sniffing a lemon tree.

Betsy gave a big wave. "You go on. I want to gather plant ideas for my bungalow."

Signaling okay, Page went to find Rosa. Turning the corner, Page caught sight of Bert and Eleanor sitting at a picnic table. She ducked behind the wood fence to eavesdrop, able to observe them through the wooden slats.

"When are you telling Ed that you're ending things?" Bert's hand stroked Eleanor's cheek.

"Not until Thursday. I don't want to raise any suspicion. Maybe I'll leave him a note since he's attending a meeting with the town's commissioners."

"Say, I rented the villa. It's classy, like us. Baby, we're going to live the life." Bert held up a photo.

"That's wonderful news." Eleanor tucked the photo into her handbag. "What about Rosa? Will she present a problem?"

"Rosa's all caught up in traveling the world with her boyfriend and could care less what I'm doing. She got what she wanted, and that's all that matters to her. Like father, like daughter, you might say. The attorney is meeting with her to spell out some restrictions I've added to her inheritance. Better to let him deal with her wacky behavior." Bert glanced at the annual greenhouse.

Eleanor applied lipstick and studied herself in the compact's mirror. "You're positive the money will get wired tomorrow because I'm not going unless you can deliver the lifestyle—"

Bert's voice went cold. "The money and liquidation of Jake's stocks and bonds are handled. Hear me for the last time, Eleanor. If you persist in chasing my hard-earned wealth and not me, I may rescind my invitation."

"Oh, I hear you clearly, but you forget what all I know about you. The way I see it, my pet, we must stay close to each other, and for obvious reasons," replied a cryptic Eleanor. Her hand leaned across the table and stroked Bert's cheek. "Darling, you know I love you."

Bert removed her hand. "Your threats could become dangerous to your health, Eleanor. While you attend that snooty party tonight, think on those words." Bert stood. "Let's not be seen together again. I'll meet you at the airport. You've got our itinerary."

Page hurried to the far side of the fencing to avoid notice. Once more, the inklings had proved valuable. She played hopscotch on the pavers to dodge the wet dirt caused by the sprinklers. Seeing the greenhouse, she relaxed. Rosa was up next.

"Hello, Page. I'm glad you told the truth and stopped by." Rosa wiped her hands on her overalls.

Page thought the girl odder with each encounter. "Of course, I came. I also wanted to tell you that Betsy and Ina used every violet petal this afternoon. Thank you again." Page paused to observe Rosa's tense body language.

"I'm glad the blossoms got appreciated. Flowers are my family. I take care of them, and they take care of me." Rosa sprinkled plant food into the nearby pots.

"That's a unique way of interacting with Mother Nature's gifts. I've never quite thought of flowers—"

"You must," Rosa abruptly replied. Her eyes flashed an intensity that she quickly quelled. "So, besides picking up your hibiscus that you shouldn't have left behind, what else do you need this afternoon?"

Page noted the troubling shift in Rosa's personality. With that awareness, she changed course. Smiling, Page ventured over to a display of herbs. "Rosa, with your amazing connection with all growing things, could you help me choose some herbs? I've always wanted an herb garden, and now that I'm settled at my cottage, well, it's time."

Rosa nodded but kept her serious expression in place. "I can help you select herbs that ask little, but only if you commit to them. Will you?"

Page felt relief that Betsy wasn't around. Her mouth and Rosa wouldn't gee-haw. The word *unhinged* popped into Page's awareness. "Yes, I will commit to my herbs; after all, they're going to feed me." Page paused, taking another read on the young woman. "You're a hundred percent correct to ask me that question."

Rosa's face brightened. "You do understand. Okay, here's a very healthy basil plant. You like basil?"

Page nodded and accepted the plant. She snagged a nearby basket.

"Take this chocolate mint. I grew this variety myself. Chives are mellow. You'll want them." Rosa grew thoughtful as she gathered a half dozen more plants for Page's basket. "There you go. Have Ray ring these up and put your hibiscus in the vehicle." Rosa turned back to her plants, dismissing Page.

"Thank you for everything, Rosa. I hope the rest of your week treats you nicely." Page added.

"I'm counting on it. You should go now." Rosa's voice held no emotion.

Page nodded and went in search of her cousin.

Betsy's cart held two lemon trees and an orange hibiscus plant. "I'm going to keep these at the cottage until I move. What took you so long? I thought I was going to need to send out a search party."

"I was spying and then chatting with Rosa. She's one strange bird, that one." Page wasn't sure how to describe the encounter with Rosa. Bert was right—calling her wacky.

Betsy twisted Page's arm to read her watch. "We need to skedaddle. You've got a hot golf date, and we haven't eaten. You can tell me more later regarding the strange bird and your spy mission."

"My gosh, I only have an hour. We'll need to grab fast food." Page felt a burst of joy that she'd evaded a meal of Betsy's. "And because you made a side trip to Plant Huggers, drive-thru dinner is my treat." *Magnanimous* would define her night.

"Can I choose the place?" Betsy's voice amped with enthusiasm.

"But, of course." Worry came calling, but Page relaxed. Fast food was fast food. Betsy couldn't possibly mess that up. Act *magnanimous*, she reminded herself. Page waited while Ray loaded the hibiscus before hopping in the passenger seat to hear Betsy's answer.

"I pick Dagwood's Dogs. I'm craving a fat, juicy hotdog with onions and relish. Besides, he's on the way home. That'll save time." Betsy started the engine.

Page could only nod. Betsy had managed to ruin even takeout by choosing disgusting hot dogs, which resembled things Page wouldn't allow herself to envision. "Dagwood's it is. Magnanimous me."

"What? I didn't catch the last part." Betsy pumped the gas pedal a few times and applied the brake for no reason at all other than that it existed.

"It was nothing." Page rummaged in her handbag for a mint. She dropped her window a few inches, anticipating the coming food aroma.

CHAPTER 20

The sun still held a position in the sky high enough to deliver intense heat as Page knocked on Steve's bungalow door. She'd chosen a yellow sundress and white sandals for their outing. The dousing of perfume was compliments of Betsy as Page dashed out the door. Starving and fragrant, she waited for the Renaissance man to appear.

Steve opened the door. "Wow, I didn't expect you to call for me. I probably should add to my Renaissance man qualities that I'm not chauvinistic. I'm cool with a woman taking charge of a date."

"Hey, I lost the bet, and that means I cover all the bases tonight. Still, it's good to hear I'm in charge." Page did a fist bump, noticing his hair was still damp from a shower. The yellow shirt which matched her dress made her smile. She doubted he'd noticed. They walked side by side down the sidewalk.

"You're driving, I see. Well, okay, I'm primed for fun." Steve settled into the passenger seat.

"As I said, I'm covering all the bases." Page caught sight of his dimples.

"Yes, all the bases." Steve cleared his throat. "Um, Page, you look nice tonight. I mean, you always look nice, but tonight, especially so. You smell really nice, too." Steve leaned over to sniff her neck. "Yeah, I like that."

She would kill Betsy later for drenching her and giving Steve the wrong signal. "You can compliment Betsy. She sprayed me down as I left. It's her bottle of 'man magnet,' as she calls it. I apologize if it's awakened, male—"

Steve laughed so hard the SUV shook.

"Oh, would you please stop? Why is it when I'm around you, embarrassment or humiliation finds me?" Page glanced in the rearview mirror. "I think we're being followed."

Taking a glance back, Steve grabbed his cell phone. "Koch, the black van is behind Page and me. I'm in her SUV. We're trying to enjoy an evening away from the crims. Got a squad car nearby, or do I need to handle this?" Steve thumped the dash, waiting. "Good plan. Thanks, man."

"What's up?" Page's worry frown appeared as she looked behind her.

"It's going to be fine. I need you to cut your speed to give the officers a chance to catch up. They'll handle things. These goons want to intimidate me. A bad move on their part, as they'll soon discover."

"If you say so." Page's voice sounded all quivery. *Get a grip*, she told herself. "Is twenty slow enough?"

"You're doing great. I see two cop cars up ahead. They've got the van pinned with no side street to cut down. Smooth and fast move on their part." Steve's expression grew serious. "You're leading them right to the trap."

The cops allowed Page to pass through but stopped the van. She took a breath. "Now what?"

"Pull over to the curb. I'll be right back. You okay?" Steve touched her arm.

"Yeah, for now. That man magnet perfume is nothing but trouble. I've attracted more men than I wanted." She watched Steve interact with the two cops and the van's driver. Why were the cops laughing with Steve when some South American bandits wanted a piece of him? She relaxed as he approached her vehicle.

"Let's go golfing." His face held amusement.

"What happened to those men? I'm confused."

"Those men were a mom taking her two daughters to

ballet class." Steve saluted as one of the cops drove past.

"Seriously?" Page felt relief bubbling up.

"Seriously. You can rest easy. That perfume ain't that potent, well, except on me."

~*~

Steve and Page waited to place their order at the food truck. After two rounds of golf and Page getting wet by the waterfall, their fun soon gave way to discussing the case. For the next bit of time, they savored their light-hearted banter.

Page stepped up to the order window. "We'll have one caramel apple—"

"With pecans," inserted Steve.

"Make that a caramel apple with pecans, a hamburger well done, no onions, an order of fries, and a small iced tea." Page grabbed her wallet only to have Steve's hand touch hers.

"Let me feed you what is obviously dinner. You treated us to golf."

Page hesitated. Her liberated side warred with her feminine side. "I'm supposed—"

"Allow me, please."

The way Steve looked at her vaporized any objections. She knew he respected women. "All right. Thank you." Page found them a clean table. While she waited, her mind intruded, cautioning her to keep things low-key. Her heart beat a different tune, telling her to *carpe diem*. Deciding both were right, she smiled as the Renaissance man joined her.

"Dare I ask why you haven't eaten dinner?" Steve stole a fry.

"Ugh, don't remind me. Just my karmic food luck, Betsy chose Dagwood's Dogs for us. I don't eat those disgusting mystery meat things...ever. Not even if I was on an island with nothing left to eat. I'd rather starve." Page made a face.

"I've got the picture. Enjoy your burger. You deserve

something good after Dagwood's and losing both games." Steve took a bite of his apple.

"Tanner, I let you win those games. I know how fragile that male ego is." Page winked and dabbed mustard from her chin. "Best burger in town."

Steve chuckled and studied his apple. "Want a bite, Eve?"

Page gave a hard smack to Steve's hand, causing the apple to fly off the stick and land on the table of an elderly couple.

"I'm so sorry," she said to the startled man and woman. She watched Steve retrieve the runaway fruit.

"The woman packs a wallop. Sorry 'bout the intrusion." Steve's friendly demeanor invited a response.

"After sixty years together, my wife can still wallop me, too." The man chuckled and pointed to his wife, earning him a smack. "Like I said."

Returning to their table, Steve sat down in front of half a burger and a handful of fries. "What's this?"

"An apology." Page chewed. "That little faux pas is just another of my embarrassing moments around you." Page dragged a fry through the catsup.

"Page?"

"Yeah? What?"

"I quit counting your embarrassing moments when the wave toppled you off Betsy's deflated float," said Steve.

"You stopped tallying my debacles way back then?"

"Yep. Can I have a sip of your tea?" Steve held out his hand.

"Hearing that you've stopped tallying, I can do better for you." Page went to the order window and returned with a chocolate malt. "For you and me." She held up two straws, realizing too late she'd have to sit next to Steve.

The older woman nodded to her husband. "See that, Harold? Those two share a happy marriage like us. Go get me one of those malts."

Steve and Page burst out laughing. They watched Harold do her bidding.

"They're adorable," added Page.

"Poor sap. Look at him unwrapping her straw and placing the napkin around the cup."

"Just adorable," repeated Page.

Steve looked heavenward. "I'll never understand women. Come on, take me home." He held out his hand to Page.

They exchanged goodbyes with the couple and did a slow walk to Page's vehicle.

Once inside the SUV, Steve reached for Page's hand. "I've enjoyed tonight."

"Me too." She started the engine. Page maneuvered out of the parking lot. "So, bet winner, I've got an easy question for you."

"This again. Okay, what's your question?" Steve loosened his seatbelt.

"My place or yours?"

Caught off guard by Page's playful question, Steve shifted in his seat, triggering the belt's tightening. "This damn restraint."

"You need restraining, Tanner, and I'm still waiting for my answer. My place or yours?" Page stole a glance.

"Well, that all depends on what you have in mind," Steve teased. "Though I expect your answer will disappoint me."

"Detective Tanner, my answer will not disappoint." Page bit her lip.

"It just did." Steve paused. "Your place. I know what you're after, Ms. Sleuth." He'd brought the humor back for them.

"That doesn't take much detecting skill. Anyway, as I recall, you were expecting reports. If you're cooperative, I might feel inclined to share some scuttlebutt after my recent accidental eavesdropping. Before you go bananas, I wasn't in any danger unless you count a close call with a splinter from a wood fence."

Moments later, Steve and Page entered the cottage and discovered Betsy in the hammock reading her novel. After a few attempts, she sat up. "Judging by appearances, it looks like you two had some fun."

Page claimed a nearby chair. "Yes, and I even let Steve win both games of miniature golf."

Steve shook his head and scooted a chair closer to the women. "You might ask her later who got soaked?" Steve peeked at his watch. "So, let's get this sharing out of the way. No doubt, Barnacle needs a walk."

Betsy cleared her throat. "I don't think so. Hey, Barnacle?"

Within seconds, the dog appeared at the porch screen door.

"He's had quite the busy night," chuckled Betsy.

Steve opened the door for Barnacle. "How did you get out again, you Houdini? And, what have you gotten into?"

"Oh, I can tattle away. He provided me plenty of entertainment. First, Barnacle has mastered the latch on his pet door, which got him to the backyard. After a respectable amount of chewing on dinghy wood —"

"Damnit, Barn, you didn't gnaw my boat again?"

"I hollered at him, and he stopped," replied Betsy. "Next, he dug the fastest escape hole I've ever seen and took off for a swim. Of course, I went down to the beach, and after ten minutes of cajoling, he came home with me."

Page chirped in. "Please tell me you didn't let him in my cottage wet with sand?"

"Nope, I know the rules. Barnacle then had a spa night with the garden hose and some of my shampoo. He seemed to enjoy that bit of pampering and doesn't mind smelling like roses."

"I'm not believing this. Barnacle, you owe Betsy a major thanks, and so do I." Steve bent down to sniff his dog. "You're a dandy, all right."

"Last, I know you forbade us to feed him, but Barnacle seemed hungry after his big doings, so we shared a bag of potato chips. That, kiddos, concludes Betsy's night with the only male companion she's allowed. Pathetic me."

Page buried her face in her hands. Only Betsy could turn dog sitting into hilarity.

"Betsy, I promise to advocate for your release from the moratorium on males. Heck, I might even introduce you to a guy from the station," taunted Steve.

"Yes, to advocating, but a no way to the cop introduction. Years ago, I went out with this undercover—"

"Stifle, Bets." Page turned to Steve. "You don't ever want to hear any past dating tales. They never end well for the guy."

"That's not entirely true," Betsy huffed, relishing the attention.

Page raised an eyebrow.

"POR," responded Betsy.

"More of this, POR?" Steve raised both hands in exasperation. "Ladies, as much as I'm enjoying your repartee, can we move on to discuss the case?"

"Right," said Page. "This time, I'll start." She detailed for Steve and Betsy what she'd overheard between Eleanor and Bert earlier and her concerns that Rosa exhibited signs of some mental disorder.

Betsy chimed in with Ina's scoop of overhearing Eleanor's chat on the cell phone. "If you ask me—and you should—I wager Bert and Eleanor possess means, motive, and opportunity to get rid of Jake. They attended the fireworks festivities. Plus, Steve, you told us they were milling around and missing for a chunk of time."

"You're right, Betsy. Maybe they weren't having a cuddle behind some tent. What if Bert decided he needed Jake's money to get Eleanor to leave the mayor? Besides, I seriously doubt his possible side hustle dealing mushrooms brought in significant moola. Eleanor isn't cheap to keep around. Money rules her world. I think those two could slide over to murder. What do you think?" Page directed her focus to Steve.

"It's plausible. We may need to bring Eleanor and Bert in for additional questioning. For the moment, Ralph stays on top of my list. The cigarillo puts him with Jake at the time of the murder," said Steve.

"Did you get the DNA report back today?" Page bit her lip. She'd been counting on this evidence to guide her.

"No, there's a delay. We expect it tomorrow. That's going to prove an important piece of information. Both Koch and I are pressuring the lab to rush it." Steve observed Barnacle try and fail at jumping into the hammock with Betsy. "Barn. Get over here."

Betsy stood. "That's okay, Barnacle. I'm going for a cold drink. Anyone else want something?"

"Sure. Would you mind bringing me a juice? Those French fries made me thirsty," declared Page.

"Fries? I thought you had candy apples?" Betsy's eyebrow lifted.

Steve came to the rescue. "I bought the fries. We shared, which makes me thirsty, too. Can you double the juice order?"

"Can do." Betsy sauntered off.

"Is her juice safe to drink?" whispered Steve.

Page grinned. "Yep, it's bottled." As soon as the words left her mouth, she heard the caps popped.

"Bottled sounds okay." Steve grinned.

"Here you go. Cranberry juice with a spritz of lime." Betsy read their expressions. "What's wrong with cran-lime juice?"

"Not one thing. I love it." Page took a big drink. "Hmm." And this time, she meant it.

"And you?" Betsy looked at Steve.

"Winning combination, just like you and Page." Steve raised his bottle in a mock salute.

"You silver-tongued devil. Let's get back on track. My novel waits for no one. The dowager's discovered some of her heirloom vases have gone missing. I need to find out if that no account daughter-in-law is the culprit because the family suspects it's the chambermaid who's with child. As for the father of her —"

"Save us, Steve," mumbled Page.

"Yes, well, we did bring Ralph back for another stay with us. We charged him with attempting to flee the country and breaking bail. He and the judge will have an encore at some point. For now, at least he's alive."

"That's good news. I'm curious about Jake's journal. Have you found anything that sheds light on the five suspects?" Page took a sip of her drink and hoped for a piece of valuable evidence.

"To sum up what I've extrapolated from Jake's entries, it's pretty much what we've already figured out. Ralph and Buck were poaching something illegal, but Jake hadn't figured out what. Bert was dealing something questionable out of the nursery, owed Jake money, and was embroiled in an affair with Eleanor. As for Rosa, Jake wrote very little but did record the days she cleaned the house and how much he paid her. He made one entry months ago that he suspected Rosa had snooped in his checkbooks. Interestingly, Jake was engaged in tidying up his finances and estate and made a note to redo his will," finished Steve.

"He probably knew his time here was short and understood his heart wasn't in good shape. Plus, I bet he decided his brother and niece were unworthy to inherit his full estate. I wager he'd decided to cut them out." Page sat thoughtfully.

"Poor guy. If I'd only known that flounder was the last he'd give me, I would have spent more time thanking him." Betsy sniffed.

"It's okay. I'm sure Jake took pleasure in giving you that fish to enjoy." Page squeezed Betsy's arm. "Anything else for us, Steve?"

"Just that Buck continues to run his charters. We've got an officer assigned to him when he's docked. He's still sleeping on the boat. Also, the goons haven't been around the marina. We didn't have a reason to arrest them. Koch and I think they're biding their time until an opportunity presents."

"You mean to mess with Ralph or Buck?" Betsy looked confused.

"Yes, because Ralph and Buck have knowledge which might get others indicted," added Steve. "Don't worry, Page, I think you and Betsy are plenty safe. That third guy, who you and I observed with Buck and Ralph, has left the country. The airport camera showed him boarding a plane the night we nabbed Ralph. We won't get him back here."

Page released a pent-up breath. "I guess that's good for us but bad for you and Koch. You lost a possible witness to the fin poaching."

Steve stroked Barnacle's ears. "We need something to break our way in Jake's case. The gun is still unaccounted for as of this afternoon. Finding that would go a long way to knowing who killed Jake."

"Wait. I thought you scored Buck's weapon and were going to have the lab check it." Page stared at Steve, struggling to understand.

"Sorry. I forgot to tell you. Buck couldn't find his gun. He and the officer looked everywhere in his small apartment. No weapon. The officer told me he felt Buck was genuinely upset and even more worried that it was missing. Excuse me a second." Steve checked his cell phone for messages. "Okay, Betsy, what's on your mind?"

"I assume you meant Buck was upset the gun was missing

because he wanted to hand it over to prove his innocence?" asked Betsy.

"Yeah, that's what the officer thought." Steve rose. "So, I need to go. You've scored some info for that hidden suspect board. I expect to hear from you if anything at all comes your way. That includes those inklings and —"

"Nudges," supplied Page. She walked him to the door.

"Night, Betsy, and thanks again for taking care of Barnacle," hollered Steve.

"Yep, he's my only guy for now," answered Betsy with a sigh.

Steve pulled Page outside with him. "Here." He put an envelope in her hand.

"What's this?" Page glanced down.

Steve smiled but didn't answer. He brushed his lips against her cheek. "Night. Come on, Barn."

Page waited for Steve to go inside his bungalow before opening the envelope and reading the homemade card:

Good for one moonlight sail and dinner aboard Carpe Diem. Must be redeemed within seven days.

She needed Betsy's fan.

CHAPTER 21

The unexpected screech of a seagull woke Page hours before her alarm. Failing to drift back to sleep, she seized the opportunity for a sunrise walk on the beach. She dressed in white crop pants and an oversized striped shirt and crept past Betsy's door more silent than a cheetah zeroed on a hare. Outside, Page grabbed a breath of personal freedom, unable to recall the last time she'd had two whole waking hours alone.

Adjusting her ballcap, Page set a relaxed pace. Stepping over two beached jellyfish, she stopped to pick up an unusual shell. She turned it in her hand to make sure no one still occupied the residence. A wave washed across her flip-flops, vying for attention. She sensed someone approaching.

"Good morning. You're out here early."

Page pivoted to see Steve holding his surfboard. "I could say the same for you."

He stared at the water. "Tide's high, and a storm offshore is sending in ride-worthy waves. In a perfect world, a surfer's day is defined by the ocean's mood."

Page's foot drew a circle in the sand as she considered Steve's words. "I get your meaning, surfer. Go claim that perfect ride." She paused, considering what she wanted to say. "As for me? I'm claiming more solitude."

"I get your meaning, as well." Steve chuckled. "If I see Betsy, I won't tell her which direction you went."

Page waved and continued her walk, with thoughts of Steve and his sailing invite dancing in her head. She paused to focus on a school of dolphins swimming parallel to the beach.

Their frolicking succeeded in claiming her attention. Reflecting on bottlenose dolphins' behaviors, Page remembered reading that they undergo different cycles in their daily activity. Traveling, feeding, resting, and their favorite activity, socializing. The intelligent tricksters liked to interact with people and could even comprehend speech and numbers. What touched Page most was how dolphins often helped people in need. "Betsy and I should plan to visit the dolphin rescue center a few miles up the coast on one of their days off," she mumbled to herself.

A young man jogged by and glanced over his shoulder, hearing her talk to no one.

Embarrassed, Page nodded to him. Time to go mindless and store up some pleasure for the day. She walked at a faster pace, making the marina her destination. An inkling came within seconds. Unsure what it portended, she forged on, bringing an expectation.

Climbing the beach access steps, Page stopped to rinse the sand from her flip-flops and feet. The nudge not to tarry caused her to shut off the sprayer and walk toward the docks. She passed fishers engrossed in outfitting their boats for a day on the water. Page experienced a pull toward the charter boat docks and saw why.

"Is his boat still docked?" A man asked with a thick Spanish accent. His dark skin and hair complemented his speech.

"Too late for our plan, amigo. The boat's about to pull out." The second man shared similar features.

Page parked herself on the bench next to the Bait Shak, listening to what surely had to be the two goons out to nab Buck. She tugged her hat lower, shading her face, and felt thankful for the wide-framed sunglasses. She didn't have to wait long for the men to speak again.

"Cerote, we missed the last chance to end our problem. Señor Jose will be *muy* mad." Goon One rubbed his face.

"*Hola!*" Goon Two pointed at a sign saying *Boat Rental.* "*Vamos.*"

Understanding dawned on Page's face. She grabbed her cell phone, hoping Steve had ridden enough waves to have his phone nearby. On the fifth ring, he answered.

"Tanner here."

"It's Page. Don't talk. Listen to me. The two goons are renting a boat at the marina and going after Buck."

"What the hell—"

"Not now. I got a nudge. You need to get the coast guard or police boat or whatever here. Buck's taking a group fishing and is readying to leave. These two are planning to follow, and everyone on that boat is in danger. Gotta go—"

"I'm on it. Come straight home. Page?" Steve dialed Koch as he ran out the door, still wearing his wet bathing suit.

Page watched a few feet away as the two men conversed with the Bait Shak employee. *What could she do to stall them?* A smile lit her face. She made her move. "Hi, there, fellows. Isn't it a great day to be out on the water?"

The three men nodded with added politeness.

Turning her focus to the guy at the Bait Shak window, Page saw his name tag. "Listen, Reggie, do you have my boat ready? It's that one painted yellow." Page pointed and added her best smile.

Goon Two stepped in. "No, Señora, that's the boat we're renting. Wait for your turn. Pick another one." His expression turned menacing.

After Page gave him her name, Reggie jumped into the conversation. "Ma'am, I don't have you down for a reservation today." He spun the computer screen around to Page. "See?"

"Well, that's your problem. I booked it last evening while I was visiting a friend who has a sailboat. Some other guy took my card and reservation. That yellow boat is my rental."

"I guess Ed screwed up. He worked last night for me." Reggie's eyes roamed the remaining boats. "Sorry, guys, I must take the lady's word. I don't have anything for you until tomorrow morning. Why don't you come—"

Goon Two pulled Reggie's upper body across the counter. With a chilled voice, he said, "Look again at the list of boats. I believe you'll find one for us. Pronto."

"Leave it, Marco. We'll find another way." Goon One sent a nervous smile to Reggie and Page. "He's waited a long time to go deep-sea fishing. Today was our only day, Señor Reggie."

Page nodded. "That's too bad. I'd reschedule, but I'm waiting for my group to arrive at any moment."

"Come on, Marco. Let's *vamos*."

Marco balled both hands in fists, trying to decide his next move.

Page backed away, wishing Steve would appear. She couldn't delay the men much longer.

The smarter goon tugged on Marco's arm. "Is bad. Come." Hearing approaching police sirens, they took off running, leaving Page to steady Reggie's nerves.

"I'm sorry for my role in all of this, but Reggie, you handled things perfectly."

"I did?" His voice trembled. "I don't understand what just happened. Did you have a reservation?"

Page shook her head. "I only said it so we could keep those bad guys from renting the boat. I suspect they were after Buck Lester. You know him."

"Oh, hell. I don't want to get tangled up in that mess. There's been a policeman here at night because of Buck's shady doings. Dumb me thought working here was safer than delivering pizzas." With a shaky hand, Reggie reached for a root beer.

Steve came running up to Page. "Are you okay? Why are you still here? What went down?" He stopped to grab a breath and take in the scene.

Reggie perked up. "She managed to stop those two badasses—"

"*We* managed to stop those two men, Reggie. You and me." Page spun to face Steve.

"Hey, there. Took your sweet time getting here." For the first time, Page noticed how he was dressed and grinned. "Sorry to interrupt your hang ten, Detective."

"If you're done, maybe you could tell me if the goons scored a boat—"

"No boat, but they did hightail it out of here because you all came with sirens blazing." Page grabbed a breath. "Reggie and I might have kept them here longer if not for your loud introduction. Right, Reg?"

"In my opinion, they overstayed their welcome." Reggie tucked his shirt back in place.

Steve chuckled and took hold of Page's hand. "Reggie, these officers behind me will take a statement from you and then get out of your hair. Try and relax. Thanks, buddy, for doing your part." Steve's frown now aimed at Page. "I'm driving you home, and you can tell me all about your little escapade with two dangerous men and why I should—"

"Devote the rest of the week to thanking me at every opportunity for saving Buck Lester's sorry mug. Take me home." Page twisted Steve's wrist to read his watch. Step on it, mister." She jogged toward Steve's SUV.

Exasperated, Steve threw both hands in the air and followed behind.

Page marched into Hibiscus with Steve on her heels, declaring he needed to get her statement yet again.

Betsy stood ready with her greeting. Hands planted on her generous hips. She huffed, "I'm not surprised seeing you with Steve. I'm not even surprised that he's standing here in swim trunks at this time of the morning. Nor am I surprised that you two can't manage to go eight hours without seeing each other. No, what surprises me is that you're so lousy at hiding these encounters from me. Furthermore—"

"Um, Betsy, you've got things wrong," interrupted Steve.

"Very wrong," added Page with hands on her hips matching Betsy's stance.

"What part do I have wrong?"

Page shrugged. "Who knows what part. You had so many. Steve, would you please inform the judge what she missed while…" Page craned her head around to the kitchen island. "While I enjoy a leisurely breakfast of gosh knows what's in that bowl."

Betsy's mouth fell open as she heard Steve recount Page's encounter at the marina.

"I can't believe you'd involve yourself with such dangerous men. This pushes the limit of your past sleuthing encounters—"

"Turncoat." Page made a face.

"Okay, ladies, let me finish. Betsy, I've brought your cousin home and need to get her statement. After that, I'm leaving Page in your capable hands. I trust you can keep her at Honey Bees?" Steve pulled his cell phone out.

"You're kidding, right? Me keep Page somewhere against her wishes? I'd have a better chance of inheriting the *Mona Lisa*. Maybe you should keep her with you." Betsy returned to her waiting bowl.

"I can't believe you two are standing here negotiating my comings and goings." Page puffed her cheeks. "Tanner, if you want my statement, plant yourself and turn on that cell phone recorder. I've got a day of work waiting for me."

"Statement time serves as my cue to disappear," declared Betsy.

Page spent the next fifteen minutes detailing the scene

with the goons and Reggie. She felt pleased that Steve had only a few remaining questions, which meant she'd done a decent job giving the facts. It was his next few minutes of lecturing her on what defined good judgment and safety that she didn't enjoy.

Walking Steve to the door, Page decided to take back control. "I accept."

Lost in thought, Steve's face showed confusion. "What do you accept?"

"The invitation for a moonlight sail and dinner." Page offered her best coy look.

Steve nodded. "Ah, that invite. You can sure turn a conversation on a dime."

"Yes, it's a gift. Like Betsy, I have many."

"I'm not going to touch that statement." Still feeling off-center, Steve hesitated.

"I like Friday night." Page took a read on his face. "Or, perhaps Saturday?"

"For sailing?"

"Of course, for sailing. Are any of your neurons firing in there?" Page tapped his forehead. "Maybe you're the one who bears watching?"

Steve rallied. "You want the job, Miss Drew?"

Page shoved him out the door and closed it. The cuckoo clock announced it was past time to pull herself together. The Perk, where gossip flowed as easily as the coffee, waited.

CHAPTER 22

Page and Betsy entered The Perk, anticipating their signature iced lattes and a quick visit with the male town crier, Mickey. The coffee shop's downtown building, with its original tin ceiling and oak-planked floor, provided the perfect backdrop for displaying local artists' paintings. The eclectic mix of comfy chairs and sofas invited easy conversation while sipping a delightful something. Soft jazz played, and the welcoming smile of the barista greeted the cousins.

"What can I make for you this morning?" The barista woke up the espresso machine's hiss.

Betsy stepped up to the counter. "Hello, I want a large iced hazelnut latte with whipped cream. Make that a lot of whipped cream."

"Got it," said the barista. "What can I start for you?" she asked Page.

"I'll have the same, sans whipped cream," Page smiled at a passing toddler.

"I've got this." Betsy slid her credit card through the machine. "Go find our honey and gossip supplier."

"I see Mickey busy wiping a table in the corner. I'll stroll over," answered Page.

Mickey waved as she got closer. "Morning, Page. How's your honey supply holding out?" His slim frame held no fat but a surprising amount of strength. His dark eyes could peruse a room with lightning speed, which meant patrons of The Perk seldom harbored a need.

"Hi, Mickey. Betsy and I were hoping to find you working

this morning. And, as a matter of fact, we do need honey and some guidance, too." Page held off, trying to tap Mickey for gossip.

"What kind of honey? What are you going to use it for?" Mickey asked. He'd pulled up a wooden chair to straddle.

"We're considering adding body products to Honey Bees' inventory. Of course, we need results-driven formulations and a company that can make the potions. Any ideas?" Page motioned to Betsy.

Mickey stroked his chin. "Actually, my papa developed some winning formulas, but I never got around to bottling them. Plus, I've got a few honeys that work well with essential oils like lavender and such. Shea butter and jojoba oil get along nicely with honey's humectant properties. Yep, I think we can work something out," suggested Mickey.

"Thanks. That sounds perfect," answered Page.

"What sounds perfect? What'd I miss?" Betsy placed both coffees on the table.

"Oh, Mickey and I were discussing our idea to add body care products at Honey Bees."

"And? What do you think, Mickey?" asked Betsy, unwrapping her straw.

"I like your idea and think you'll have success if the containers are attractive. I even told Page you could use my recipes. I'd think you'd want to have a few testers made up and see which ones perform the best on your skin."

"Now, that's a great idea. Page has combo skin, and mine is dry, so we'd make good guinea pigs, huh, Page?" Betsy shoved a napkin over.

"Outstanding guineas," nodded an amused Page. "Do you have someone who can bottle that's close by?"

Betsy jumped in. "Oh, that would make things so much easier for us if you do. Honestly, Mickey, if not for you, Honey

Bees might never have happened." She squeezed Mick's hand.

"Ah, Betsy, you give me too much credit, but I admit my bees' honey opened Honey Bees doors for you two. And, yes, it so happens I'm connected with a bottler in South Shore." Mickey stood. "Back in a minute. I'll get you their card."

"I do believe this endeavor is destined," said Page. "We need to get Mickey a thank you gift. Don't you think?"

"I do. Let me ponder what, since I know Mickey a little better." Betsy winked.

"Here you go. Give the folks a jingle. Maybe have a meeting and see what you think of their operation." Mickey paused. "Yep, that's a good next step, ladies."

"You're right, and that's what we'll do. Thank you so much," Page tucked the business card into her wallet and signaled Betsy.

"Before you have to deliver another tray of drinks, what scuttle do you hear around Jake's death? Page and I can't believe this happened during the festival." Betsy shook her head.

"No one can believe it. No one," answered Mick, staring out the shop's picture window.

An inkling came to Page just as an all too familiar flashy female entered The Perk. Page cocked her head for Betsy to take note. The sighting provided the sleuths an opening to question Mickey.

Betsy rolled her eyes. "Geez, it's that affected Eleanor. There's something about her—"

"Oh, there's a lot about her, starting with pretending to have class. She doesn't. She's a street cat, and I can prove that statement." Mickey made a face, watching her.

"Tell us. How can you prove Eleanor's a street cat? That paints quite an image." Page gave him a grin.

"I call 'em like I see 'em. Here's your proof. I overheard Eleanor and Jake going at it last Thursday right at this very table."

Mickey thumped the top.

The three nodded as Eleanor passed, holding a bottle of juice. She settled in a corner chair and pulled out her cell phone.

Betsy leaned in. "So, what did she and Jake fuss about?"

"I heard Jake accuse her of trying to use her husband, Ed's, clout to get the bank manager to disclose Jake's assets. Eleanor told the bank guy that Jake had asked to borrow money from her husband, and she wanted to get a sense of his net worth. See what I mean? She's plenty brassy."

"That's brassy, all right. What did Eleanor say to Jake?"

"She told him the banker must have confused her with someone else because she couldn't care less what assets Jake had in the bank."

Page was intrigued. "Then what transpired?"

Mickey stole a glance at Eleanor and sneered. "Jake got right in her face and said he'd figured out her motive, and she could forget any notion of Bert getting further loans to buy her baubles and whatnot."

"Baubles? She's brassy and a man user," interjected Betsy.

"Yes, then Jake went all moral on her. He told Eleanor the next time their paths crossed, he expected her on the mayor's arm and not his brother's, or he might feel inclined to tell her husband about the bank visit and the dalliance with his brother."

"I bet that set her off," whispered Betsy.

"Yep, she got all huffy and told Jake that he'd be wise not to involve himself in her life. Get this last piece. Eleanor said she hoped it wouldn't prove necessary to let a few men know that Jake had become a problem."

Page's eyes narrowed. "She's a cold and calculating one. Two dangerous personality traits."

"You're right about that, Page. Her threat caused big Jake to storm out of The Perk. As I told Koch last night, that's the last time I saw Jake alive."

"That information was super important to give, Mickey." Betsy swirled her straw around.

"That's what Koch told me, too. He asked if I thought Eleanor capable of murder." Mickey sneered. "I told him any woman who got her tailfeathers up as high as Eleanor's was capable of killing."

Page and Betsy exchanged looks.

"Mickey, you're one terrific fellow. Page and I knew you'd have some valuable insight into Jake's death."

"Thanks for that. Listen, I've got drinks waiting for the book club ladies over yonder—what a feisty bunch of hens." Mickey looked at Betsy. "Guess I'll see you at the bowling alley. The Mermaids seem to have a winning streak going."

"We sure do. Thanks again for the info. All of it," said Betsy.

"Yes, thank you, Mickey." Page shifted her attention to Eleanor talking on the cell phone. "Excuse me while I sort through that stack of magazines near a certain someone." Page nodded and went to eavesdrop.

"Would you shut up and listen? Koch is suspicious and wants us at the station tonight. How am I going to explain being interviewed to Ed? He's not that dumb. Can't we get out of Shell now?"

Page moved to where Eleanor's back was to her.

"Fine, but one way or another, we fly tomorrow night. At least we've got our stories straight. I doubt Koch can find a reason to charge us as long as we don't deviate. We must play things cool. Later." Eleanor disconnected and grabbed her handbag, ready to leave. Noticing Page, she frowned.

Page plastered an uninterested expression on her face, thumbing through the magazine. She could only hope that ruse assuaged any of Eleanor's concerns.

The mayor's wife stole one more look Page's way before

leaving.

Whew, thought Page. She'd played her clue gathering too close, but it once again proved her inklings' power. She and Betsy had scored two important bits of information for the suspect board.

Betsy came up beside Page. "We need to go open the shop."

"Gosh, you're right." Page saw the clock. "We also need to invite ourselves to Eleanor and Bert's questioning tonight."

"What? That's what you just overheard?" Betsy pushed them toward the exit.

"Sure did. What's more, Eleanor seems plenty worried about Koch's interest in them. She and Bert are in big-time cahoots." Page fished in her bag for the vehicle's keys, letting her mind wander about Eleanor's motive.

"How do you plan to finagle us back into that feng shui needed observation room, Sherlocka?" Betsy yanked open the passenger door.

"I haven't gotten that part worked out, but I will."

CHAPTER 23

The morning rush at Honey Bees had subsided, allowing Page the chance to engage Daisy. She found the young woman bent over a catalog. Page lingered a moment to study Daisy. Her strawberry blonde hair framed a round face, and her dazzling green eyes missed nothing. But it was Daisy's effervescent personality that drew others to her. With no effort, Daisy could generate easy smiles from Honey Bees customers. Page counted Daisy and Ina as cherished gifts to Honey Bees. "What has you so engrossed?"

Daisy held up the page showing various body care products. "Betsy told me you decided to move forward, offering lotions and whatnot. That's exciting news."

"I'm pleased you agree. We want the products to appeal to all age groups." Page scanned the pictures before laying the catalog aside. "With your college knowledge of marketing, do you think we can successfully target a broad market?"

"I do, Page. I mean, who doesn't want a lovely lotion or body butter? Right?" Daisy's expression lit her next words. "My dad has always said never dismiss an idea until fully explored."

Page smiled. "And, do you have an idea you wish to explore with me?"

Daisy gave a quick nod. "Since baking isn't my thing, I'd love to help with the body products endeavor. Assuming you'd want me?"

"Your dad gave you sound advice, and you're about to get the proof." Page loved the girl's verve. If Daisy's eyes sparkled with any more anticipation, they'd ignite the plate of honey ginger cookies. "Grab your backpack. We've got an appointment to meet a supplier in South Shore."

Daisy spun around. "Wow, totally cool. I'm ready to help you slay this meeting. I've been brainstorming all morning. How about soaps? I can design their shapes, and then there are hair care products."

"I love your enthusiasm. Bring it along." Page waved to Bailey as he passed the window carrying a delivery.

Daisy started toward the back but halted. "Thank you, Page. I promise you and Betsy won't regret hiring me," she said, before disappearing.

Betsy came out laughing. "You must have invited Daisy to tag along. Are you leaving soon?" Betsy stacked a batch of freshly baked blonde brownies.

"Yes, and yes. If her enthusiasm is any gauge, Daisy will run with our project and need minimal supervision." Page placed a glass dome over the bars.

"I agree. May I offer a suggestion?" Betsy broke off a piece of cookie and popped it in her mouth.

"Suggest away, partner."

"After your meeting, go to Hibiscus. You want to update our suspect board. Use the quiet time without me there yammering to do that. You like?" Betsy lifted her eyebrow.

"That's a splendid idea. And, Betsy, your yammering keeps my funny bone awake. Don't you dare change." Page went around the counter and hugged her cousin.

"Really?" Betsy's carriage lifted.

"Really. I couldn't find a better or more loyal cousin to get paired with in this lifetime."

"Well, since you see me in such a good light at the moment, would you consider removing the no men force field —"

"Nope. You're still in lockdown. Here comes Daisy. See you later at Hibiscus, and don't forget we're going to watch that interview tonight," volleyed Page over her shoulder.

"Yeah, right, good luck with that one." Betsy darted behind the counter as two customers entered.

~*~

Upon arriving home and seeing Steve's SUV parked next door, Page hurried inside to change into her one-piece black bathing suit. She admonished herself again for the purchase. What fool wears a dark color in the heat of summer? A too chilly fitting room caused her to forget that rule. Returning her thoughts to the mission, she'd bet her favorite bed pillow that Steve Tanner was on the water straddling a yellow surfboard.

Beach bag in hand, Page walked out toward the ocean. Her ever-observant prey waved from his surfboard. She spread out her tropical flowered towel, noting that Steve wasn't giving up any rides to visit her. Fine. She'd swim out to where a dozen surfers congregated and deliver her barter scheme to the one who bothered her pulse rate.

Smile in place. Page came alongside his surfboard. "Hiya."

"Hiya." Steve's eyes took a read on her. "What brings you out to the sharks' habitat, Miss Drew?"

Page slowed her legs' movement and looked for fins.

Steve laughed, along with the two surfers on each side of him.

"You're awful. All I want is a minute to make you an offer." Page did another scan for sharks.

"Hey, Steve, you should take her offer. A man your age doesn't get many of those," teased the blond surfer closest to him.

"Stow it, Finn. You might be surprised at what offers come my way," countered Steve with a devilish grin.

Page didn't know which troubled her most, Steve having women after him or why the guy's name was Fin. She slowed her treading and asked. "Um, why are you called Fin?" She moved closer to Steve's board.

"Because that's his name." Steve hoisted a grateful Page

out of the water and onto his surfboard.

"Thanks." Page turned toward the young man. "Your mom named you Fin?"

Steve signaled the surfer to take the wave. "His last name is Finn, with two n's."

"Ohhh, that's actually funny."

Steve wiped the salt spray from his face. "Page, what's your offer? I'm out here trying to capture a few waves before work pulls me back."

"Yes, my offer. Actually, it's two offers I bring. One, how about we go sailing Saturday evening?"

"Sure, Saturday works, at least right now. Next?" Steve maneuvered the board to miss the break.

"Next, I offer a barter, so to speak. I happened to overhear —"

"Page, you never happen to overhear. You find a way to shimmy yourself into eavesdropping on others. Start over and tell me straight."

Steve's smile messed with her pulse. "Okay, sometimes I shimmy, but sometimes I don't. Do you want to hear this bit or not?"

"At this slow pace, I'm listening for the cows to come home," Steve teased.

"If you invite Betsy and me to your soiree tonight with Eleanor and Bert, I'll tell you what I learned at The Perk." Page swiped at the water stinging her eyes.

Steve pondered. "Okay, if this gossip isn't valuable, I reserve the right to rescind your invitation."

Page recounted Mickey's story and ended with what she'd overheard Eleanor telling Bert. "I don't know what those two did regarding Jake, but clearly, Koch has them worried and wanting to leave Shell earlier than planned."

"Don't forget leaving with a big chunk of Jake's money,"

added Steve.

"Yes, siree." Page noticed Finn back bobbing next to them. "What time?"

"Are you asking me what time the interview is?" Steve pointed Finn to a coming swell.

"I am."

"This is a scary thought, but maybe I'm learning to interpret your shorthand language. Seven o'clock."

"Looks like you're able to speak it, too." Page slipped off the board. "See you later, Finn."

"See you. Hey dude, notice how she told me goodbye and not you?" Finn snickered.

Page swam to shore and stretched out on her beach towel until Betsy came to wake her for dinner.

~*~

Switching off the kitchen light, Page went to join Betsy on the porch. "Thanks again for getting us barbeque and not trying to cook tonight."

"I love Bailey's hot sauce and ribs, so no sacrifice here. Besides, you paid for our meals. In case you're sad about missing my duck and oxtails, I ended up cooking and freezing them. We'll enjoy them another night." Betsy set the hammock in motion.

Page's expression looked questioning, "Why are you—"

"The swaying helps digestion. You should give it a whirl," suggested Betsy.

"I should. Listen, we've got thirty minutes before we should leave. Want to review the updated suspect board?"

Betsy sighed. "Can it wait until after we observe tonight? That way, it's all current."

Page nodded. "That's a logical plan. You keep digesting while I check international flights leaving tomorrow night. I have to guess which country has Bert's villa waiting."

"With my extensive travel experience, I say focus on Spain.

Eleanor and Bert strike me as people who'd like that lifestyle most. Besides, being blond, Bert blends best in Spain."

Page did a deep bow.

"Did you drop something?" Betsy tried and failed to peer over the hammock.

"No, silly, that was me bowing to your keen deduction skills. Meet you at the front door in twenty minutes." Page left the porch, hearing Betsy telling herself that she had keen deduction skills.

~*~

Koch escorted the two sleuths back to the observation room. "Sorry I had to slip you in a different door, but I didn't want to risk Bert or Eleanor seeing you. It's for your protection. Daisy would chew me a new one if one hair were rearranged on your heads."

Page nodded. "We understand and appreciate your keeping our presence quiet."

"As for Daisy, we're ready to adopt her as a permanent Honey Bee," chimed in Betsy.

Koch's normally staid face made a slight grin.

Page thought Koch was a steadfast and loving father. She bet he left his gruff demeanor at work. "When you see Daisy next, make sure you ask her to share news on how we're putting her education to use."

Koch opened the door. "Will do. Enjoy the upcoming show. If you play your Tarot cards right, I may have a surprise bonus showing later."

Betsy turned to Page. "Whatever did that man mean about Tarot cards and a bonus? I swear men at Shell speak in tongues."

Page struggled to contain her laughter. "I think Koch's reference to Tarot was his way of teasing me about my intuiting gifts. As for the bonus show, you got me, kiddo. Guess we'll need to wait and see."

"Moving on, where's Dreamboat?" Betsy craned her neck to see around the two-way glass.

"Who is Dreamboat?" asked Steve, appearing at the open door.

Page sent a dagger stare to Betsy.

"I…was referring to…Page, who was I referring to?" stammered Betsy.

"The prisoner that officer paraded down the hallway." Page switched focus to Steve. "You know Betsy and her eye for men."

A puzzled Steve glanced outside the door. "I don't see any dream—"

"Look, Bert is sitting down. You'd better go," encouraged Page.

Betsy waited for Steve to leave. "A prisoner? You paired my roving eye with a criminal? Steve's opinion of me may have hit an all-time low," Betsy sighed in disgust. "A prisoner."

"Hush, I'll fix things later. It was the best I could do on short notice. May I remind you this is your fault, nicknaming him my Dreamboat." Page released a breath and gazed at Betsy.

They both broke out laughing, forcing serious expressions back to their faces when Koch and Steve entered the interrogation room.

Detective Koch spoke first into the recorder, noting the date, time, and who was present. "Over to you, Detective Tanner."

"Bert, we appreciate your cooperation as we try and tidy up some loose ends around your brother's death. Again, please accept our condolences over your loss." Steve waited.

"Thanks. I hope we can get this over fast. I don't know what I can add to my previous statement." Bert fidgeted in his chair.

"See that? Fidgeting is a sign. He's guilty," said Betsy.

Page nodded. "Yes, guilty of something."

Steve glanced at his notes. "To recap, you attended the firework festivities and mingled around that evening. That being your description for your movements."

"Yes, I mingle. It's good for my business."

"Look, Bert, here's where my deduction has taken me. Coincidentally, you and the mayor's wife, Eleanor, have a block of — say — twenty or so minutes you can't account for and where no one saw either of you. That's plenty of time to take out Jake."

"What? Why in the hell would I want to shoot my brother?" Bert jumped up. "You're going the wrong way with your so-called deduction, Detective Tanner."

Steve sent a sharp look. "Take a seat. As I was saying, twenty minutes allows you time to commit murder. As for the why? That gets to motive, and yours happens to make the top three reasons to kill. Money, Bert, lots of money. You and your daughter were Jake's only beneficiaries."

"You're crazy. I own a lucrative business. I didn't need Jake's money." Bert rubbed his forehead.

"We think you did need his money. After all, you borrowed some and refused to pay it back." Steve waved Jake's journal.

"What's that?" asked Bert. His voice went up an octave.

"He's progressed to squirming," announced Betsy, rubbing her hands together.

"Yes, and good observation." Page stayed focused on the unfolding scene.

"This is Jake's journal. Did you know he kept one? Probably not," answered Steve. "On this page, your brother shows an outstanding loan to you for twenty thousand dollars."

"Oh, that. It slipped my mind. I needed some cash for this bulk shipment score of trees and various nursery embellishments. I'd planned to cut Jake a check next week."

"According to Jake's entry and a few witnesses who overheard you two arguing, you had no intention of paying back that loan. In fact, you threatened to tell something on Jake if he didn't forgive it. The witnesses told us you were bested when Jake said he had something far worse on you. Want to tell us about that?"

"Nothing to tell. Whoever those witnesses are, they got things twisted. People aren't that smart."

"These witnesses are respected residents of Shell Isle. To continue, we're starting to piece together that you and Eleanor have a thing going on the side."

"Ridiculous. She's a married woman. I don't do married women. I have the pick of the litter in this town." Bert attempted a suave move and pushed back his hair.

"Well, it seems that you picked Eleanor from said litter. Don't waste my time denying this. The witnesses—"

"They're wrong, I tell you." Bert's reactions were colored with guilt.

"Bert, you're dodging every fact that I'm throwing you. Did you or did you not talk to Eleanor on the phone this morning and discuss having matching stories and leaving the country tomorrow evening? Face it, man. We've got you boxed."

Bert's face turned whiter than the walls surrounding him. He said nothing.

"Do you own a gun?" fired off Steve.

"A gun? No, of course not. And I'm telling you that I didn't shoot Jake."

"Your daughter told us you own a weapon. She even brought us some extra bullets from your box. You probably heard nine-millimeter is what killed Jake. You shoot nines. I think every gun owner linked to this case shoots them." Steve raised his arms in the air. "But, hey, I only need one of you to make this case. Your daughter helped us out."

"She's setting me up. That detestable little—"

Koch moved into Bert's face. "I have a daughter who's

precious to me. I'd never turn on her like you're doing. A father who's capable of that is capable of anything. They don't come lower than your type, Mr. West."

"Where's your gun?" demanded Steve. "We have a search warrant. Answer now, or I'm sending the guys to comb through your house and the nursery. They tend to make a big mess, but they always deliver us…something useful." Steve pulled a chair up to Bert and tapped him on the shoulder.

Bert made brief eye contact.

"I wonder what else we might find at the nursery?" Steve's final blow broke Bert's will.

"So, okay, I own a gun. I never think about it. It's in my floor safe."

Steve signaled Koch. "Have you fired it recently? There's no reason to lie because the report will tell the truth."

Bert exhaled. "No, I haven't fired it, but I'd like to use it on these supposed witnesses."

Steve's expression changed to anger.

Bert fumbled. "Wait, that came out wrong. I meant it as a figure of speech. Forget I said that."

"Like that's going to happen," interjected Betsy.

Page grinned. "Bert's puddling. Steve's going to put a decorative bow on his story soon."

Steve moved a piece of paper toward Bert. "Write down the safe's combination and give me your house key."

"Here. Can I go now?" begged Bert.

"We'll see." Steve handed off the items to a waiting Koch. "So, here's where I am with you and Eleanor. You're having an affair with a woman who demands the finest. To deliver that, you needed Jake's money. You've achieved that by hurrying him to his grave a few weeks early."

"What do you mean a few weeks early?" Bert's face registered surprise.

"You didn't know Jake had a bad heart? The ME's report stated his death was imminent."

Bert could only stare at Steve.

"So, if you'd only waited a bit longer, Jake's money would have come to you. You didn't need to kill the guy. Unfortunately, you chose the wrong path to that money."

"None of this is true. You don't have real proof. So, what if I owed Jake money, and I'm having a fling with Eleanor? Big deal. No crime there. I have nothing further to say without an attorney." Bert stood.

Steve pressed Bert's shoulder down in the seat. "Hold on. We're not done here. First, the ballistics on your gun will provide information that you won't. Second, we know you and Eleanor made plans to leave the country tomorrow night."

Bert flustered. "I'm free to do as I please. You can't keep me—" Bert came out of his chair again.

A much taller Steve looked down at Bert. "Understand this. You're a suspect in a murder investigation. Try and flee, and we'll arrest you. Now, get out of here. I've got your Eleanor waiting. Once I tell her how you chattered, I expect she'll cave fast. Who can say? Maybe she'll spill it all to avoid jail time, assuming she's innocent of wrongdoing. You might want to take that worry home with you, Mr. West."

CHAPTER 24

Betsy waited for Bert to leave before putting her head outside the door. "Hey, Koch, could we have a couple of colas?"

Koch nodded, telling a sergeant to fetch the drinks. He continued talking to the bailiff.

Betsy placed a can in front of Page. "Here you go, Toots. It's intermission. Drink up."

"Thanks. I was thinking about Eleanor. I'm at a loss how she fits into—" Page got an inkling and her answer.

"I know that look. You got a thump," declared an excited Betsy.

Steve entered the room. "Who got a thump?"

"Page, of course. See that elfin grin? That's the sign she's going to stir up trouble for somebody." Betsy sipped her soda.

"Um, Page, if you have something for me, I'd appreciate hearing it now before I start with Eleanor." Steve waited.

Page watched Eleanor coming into the interview room. She'd dressed in a sleeveless designer black dress. Her dark hair pulled into a tight chignon, tried to create an image of control. But it was her contoured cheekbones and false eyelashes that failed at sophistication. Words like *ruthless* and *conniving* entered Page's mind. She turned her attention to Steve. "You might want to ask if she paid Jake a visit at the point."

"You're aces, Miss Drew." Steve hurried out.

Betsy leaned back in her chair and shook her head, absorbing Page's words. "Wow, she was at the cannon site on July Fourth. Eleanor could have killed him. I knew that la-de-dah lacked scruples."

"Let's see what Steve can discover. Koch has finished the intro part. Here we go." Page scribbled a note to herself. Another inkling confirmed Eleanor's worry that Jake had blabbed about her affair.

Steve opened the interview wearing his friendly face. "Thank you for making time this evening. We'll try and get this wrapped up quickly."

"I'm sure the mayor would appreciate hearing this. You were wrong to bring me down here." replied an icy-voiced Eleanor.

Grabbing a file, Steve sat down next to her. "Let's begin, shall we? You might like to hear that we had a productive session with your…what would you call Bert?"

"I'd call him Mr. West. Why are you bringing him into our discussion? Honestly, I've yet to feel impressed with this department's abilities. You might like to hear that I've told Ed that a housecleaning of this station is in order. Please keep that in mind as we go forward, Detective…?" Eleanor squinted at Steve's badge. "Yes, it's Tanner. I must remember that."

"Now, Eleanor, I'm disappointed. I pegged you as smart, maybe even cunning. You've managed to turn things adversarial in a few sentences. That miscalculation could prove costly. Your veiled power threat carries no weight with me. None," seethed Steve. "So, let's return to my question. I'm going to give you the answer so we can get things moving along. You're having an affair with Bert West."

"That's preposterous." Eleanor acted bored and smoothed a wrinkle from her linen dress.

"Tell her," invited Koch, wearing a smirk.

Steve nodded. "Bert's already confessed to your dalliance. I was providing you the opportunity to prove my assumptions about you wrong. You failed. Now, I'm forced to distrust all future answers coming from your mouth." Steve sighed. "Goes with the job."

"Bert would never tell you we're involved. It's simply untrue. You're the one lying." Eleanor managed to lift her chin higher.

"Ah, Eleanor, you called him Bert, and that's personal. I'm moving on. Fact one, you are involved in an extramarital affair with Bert West. Fact two, you and Bert made plans to adios the country tomorrow night. Fact three, that ain't happening." Steve's sent an intense look toward Eleanor.

"You can't tell me what I can and cannot do. I have rights and—"

Steve ignored her. "Fact four, you're a suspect in Jake's death, which means I have every right to detain you." He held up all fingers in front of her face. "Fact five, I have witnesses that overheard you asking Bert if he'd deposited Jake's inheritance. Fact six, I have a witness who listened to a phone call where you confirmed with Bert the flight departure time and your matching stories for the police."

"This is absurd. I've heard enough." Eleanor stood.

"I'm sorry, ma'am, but Detective Tanner isn't finished." Koch extended his arm toward her chair.

"I'm going to finish making my points. You can refuse to answer and seek legal counsel. I thought if you were innocent of having any involvement with Jake's death, you'd gladly cooperate. It seems I was wrong." Steve frowned. "Fact seven, we have Jake's journal, where he recorded a lot of fascinating observations and notes on conversations. You made the journal. Jake met with you and encouraged you to end the affair, or he'd go to your husband with the information."

"Jake was a nobody busybody. I detest—" Eleanor clamped her hand over her mouth.

"Yes, well, that's helpful to know." Steve gave a knowing smirk. "However, the last two facts really throw guilt your way.

Fact eight, Jake made an appointment with your husband for July fifth. You knew about this meeting and what it could mean to your future as the mayor's wife. Everyone knows how much you covet playing high and mighty. No, you couldn't risk Jake talking with Ed, which leads me to the last piece of incriminating information. Fact nine, you confronted Jake after he fired the cannon. You see, Koch and I suspect your conversation went badly, and filled with rage, you shot him."

"You're saying that I shot Jake?" Eleanor laughed hysterically. "This is rich. Me, the mayor's wife, shooting a measly little charter captain because he thought my morals unacceptable. Like he was judge and jury of other people's behaviors? I think not, you, inept detective."

"Sorry, but that's not how we see things. Right, Detective Koch?"

"Sure isn't, ma'am. With *no* due respect, we think you're a most capable murderer type. Steve, since she's refusing to answer our questions tonight, can we wrap? My wife's made my favorite lemon crème pound cake, and I'd like to get home."

"Can do." Steve cocked a grin. "I'm almost done. I can't allow Eleanor to leave without extending her our congratulations."

Eleanor rolled her eyes and grabbed her Italian handbag. "What congratulations?"

"Oh, we're congratulating you on making the final cut of suspects who had means, motive, and opportunity to murder Jake. It's an elite list, which should please you — the elite part and all. Last, we're working around the clock and remain confident in solving this case with or without the gun. Feel free to take yourself home to the mayor." Steve bestowed a confident smile on Eleanor and walked out of the room.

"Holy smoking guns. Jake had set a meeting with Ed. We don't have that tidbit on our suspect board," said Betsy. "I hate this room. It's so hot." She pulled the fan from her tote.

"You're right. Steve held that piece back, or maybe he only just discovered it. Either way, things aren't looking too rosy for snooty Eleanor. Sleep won't come easy to her this night, and there's satisfaction in that fact." Page tilted the soda can to drink.

"Plus, your inklings helped Steve press in on Eleanor. Your gift never ceases to amaze," added Betsy.

"You know that I don't take my intuition for granted. I'm honored to play a role in solving mysteries, even if they often mean a murder happened. Aim that fan my way. It's unbearably hot in this joint." Page leaned her face toward Betsy's fanning hand.

"Koch told us he had a surprise show. Wonder if that's next?" Betsy tossed Page the fan and peered into the hallway. "Intermission is over. The next show stars Ralph Owen."

"I love a trifecta. This one should make a fine finale. Come sit." Page patted the chair next to her.

Steve opened the door. "Okay, my two favorite snoops… sleuths, we've got Ralph in the hot seat to close out tonight's soiree. Got more for me, Page?"

"Sorry, nothing." Page made a pouty face, which brought a smile to Steve.

"How about you, Betsy?"

"You're asking me for insight? Me?" repeated a shocked Betsy.

"Well?" Steve stood, watching amusedly.

"All I can tell you is this room is hotter than the fires of hell." Betsy snagged her fan from Page.

Steve winked. "Duly noted. See you two soon."

Ralph's face looked haggard. His nervousness was evident with each jerky body movement. The suspect's beady eyes darted around the room as if he expected trouble to visit at any moment. Gone was Ralph Owen's cocky attitude. Present was a subdued prisoner, unsure of his fate.

The attorney wore a three-piece navy suit and a worried expression. His open briefcase meant to convey preparedness, rested on the table between him and Ralph. He released a heavy sigh when Steve entered the room. Koch stood only in a support role.

"Evening, Ralph. I hope you're finding our accommodations to your satisfaction. At least your poaching friends can't get to you in here, right?" Steve's eyebrow rose.

Ralph waved the question away like it was an annoying gnat.

"Jim, I see you're representing Mr. Owen. Thanks for coming to the station tonight. We've received reports that necessitate this meeting."

Koch passed an envelope to Steve.

"We have two reports to share, which concern your client's smoking preference and how it relates to this case. Jim, these copies are for your file." Steve passed the envelope. "Basically, we know now that Ralph's name is an alias. He's in the U.S. illegally. Here's the big piece of evidence. His DNA matches the cigarillo found at the murder scene. As an aside, none of the other suspects smoke. Additionally, Ralph owns an unregistered gun, which fires nine-millimeter bullets. The same size that took Jake's life. Your client was unable or unwilling to produce said weapon for us."

"I'm telling you, my place got ransacked. Someone stole my gun."

The attorney cautioned Ralph to remain quiet.

"So, those facts lead to a few questions which we hope your client will see it's in his best interest to answer. Okay, if I continue, Jim? I'm going to direct my questions to Ralph," stated Steve.

"Sure, you can ask, but that doesn't mean you'll get anything." The attorney's expression remained friendly.

"Ralph, let's start at the beginning when Jake came around saying he suspected you and Buck of breaking the fishing laws. We know that you're involved in selling shark fins to a conglomerate out of Central America, probably tied to your birthplace. You'd brought Buck in because he needed money to cover bad gambling debts. Things were rocking until Jake showed up, tapped into his past law enforcement experience, and told you and Buck to mend your evil ways. You had a decision to make. Either take out Jake or risk your partners taking you out. That's what we call back to the rack. How am I doing?" asked Steve.

Ralph shrugged.

"You do an impressive recount, Detective Tanner," said Koch. "Plenty of facts and logic. The jury will appreciate that."

Steve gave a solemn nod. "So, continuing, now you have a problem that needs remedying fast. Don't you, Ralph? Yep, Jake must go, and you hatch an almost brilliant plan to take care of your problem when Jake is alone firing the cannon. Here's my theory. When Jake shoots the cannon for the third time, you fire the bullet at that moment. The cannon hides the sound of the gun. Like I said, a brilliant plan, except for the one thing you left behind. That damn smoking habit and the cigarillo busted you." Steve slid his closed file across to Koch and waited.

The attorney leaned back and folded his hands. "Are you ready to charge him with murder?"

Ralph popped out of his chair. "No way in hell."

"What was that, Ralph?" Steve moved closer to Ralph, blocking him from the exit.

"I said, no way in hell. I didn't take out Jake. I admit the thought was in my mind, but I hadn't acted on it." Ralph swiped at his forehead and paced the room. "Do something." Ralph glared at his attorney.

"Could you give me five minutes with my client?" asked Jim.

Steve stepped aside. "Five minutes. Take the empty room across the hall."

"Come on, Betsy. Let's get some fresh air. This case is crazy confounding." Page held the door and noticed Koch and Steve weren't around.

Standing on the deserted sidewalk, Betsy fluffed her flowered shirt, inviting air movement. "Answer me something, will you? Why do I feel like every suspect Steve interrogated tonight is guilty? Bert, Eleanor, and Ralph. They each did it. Poor Jake should have three bullet holes."

Page nodded. "Truthfully, it seems that way to me, too. I'm hoping once we put more info on the suspect board, clarity will come. I do sense the circle is tightening on the guilty one."

Betsy's face flushed with pent-up emotion. "All I want to do is bake sweets and sample a few each day. I don't want to sit in the police station starved for air and listen to people lie." Betsy paused for a breath.

"Are you gearing up to have a hissy fit? Because if you are, it needs to be a quick one. We've only got two minutes. Here, let me fan you," offered Page.

Betsy's happy nature returned. "Forget it, if I only get a two-minute hissy. Let's go suffer more from murderer number three."

The women found a pitcher of ice water and cups waiting in their room.

The attorney spoke first. "My client wishes to explain why his cigarillo was found at the scene of the murder. It's his hope this truthful information will exclude him from suspicion."

Steve nodded. "Let's hear it, Ralph."

"You're right. I did see Jake that night on the point. I wanted to scare him off reporting us." Ralph's voice cracked. "He was already dead when I got there. I swear it, man. I dropped my smoke and ran off. Someone else got to him. It wasn't me."

"Well, Ralph, we appreciate your adding to your story, but here's the deal. Liars lie. You are one of those. This could be the truth, but it could also be a lie to cast suspicion elsewhere. You, like others, had the means, motive, and opportunity to commit this murder. We've placed you at the scene, and once we find the gun, we'll know if you've told the truth. No further questions."

Steve went to where the two sleuths waited for dismissal. "I'm sure you're past ready to leave. Come on. Let me walk you out."

"I was sort of hoping you'd treat us to another banana split before the place closes," said Betsy.

"Page, are you in on this buy us more splits?" Steve held the front door for the women to pass.

"Nope. Betsy flew solo on this one, but I'm open to the idea."

"To your point, I find myself a fan of Betsy's ice cream idea. My vehicle is back in the garage, so I'd planned to bum a ride home. I see no reason why I shouldn't indulge the three of us in splits. To show my appreciation for your help tonight, I'll even take the back seat."

"Steve, I need to ask one question regarding this case, and then I vote we ban further discussion. My banana split gets my undivided attention." Betsy flicked the button to get more air conditioning.

"Ask away. I'm in a good mood."

"Why doesn't Jake have three bullet holes in him from Ralph, Bert, and Eleanor? Maybe someone missed counting?" Betsy's grin was hidden.

Page flashed Steve a dismissive blink in the rearview mirror.

Steve blinked back. "Only you, Betsy Ross, could find a way to deliver humor while discussing a murder. But there's logic to your question. I think this trio is capable of the act, but I'm working with a lot of circumstantial evidence. Unless someone squeals or that missing gun is found, I've taken things as far as I can for the moment. We need a break, and soon. Enough said."

~*~

Betsy's chattering non-stop about every unique banana split she'd ever eaten traveled home with a subdued Steve and Page. They gave the appropriate responses to Betsy, but their thoughts remained on the investigation. Pulling into Hibiscus's driveway forced everyone's attention back to the present moment.

"Thanks for the ride. No doubt, I'll see you tomorrow." Steve hopped out.

"And thank you for the ice cream and letting us attend tonight's interviews. I'm awash in confusion." Page stood next to her SUV.

"Yes, to all Page said," hollered Betsy, already halfway up the sidewalk. "Say goodnight, Page, and come inside."

"She sounds like your mother," laughed Steve.

"Yep, Betsy likes to wear many hats. Well, goodnight, Steve." Page moved toward the cottage's front door.

"Night," Steve tossed over his shoulder.

Page turned the lock and exhaled. The exhausting day wasn't yet over.

"I call dibs on the shower." Betsy appeared from her bedroom, waving her nightgown.

"Okay, but would you please not turn your shower time into a spa day?"

"Very funny. If you'd up the size of that water heater, we wouldn't run out of hot water."

While Betsy did her ablutions, Page strolled out to the deck. The breeze felt like a caress against her cheeks. Gazing at the ocean, she could see the waves breaking. A handful of people holding flashlights were scattered around the tidal pools, studying what high tide left behind. She inhaled the salt air and closed her eyes. Despite the busyness of her life, Page felt anchored to her joy living at Shell Isle. No place she'd lived before ever offered such peace, such happiness. To claim more of those feelings, she needed to solve this case. The suspect board awaited.

CHAPTER 25

Page brought the suspect board into the living room and propped it against the wall. "Here's our trusty friend. Where's that cocoa you promised me?"

"Coming. I had trouble separating the mini marshmallows. This humidity—"

"Don't doll up my mug with anything. Plain cocoa is fine." Page craned her neck to see what addition Betsy had sprinkled into the cups. "Too late for me," she muttered. Seated on the floor crossed-legged, Page smoothed her coral nightshirt around her thighs and waited for spicy liquid chocolate.

Betsy came into the living room, bringing a wide smile and two cups of pride. "You must taste this. It's my best concoction yet."

"But I wanted—"

"I know you requested plain, boring hot chocolate. Take one sip, and if you hate it, I will go make the humdrum version." Betsy passed the mug.

Page sampled the liquid while looking at her cousin. Surprise found her taste buds. "Why, Betsy, this is delicious. The cocoa gods found you."

"Cocoa gods. Now, that's funny. Want to know the recipe?" asked Betsy. She moved aside a throw pillow and sat in the upholstered chair closest to Page.

"I'd love to hear the recipe. I can't make out if there's raspberry or—"

"It's my latest favorite secret ingredient. Muddled cherries. So good." Betsy smacked her lips.

"Muddled cherries? Well, whatever they are, I approve. Let's get after these suspects." Page pointed to the board and grabbed the marker.

"I'm raring. Tomorrow's a workday, so hopefully, we can do this update fast. Name the first baddie."

"Ralph is listed first." Page began writing. "He owned the cigarillo, and he visited Jake that night to try and stop him from blowing the whistle on fin fishing. We can now check all three boxes for motive, means, and opportunity—Steve's right. We need the gun. Anything else about Ralph?"

"Other than I think he's more afraid to get out of jail and face what the goons have in store. Next." Betsy blew into her cup.

Page pointed to Bert. "We know this guy is dealing magic mushrooms, so he's willing to break some laws for profit. Bert's chasing money and love, which is a powerful motivator for murder. He certainly gets an F as a father. What we're waiting for next is the ballistics report. The police went tonight to retrieve his weapon. That will likely tell Bert's story." Page checked the three boxes. "Bert stays at the top of our suspect list. Agreed?"

"For sure. You remember I think Ralph, Bert, and Eleanor killed Jake." Betsy grinned.

"If you can prove that, I'll—"

"Hush. Keep going. That doll Eleanor is next." Betsy wrinkled her nose.

Page grew thoughtful. "Eleanor's conniving and selfish. Her desires are charged around living the good life, as defined by her. I believe Eleanor sees that as a ladder. She's heartless in stepping on each rung. She must have grown bored playing the mayor's wife and now sees Bert's inheritance as the next rung to good fortune on all fronts. If Jake threatened to expose the affair before she could feel confident in her exit, would Eleanor kill him?"

"I say she would. Go ahead and mark the three boxes so

that we can move on. I can't stand discussing her." Betsy crossed her arms. "Loathsome woman."

"We come to Buck. Steve said he's running the charter boat and staying clean. He's kept an officer around for protection. Buck's motive matched Ralph's; however, I imagine Buck lacked knowledge about the risks of their poaching enterprise. Buck's alibi is solid, according to Steve, which means opportunity and means stay blank."

"He's another one with a missing gun," added Betsy.

"That's true. Two of our suspects' guns have gone missing, and one is supposed to get picked up." Page tapped the marker against her palm.

Betsy yawned. "The last one is crazy, Rosa. Tell me her bedtime story."

Page offered an uneven smile. "Why we still have Rosa as a suspect remains a bit of an enigma for me. Of course, she wanted money to fly the coop, and Uncle Jake denied her. I agree she's got a disconnect in her social brain."

"A big disconnect." Betsy placed her empty mug on the coffee table. "She did possess the motive and opportunity to snuff out her uncle." Betsy grew thoughtful. "Who knows. Maybe she used her father's gun. Go ahead and check means. I want to turn in."

"I suppose you're right about her using Bert's gun. She did give Koch bullets from the weapon. But no, why would Rosa do that if she fired the weapon?"

"Because she's a fruitcake with extra nuts. I'm telling you, Sherlocka, keep means checked for this one." Betsy stood up and returned the throw pillow to its rightful place. "Say goodnight, Betsy."

Page laughed. "Goodnight, Betsy. Thanks for adding valuable input tonight, no make that today." An inkling surprised Page. She chose to let Betsy retire without that news.

She spent the next few minutes tidying up around the cottage and screen porch. It amazed her how two women could leave so many imprints of disorder scattered around. Page replaced the coasters in the tray, fluffed all the cushions, and put the suspect board in the closet. Taking their mugs to the kitchen, Page peeked out the window. The inkling's validation came with flashing blue lights as a squad car pulled into Steve's drive. She grabbed her parka from the coat hook and ran out the door barefooted.

Steve was jogging to the vehicle when he caught sight of Page approaching him at Mach speed. He held up a finger to the officer. "Miss Drew, you don't miss much. Nice outfit."

"Flashing lights at my neighbor's house does get my attention. What's up?"

"Since I don't have my SUV, I'm bumming a ride to Bert's home." Steve adjusted his ball cap.

Page gulped. "Why go to Bert's home at this time of night?"

Steve paused a tick. "Because he's dead."

CHAPTER 26

Sleep never found Page. Only swirling visions of Bert claiming his innocence. Page had stalked her side windows most of the night, hoping to catch Steve's return. She couldn't determine if he was home or not without his vehicle in the driveway. Barnacle dug in the backyard, but his presence meant nothing, as Steve often left him outside. Rather than knocking on Steve's door asking for details of Bert's death, she'd keep watching. After thirty minutes of nothing, Page abandoned her post to shower and dress for a day devoted to Honey Bees.

Hearing oaths coming from the dining area, Page left the bedroom to explore. Shock, along with a print skirt and mint green blouse, dressed her. "Whatever are you doing?"

Betsy teetered on a step ladder with duct tape in one hand and scissors in the other. "Morning. I'm solving my insomnia. This blasted cuckoo bird has chirped for his last time," declared a breathless Betsy.

Page's jaw dropped, watching her cousin tape the bird's door shut. "You can't shut him up that way—"

"I can, and I did." Betsy stepped down and dusted her hands on her violet-patterned muumuu. "Last night was the final straw with that bird cuckooing. Just as I dropped off, he'd come alive. Enough. Aunt Tilly can channel her spirit down here and give me a lecture. I'd rather have the ghost of our Tilly messing with my qi than some ceramic bird."

A knocking on the door broke Page's inability to speak. "Steve. Am I ever glad to see you. Come in."

"Thanks. I figured you were past antsy." Steve noted

Betsy on the step ladder, plastering more duct tape on the clock. He looked at Page with raised eyebrows.

"She's renovating," said Page, resigned to the cuckoo's fate.

"Hi, Steve. I'm more than renovating. I'm problem-solving. Why visit us so early?" Betsy accepted his steadying hand as she descended her perch.

"I left Page hanging last night with news of Bert. I wanted to fill in some blanks." Steve poured himself a cup of coffee, shaking his head at Betsy's offer of an odd colored cream.

Page topped her cup off and motioned for them to sit on the porch.

Betsy tagged behind. "What happened to Bert? I haven't heard this piece of news. Page, why didn't you tell me?"

"Oh, I was planning to, but when I came out, you and Aunt Tilly's clock—"

"No matter. Tell us what's happening," interrupted Betsy.

"I'll start with Rosa calling 911, stating she'd discovered her father dead in his study. There was a suicide note next to Bert. We're waiting on the ME's report as to the cause of death, but he suspects pills."

"He left a note?" asked Page.

"Yeah, it was typed on a computer. I took a picture with my phone. Here you go. Read it out loud," said Steve.

Page nodded and took the phone. *"Dear Rosa, You're a wonderful daughter, and I'm sorry to leave you this way. I can't live with myself any longer. I shot Jake. I didn't mean for it to happen. The reason doesn't matter now. I leave everything to you. Love, Your Father, Bert."*

"That's the lamest suicide note I've ever heard," voiced Betsy.

Steve turned. "Your thoughts, Page?"

"Oh, I concur. The words chosen are feeling words, but the

tone is frigid. Of course, you can't compare Bert's handwriting because it was typed. Even that gives me pause." A fresh inkling hit. Page's face brightened.

Betsy jabbed Steve's arm. "She just got something. I can read her like a book. Tell us, Page."

Page looked askance. "Bert didn't write the note. Either Eleanor or Rosa did. The question we need to be asking is, did one of them write it before or after Bert died? Still, he remains a suspect, though now a dead one."

Steve slapped his knee. "Of course, you brilliant woman. I've got to dash." He headed toward the door. "I'll try and stop at Honey Bees later."

Betsy stood with hands, clasping her hips. "Well, aren't we having ourselves an invigorating morning in the quaint seaside town of Shell Isle, where life is supposed to be congenial?"

"Cuckoooooooooooooooooo—"

"That didn't sound good." Page covered her grin.

"Not him again. I taped—" Betsy hurried to the dining room. "Defective tape. The glue must be old."

"Either that or he's one determined cuckoo." Page watched as Betsy pulled out the ladder and stripped away the dangling tape.

"Well, he's met his match with Betsy Ross. I'm buying new tape before the sun goes down today. Tonight, we sleep in quiet solitude."

~*~

All hands were on deck at Honey Bees. Ina and Betsy's baking aromas traveled out to where customers waited to order. Daisy and Page accepted compliments for the bakers, as noses sniffed inside bags of honeybuns and scones. Shelves emptied faster than could be replenished. The appreciated lull finally arrived at eleven o'clock.

Page stood back, amused, as Ina and Betsy peered inside

the displays. "That's all we have left, ladies. Three honey donuts and one broken scone. Oh, and here's a custom order for one of your now-famous hibiscus decorated cakes." Page passed the ticket to Ina.

"Oy, if we aren't a hit, Betsy. I need to clone myself."

Daisy leaned against the counter. "Here, we are thinking about adding body products. The last time I hustled this hard was when my dad promised me an allowance bonus if I could clean my room in an hour."

Page winked at Betsy. "Tell you what, ladies, lunch is on Betsy and me today."

"I vote deli. Pastrami on rye with a sour pickle. Toss in a knish," said Ina.

"I'll have almost what she's having," echoed Betsy. "Only add a bag of chips. Hold the knish. Come on, Ina. We've got cookies and cupcakes to bake for the afternoon crowd."

Page read a text and then turned to Daisy. "Would you handle calling Maury's Deli and ordering lunch? I wrote down what the girls wanted. Choose whatever you like. I'll go pick it up." Page replied to the message and hurried to the kitchen.

Betsy saw Page motion for her to come to the door. "What? I'm scooping cookie dough. We've come up with another new recipe. Ina and I inspire each other."

"Treat yourself to a breath and listen. Steve texted me moments ago. He's got the tox report back on Jake and some other news to share. I'm going to meet him at the park after I drop off your deli lunch. Don't you think Daisy can handle the early afternoon customers?" asked Page.

"Of course, she can. Get this case solved so we can get back to fun in the sun." Betsy put her head in the doorway. "You do know meeting Dreamboat in the park qualifies as a romantic encounter."

"Enough with that name, or I might sabotage your

pastrami sandwich with mayo," threatened Page. "I'm off to the deli."

~*~

Page walked the few blocks to the park. She was hungry but let her hunger for information trump her body's desire for food. Her eyes had no problem locating Steve sitting on a bright blue spread, with food containers surrounding him. Her pulse quickened. *How could he look so rakishly masculine seated on a worn throw?* "Focus on the case. Ignore your hormones. And, for goodness sakes, don't look at his dimples," she reminded herself.

"Hi there. Hungry?" Steve gave Page a look that could melt Honey Bees icing.

She wilted down to the blanket. "Past hungry, Detective Tanner. What are you serving?"

Thankfully, Steve's cell phone rang, breaking their moment. "Tanner. Right. Neither has a strong alibi. Let's meet late afternoon and strategize. Thanks, Koch." Steve tucked his phone away and turned to Page. "Where were we?"

"I imagine still hungry. Thanks for feeding me. May I?" Page held up a carton.

"By all means." Steve reached in the sack for the utensils and plates and set them on the throw.

Page broke out laughing as she lifted lids.

"What's so funny about Maury's lunch? Everyone loves deli. Don't they?" Steve lifted Page's chin to see her face. "Women. I'll never understand them. A guy tries to be thoughtful—"

Page covered his mouth with her hand and ignored the way his lips felt against her skin. "Nothing is wrong with deli. In fact, the three Honey Bees are dining on deli as we speak."

"Oh, so it's a coincidence kind of thing?" Steve paused. "Why's that funny?"

"No, listen. What's funny is you ordered what I always choose. Roast beef on pumpernickel, slaw, and a chocolate egg cream."

"That's not funny. That's weird. What kind of spell have you cast on me now, Calypso?"

Page leaned in to whisper. "Take me sailing to the island Saturday and find out."

"Let's get about solving this case so we can make that date. Eat up while I share the latest surprises." Steve took a swig of his cream and a bite of his matching sandwich. "Here goes. The police station got a special delivery of sorts this morning. Some teenage boy dropped off a grocery bag containing Ralph and Buck's guns."

Page swallowed. "Who had them?"

"Probably the goons. Koch and I presume they've given up capturing Ralph and Buck and left the country. They'd rather have them behind bars than out and about."

"Those men must think Ralph and Buck killed Jake," added Page.

"I agree. The goons want Ralph and Buck arrested. Someone on the inside will take them out fast. It's probably already arranged. A prison is often an unsafe place." Steve took another bite. "How's your sandwich?"

"Excellent. Thank you. So, now you wait for ballistics to come back?"

"Yep, and I'm hoping we get that report this afternoon. The lab understands time isn't our friend. Koch told me earlier that he's convinced Ralph's our man. I admit it's hard to disagree. Buck wasn't at the scene that night, but he could have been an accessory."

Page shrugged. "I suppose."

"Here's an aside you'll appreciate. I heard the local charter boat captains chipped in money and are offering a reward to anyone with information on Jake's death. Let's hope we get a taker."

"Obviously, those guys thought highly of Jake."

"A lot of good people liked Jake West. Anyway, the next piece of evidence to share is the baffling tox report on Jake. I need you and your inklings' help with this."

"We're making progress. At least you've quit calling my intuiting tinklings." Page reached for the other sandwich half.

"I'd like to think so." Steve's expression shifted to playful.

"Please, Detective, stay on track," Her traitorous pulse had amped again.

"Around you, Miss Drew, that's not always so easy." Steve tucked Page's hair behind her ear before shifting back to being a serious-minded investigator. "The tox showed Jake was being poisoned by something that causes heart damage."

"What? No way. So, was Jake's heart condition caused by the poison?" Page struggled to absorb this news.

"No, the pathology showed a congenital valve problem. The poison had sped up his demise. The ME maintains it was a three-way race between bullet, poison, and disease. This time, the bullet won. They usually do if aimed to kill." A young boy's ball rolled toward Steve. He stood and tossed it back to his mom.

"What's this poison called?" Page's brow furrowed.

"Foxglove. Do you know anything about it?"

Page shook her head. "Look, I know Shell's police department is tiny. Having someone like you working part-time is a huge asset. Will you allow me to take this ball and run with it?" Page grinned as the kid's symbolic ball landed at Steve's feet.

Steve handed Page the red ball. "Go for it, but safely."

Page chose to walk the ball back to the little tike. She returned to Steve, "Safe enough for you?"

He chuckled. "Can you spare me another few minutes?"

"Sure. What else?"

"What's your favorite color?" Steve's expression went playful.

Page leaned backward. "What?"

"Your favorite color? What is it? I'm curious. Can't we go off-topic for a second?" teased Steve.

"Yellow. I love yellow. And you?" queried Page, wondering where he was going with this inane subject.

"Yellow. The proof is my surfboard."

"Also, your wardrobe of yellow shirts. You own a lot."

"I'm pleased you took notice of what I wear. That's a hopeful sign of —"

"That's a sign of an observant sleuth," chided Page. She felt proud of recovering control so quickly. Of course, sitting in the park surrounded by people helped her focus. "Back to the case. Do you have more?"

Steve nodded. "Yep, the call a few minutes ago was from Koch. He said Rosa and Eleanor's alibis were useless. Around the time of Bert's death, Eleanor claimed to have taken a nightly stroll alone. Rosa stated she was cleaning Jake's house since we'd finally given her access. She's the one who discovered her father. If Bert didn't take his own life, then maybe it's someone else who wanted Bert dead. One of his dealers?"

"That's possible. Is your gut saying Bert didn't commit suicide? If so, who benefits from him being dead?" prodded Page.

"My gut says something's wrong with that suicide note. If I can discern what that something is, then my next step will become clear." Steve massaged his neck muscles. "Do you have anything more to add to this hodgepodge?"

An unexpected but long overdue nudge arrived. Page's expression turned mischievous. "Not at the moment, but soon, very soon."

CHAPTER 27

Page devoted the afternoon to Honey Bees' customers and educating herself on the legalities of selling body products. Convinced of the idea's viability, she rang the bottler with instructions to proceed with drawing up a contract. Even her ambitious goal to have inventory for the Christmas season seemed doable. Page agreed with Betsy. Honey possessed some magical powers. Her face beamed as an idea arose to support the earlier nudge.

A proud Daisy appeared at Page's side. "Look what I've fashioned for us." Daisy held up a poster board with a flow chart of tasks. "Do you have time for me to explain?"

"Indeed, I do. This looks fantastic." Page leaned against the counter, studying the poster.

"Super." Daisy propped the board on a stool. "So, my undertaking represents each step necessary to bring Honey Bees' assorted potions to market. I don't think I left out anything. Oh, and I made sure to factor in unexpected delays because they always happen. What do you think?"

"I'm awed and appreciative that you took the initiative to create this. It's amazing, Daisy. You'll be tickled to hear that I just called the supplier we met yesterday and told them to send the contract. Honey Bees is going to spread more honey love." Page snapped a picture of the poster with her cell phone.

Daisy clapped her hands and hopped around. "That's so cool. What do we do next?"

"How about we divvy up the tasks you've got listed here." Page pointed to the board. "I'd like you to choose the ones that excite you, and I'll do the rest."

Daisy's fingers tapped her chin as she studied the list. "I like them all."

"Ah, a natural-born entrepreneur. Lucky Honey Bees. Why don't you take a day or so and look for a logical division of the tasks? In other words, make categories for our enterprise. Once you do that, we'll see how to work in tandem. Okay?"

"Absolutely, okay. Thank you and Betsy for giving me this opportunity."

Page began closing out the cash register for the day. "It's our pleasure. Now, take those empty trays to the kitchen. It's time we all find some fun this evening."

~*~

Inside Hibiscus Cottage, Page scurried to change into her white clam diggers and a lilac cotton tank. The quiet should have felt welcoming, but something didn't sit right. Betsy and Ina had morphed from Honey Bees to Mermaids at closing time. Page didn't expect her cousin home until ten o'clock, which meant she had a few hours to loll around, but doing what? The nudge she'd gotten earlier didn't require her attention until tomorrow. For some unknown reason, being on her laptop and researching foxglove held no interest, yet.

Page felt a tug to the window. She peered at Steve's bungalow as his SUV pulled in. "Drat, he saw me." Page felt her face flush. "Is that what a hot flash feels like? If so, I don't like them." She stole another peek. Great. The guy had her number.

Steve stood in the same place, wearing a humorous grin. He motioned for Page to come outside.

Like a moth drawn to light, Page abandoned the protection of Hibiscus for Odysseus's charms. The only solace she took as she walked out the door was that Betsy wasn't around to witness such weakness. Was she becoming an easy woman? That question made Page do a U-turn. Backbone straight, and without a glance back at Steve, she walked up her sidewalk.

"Where are you going?" hollered a confused Odysseus to his Calypso.

"Home, where I belong." Page shut the door and went in search of Betsy's spare paper fan.

Within a minute, Steve rapped on the door. "Page? Are you okay? Open the door."

She had no choice. That's what she told herself as she hollered, "It's open." And so was the hand fan.

Steve came out to the porch, taking stock of Page, and burst into laughter.

"Shut up, Tanner. I hate you." She sounded sixteen.

"No, you don't. And I'm about to prove that statement." Steve moved toward her.

Page sat swinging in the hammock, waving her fan. "Are you crazy? Don't you dare get into my —"

Steve's frame collapsed into the hammock as his arms wrapped around Page. He brushed his lips lightly against hers. "Still hate me?" he teased.

"Yes," she pouted.

He kissed her once more. Their lips lingered a few seconds longer. "Still?"

"Perhaps a little less." Yep, she was fast becoming an easy woman for Steve Tanner. Her turncoat inner voice said, kiss him back, so she did.

"Wow, that was unexpected. Does that mean you're back to liking me? Us?" Steve stood and pulled Page out of the hammock.

She managed an almost imperceptible nod. "But, with a lot of stipulations." Gaining composure, she rearranged her clothes.

"Unfortunately, I'm going to need a raincheck on hearing those stipulations because duty calls us, Miss Drew. That's what I wanted to tell you a few minutes ago, though I enjoyed the surprise side trip." Steve's dimples appeared as he steered Page toward the living room.

"Where are you taking me?" probed Page. She'd have a dress-down chat with her body's betraying behavior later. For the moment, thankfully, her mind had regained control.

"First, where's Betsy?" Steve listened. "I don't hear her."

"Being a Mermaid, until probably ten. Why?" Page noticed Steve was wearing her coral lip gloss and turned away to avoid giggling.

Steve touched her arm. "Hey, why'd you spin around? Did I say something?"

Page eyeballed his mouth and lost her coolness.

"What now?" Steve lifted his hands.

"My gloss shade really complements your—" Laughter overtook her. She watched Steve grab a napkin from the kitchen and wipe his mouth.

"Marked by Calypso." He tossed the napkin in the trash. "Just so you know, ma'am, you've got your own issues with makeup, but I was too gentlemanly to point it out until you taunted me."

Page ran to the hall mirror, staring mortified at her reflection. Her dark mascara had traveled from her lashes to under her eyes. She looked like someone had sprinkled black pepper on her face. "Oh my gosh. I look hideous."

A grinning Steve handed a fresh napkin to Page. "Hey, you still look cute and sassy to me. We're lucky ol' Betsy wasn't around for our make-out and makeover."

"Enough of your wisecracks." Page kept wiping. "Would you please tell me where we're going once presentable? And, mister, you're still glistening." Page pointed to his lips.

"For starters, if you haven't eaten, I can grill something easy for us. I've got chicken marinating and corn on the cob. After we eat, you're welcome to join Barnacle and me for a walk on the beach. Then, the grand finale happens at eight o'clock. Are you on board so far?"

Page hesitated, but only for a few seconds. "I'd love to compare your cooking to Betsy's, and I could use the exercise."

Steve chuckled. "Oh, I don't see Betsy Ross as any competition when it comes to me at the grill. We're *muy simpatico.*"

"What comes after those two activities?"

Steve took Page's hand and led her out the door. "The captains got a bite on the reward money. The guy's coming to the station to give a statement. Also, the ballistic reports came in, but I'm not telling you anything else. I'd rather you watch what I hope is a wrap on Jake's murder."

CHAPTER 28

Page stood at Steve's kitchen sink. "If you're bent on acting a tease, Detective, and not clueing me on whom you may arrest tonight, dinner better taste outstanding." Page accepted the washed corn and pieces of foil to wrap the ears.

"Lady, I specialize in outstanding." Steve kissed the top of her head. "Barnacle and I are headed for the grill. We'll see you out there in a minute. The pitcher of tea is in the fridge. Don't worry; it's plain, unadorned tea. None of Betsy's additives. Help yourself."

"Aye, aye, captain." Page returned a salute and told her body to ignore the kiss. While she wrapped four corn cobs, her eyes surveyed the kitchen. The layout wasn't as large as hers, but the design was efficient. The pale aqua quartz counters complemented the stained driftwood cabinets. Page noticed the fireplace mantle displayed a newly completed vintage sailboat model. While Steve's interests varied, the solidness of the man did not, and that quality Page admired. Months ago, she'd labeled them as friends with possibilities. That label had worked, and she wasn't near ready to change it. She sensed Steve felt the same. Her self-imposed stipulations would keep things in check if she'd just honor them. Page took the corn and those mental reminders outside to enjoy male company.

~*~

"Chef Steve, please take a bow." Page placed her napkin next to the aqua ceramic plate. "What a delicious grilled dinner."

Barnacle gave a woof and caught the last morsel of chicken tossed by Steve.

"Thanks, and I'm glad to provide meal relief from Betsy. I can't have my favorite sleuth running on empty. Speaking of running? Let's pound some sand after I put these plates in the dishwasher. Well, maybe not pound," laughed Steve.

"Yeah, I opt for fast walking. I'll wait at the picnic table unless you need help?"

"Nope. Back in a few." Steve disappeared.

Barnacle appeared with a leash hanging from his mouth and dropped it at Page's feet.

She stroked his head before attaching the leash to his collar. "Barnacle, you need to stop chewing on Steve's dinghy, find a nice lady, settle down, and have a family. I'd take a spaniel puppy from you in an instant."

Barnacle's tail thumped against Page's leg.

"Did I hear, right? You'd like a dog like Barn?" Steve took the leash.

Page nodded. "Absolutely. I've been considering a pet once Betsy moves into her new digs, and we have Honey Bees seamlessly operating. We'll see if those stars align."

"Maybe they will in time. Let's get some exercise and breathe in the ocean's negative ions." Steve grabbed Page's hand.

~*~

Before riding with Steve to the station, Page popped in her cottage to grab a matching shirt to go over the tank. She jotted Betsy a note and left it on the one place she knew her cousin would go to first—the refrigerator. Turning on the shell lamp in the foyer, Page walked toward what she sensed would bring the missing puzzle pieces around Jake's death.

Steve was chatting on his cell phone when Page got in his vehicle. He gave her a wink and started the engine. "Sounds good, Koch. I think we've got things staged well. See you in five."

"Big night, huh?" Page's hands were balled into fists.

Noting her body language, Steve asked, "What's got you,

uptight?"

"Uncertainty, Tanner. I'm trusting your so-called staging delivers the results you expect." Page unwrapped a stick of gum.

"Relax. If nothing else, trust in my experience. I didn't know you chewed gum."

"Only when I'm uncertain. Want a piece?" Page held out the pack.

"Nope, I'm feeling certain. Don't need any." He clasped Page's hand.

Minutes later, Steve left Page in the observation room with a can of soda. "I'm making you two promises. First, you'll get rid of that gum soon. Second, you'll celebrate with me that Jake can finally rest in peace."

"Then go razzle-dazzle me, Detective." Page opened the soda's tab and wished Betsy was sitting next to her, complaining. She expected a chapped Mermaid upon hearing she missed tonight's events. Page turned her attention to the disheveled man entering the next room. His face looked like a razor made the rounds only once every blue moon, but what struck Page most was his keen awareness of his surroundings. If eyes could look intelligent, his did. The slumped shoulders demonstrated he'd given up on life going his way. Page felt a deep sadness enter her being and something more, protectiveness toward the man. Her curious self waited to hear his voice.

A weary faced Detective Koch assumed his standard role and deferred to Steve.

"Mr. Townsend, or do you prefer Major Townsend?" Steve took a seat across the table from the man.

"Either is fine."

"As an ex-Seal, I'm respectful of any officer who served our country. So, Major, thank you for having the courage to come forward and tell us what you witnessed. I understand that in your current situation, this might feel unsettling. Don't let it. We owe you a huge debt of gratitude, and tonight, I plan to send you out with a nice check. Is that sounding okay so far?"

Page noticed Steve consciously kept his voice low and relaxed. He must have received background information on Townsend. He was customizing the interview to fit the man's distrusting nature. By telling him what he could expect and building trust, Steve might get the major to open up.

"That all sounds fine. Could we maybe get on with it? I don't like being in a closed room for very long." Townsend's expression changed to that of a caged man.

"Oh, I can help that, Major Townsend. Let me open this door." Koch moved quickly, "I'm a little claustrophobic myself."

Steve relaxed his face. "I'd like to make this brief. In my preliminary notes, it says you were at the park the evening of July Fourth and observed Jake at the cannon firing. Does that sound right? Could you take it from that point and tell us what you observed, Major Townsend?"

Finding his best military posture, Townsend cleared his throat and began. "I was stretched out on my favorite park bench close enough to see that man Jake preparing things. It was growing dark, and the trees kind of hid me. That's why that bench and I like each other. Anyway, Jake must be popular because he had a few visitors."

Steve chuckled, along with Townsend. "He was well-liked. Please continue."

"I recall the first people who came were a couple. The fact is, I recognized the mayor's wife. I see her all about town. She and this guy were telling Jake to mind his own business, or they'd find a way to make him sorry. I saw Jake wave them off. They eventually left." Townsend stared off.

"Who came next?" prompted Steve.

"Yeah, the next person came in a small dinghy. I got a big howl from his arrival."

"What happened?" Steve grinned.

"When the guy went to get out of the boat, he lost his footing and fell in the water. So, here he comes to see Jake dripping wet, which likely got him even more fired up. Know what I mean? Ego and all?"

"Yes, Koch and I know that type well. I bet you did get a howl."

"So, this one tells Jake he's gone too far meddling and said he'd warned him once before. Jake says he aims to stop their poaching and see them in jail by week's end. That set this guy off in a bad way. He got all nutso acting and pulled a gun from his pocket. He started waving it around, telling Jake he'd kill him on the spot unless he backed off going to the cops. Sorry, I meant no disrespect to you."

"None taken."

"I was quoting. Otherwise, I'd say law enforcement. Where was I? Oh yeah, Jake tells him to put the gun away, but the guy refuses. He's waiting on Jake to agree to leave things alone, which Jake doesn't do. Instead, Jake tries to grab the gun, and they started wrestling. I hear the gun go off. By that time, I'd gotten up and was heading over to try and break things up. I stopped once the shot was fired and went back to my hidey-hole."

"Understandable. There wasn't anything you could do, and you didn't want to risk getting shot, too. What happened after that?"

"Well, I could tell that Jake died instantly. And, here's the craziest part. Do you know what that man did? He stayed and fired the cannon before getting in his boat and leaving."

Steve stood up and went around the other side of the table, taking a seat next to Townsend. "Are you telling me this man set off the cannon for the start of our July Fourth celebration?"

"I am, Detective. I certainly am. It was like the fool felt

some patriotic duty to fire our cannon. If I hadn't quit the sauce, seeing that would have gotten me a jug. He gets back in the boat after doing both deeds and cuts out. I was going to hunt one of you guys, but I heard someone else approaching. This was Jake's last visitor. He's a mean one with the name of Ralph. He finds Jake lying dead, throws one of those small cigars on the ground, and literally runs off like his pants were lit."

"That's a great image of that lowlife," said Koch.

"I left after Ralph. I found another bench and stayed there for the rest of the night to try and clear my head. I'd gone to a dark place, if you know what I mean."

"I imagine you had a lot of thoughts racing in your head, Major." Steve waited. "Why didn't you come to us right away?"

Townsend put his head in his hands. "I was afraid of that, Ralph. He's a bad one. I used to have bravery in me, but three tours in Iraq left me...like this. Every day, I wake up outside somewhere and say I'm going to get it together. Find a job. Earn my wife's respect again. When the charter boat captains came around asking if I knew anything about their friend's death, I knew today was my last chance to rally myself. I didn't know about the reward until later on. I'd still have come tonight."

Steve squeezed Townsend's shoulder. "I'd bet my life on that truth, Major. I also bet your life's about to get a whole lot better. Do you know how much the reward is?"

"Maybe five hundred?" Townsend pulled out a dirty handkerchief and wiped at his eyes.

"Try twenty-five thousand dollars," replied Steve. "You can do a lot of getting it together with that much money, right?"

"Holy smokes. Twenty-five grand? I can afford to rent me a place and act respectable. Get a job here at Shell and invite my wife to visit, if she will."

Page watched happiness bubble out of the man. His demeanor changed. Hope embraced his face. Page wiped away her tears. One way or another, she and Steve would help the major thrive.

"Twenty-five grand. Are there no strings other than I testify? And, about that, Ralph—"

Koch chuckled. "Don't worry about Ralph. He's already a guest here and bound for prison far away. The government agents plan to grab him tomorrow. Sir, you're as safe here in Shell Isle as if you lived on a desert island. You've become a friend of ours this night. No one will dare touch you."

Townsend's body relaxed. "Well, I like the sound of that."

Steve opened the file and pulled out four photographs. The last thing I need from you tonight, Major, is to look at these photographs and tell me if you recognize any of these people."

"Sure. No problem. This is the easy part for me."

Steve placed Bert's photo down first and waited.

"He's half of the couple. One hundred percent."

Ralph's picture came next to the table.

"That's the lowlife, Ralph. I'd know his mug in the pitch dark."

Steve handed the major Eleanor's photo. "Know her?"

"Yes sir, that's the mayor's wife. She came with the other one you called Bert."

"You're sure?" asked Koch.

"One hundred percent," answered Townsend. "Saved the worst for last, huh? Show me."

Steve nodded and placed Buck's photo next to the other three. "Take your time, major."

"I don't need to. That's the man who killed Jake."

"How sure are you about him?" asked Steve. He took in a deep breath.

"Twenty-five thousand percent sure. Is that good enough?"

Steve put out his hand. "Major Townsend, that's more than good enough, and so are you, sir. It's an honor to know someone who took three tours over in that fire hole. I hope you and I can become friends."

Townsend stood up, shook Steve's hand, and then tendered a smart salute. "I'd like that, Seal."

"Major, if you'll come with me, I need your signature on this statement. We recorded it, but it's also being typed up. I've been authorized by the charter captains to release the check to you if the information met our criteria. I think you know it does."

Townsend stopped at the door. "Thank you again, Detective. I'll make you proud."

"I'm sure you will. Go start that new chapter." Steve nodded.

CHAPTER 29

Page sat silently in the observation room, trying to process what had transpired. There were so many levels of emotions that touched the three men in that room. Those emotions came through the glass and found her heart, too. A soldier, broken by war, had found enough courage to walk through an unknown door and discover freedom on the other side. By doing good, Major Townsend had become good, become whole, once again. Page dabbed more tears. And, hadn't Steve and even Koch treated the man with deserved respect, not judging his appearance? How Page wished Betsy could have been present for this life-changing interview.

The door opened, and Steve came in, collapsing in the empty seat next to Page. He put out his hand.

"What's your paw out for?" Page tried to engage with her humor. She desperately needed a dose of that, and she suspected that Steve did too.

"Spit it out." His hand moved nearer to her face. "The gum. Lose the gum. No more uncertainty."

"I am not spitting my wad of gum into your bare hand. Besides, I added two more pieces before you showed the suspect pictures." Page shoved his hand aside.

Steve grabbed a napkin from a stack near the water pitcher. "Out with it."

"There." She waited for Steve's attention to return. "If you promise not to get a big head, I'll tell you how awesome I think you handled that broken man. You helped him see the potential for a new life and gain a friend, too. You're almost irresistible,

Detective Tanner." What made her utter that last sentence? Trouble headed her way.

Steve did an exaggerated swagger over to Page, invading her personal space. "Irresistible, huh?" Steve kneeled, his grey eyes melding with her aqua ones.

Page sucked in a breath. "Almost. I said almost, Detective." Surely, he wouldn't risk kissing her in the police station.

"I'll take an "almost" irresistible. The fact is, I know how to work with almost. I like to start with this." He closed the three remaining inches, separating them only to have Koch open the door.

"Geez, can't you two wait until you're home to carry on? I've got our next guest waiting." Koch disappeared.

"Now, that was embarrassing." Page felt her cheeks flush.

"Forget Koch." Steve waved his arm dismissively. "So, to keep our tally going, I owe you what an almost irresistible looks like, and you owe me a description of those stipulations regarding us. I think Saturday night will give us the uninterrupted time to —"

"Get out of here and leave me alone. Go talk to your guest so we can go home." Page glanced through the glass. Shock colored her features.

"That's right. You're about to witness Buck's takedown. Then, we'll go home." Steve left the room.

A glum-faced Buck sat in the metal chair.

"Buck, I'm afraid we don't have good news for you tonight. In fact, the news we have is quite troubling. Troubling enough that we've extended your cell reservation." Steve's voice lacked emotion.

"I don't understand what you mean. And I don't know why I've been hauled in here."

"Koch, has he been Mirandized?"

"Sure has. I even got a signature stating such." Koch

waved the paper.

"For the record, Buck Lester, would you care to make things easier and confess to killing Jake West?" Steve watched the shock hit Buck.

"What? Of course not. Have you nimrods forgotten that I've got an ironclad alibi?" Buck shifted in his chair.

"Your alibi sprung a major leak tonight. We're ready to wrap this murder case with or without your cooperation." Steve stared at the ceiling, collecting his words. "Here, it is neat. We have your weapon. Our lab matched the bullet removed from Jake to your gun. Plus, we've got yours and Jake's fingerprints on the weapon. That's pretty convincing."

"That's easy to explain. Someone shot Jake with my gun. I'd say they wore a glove. I told you my gun was missing." Buck's confidence lifted.

"Nah, that's not how this went down. Want to know how we know?" invited Steve.

Buck stared.

"We've got an eyewitness who gave his statement and identified you. Yes, he entertained us with the story of your arrival by dinghy. We especially got a kick hearing how you fell overboard."

Buck's face paled.

Steve sat down. "Want to hear more? Koch, you were especially curious about one thing ol' Buck here did."

"Yeah, Buck, what made you stay and fire the cannon after you shot Jake? I mean, are you some patriotic guy or what?"

"I had to fire it to give me time to leave. Otherwise, someone would have come around—" Buck stopped, realizing what he'd done. "Forget what I said. I was confused. I'm not admitting to anything."

Steve looked indifferent. "That's fine, Mr. Lester. There's plenty of time for you to change your mind. Either way, the jury will decide what happens to you. Koch, charge this piece of nothing with the murder of Jake West."

~*~

Steve and Page exchanged few words on the way home. Being in the presence of a murderer had cast a pall on the rest of their night. Not even their banter dared make an appearance.

There should have been a sense of peace that came with the resolution of Jake's case, but neither felt it. And they knew why.

Saying goodnight to Steve, Page entered the cottage. Waiting was a note from Betsy, saying the Mermaids had gotten skunked. She'd taken her snit to bed. Page saw no reason to disturb her cousin with the arrest news. Besides, at the moment, she felt depleted.

Page walked out to her deck and grabbed a cleansing breath of sea air. A fresh resolve found her. Steve had found Jake's killer. Now it was her turn to uncover who poisoned Jake and why. And there was Bert's troubling death.

CHAPTER 30

Awakening minutes before sunrise, Page threw on her bathing suit and let her bare feet take her to the ocean. How glorious to float on her back while the sun appeared over the horizon. Waves of gratitude mixed with the waves washing over her. She thought of Jeff and the four years since he'd passed. They'd shared a wonderful life and brought their daughter into the world. Of course, she was proud of her daughter's career accomplishments and cherished her visits to Shell Isle. Still, there existed a hollowness in Page's heart that begged filling.

"The ocean's like a sheet of glass this morning. You picked the ideal time to enjoy a float." Steve relaxed on his back and let the saltwater buoy his body over each wave's crest.

Eyes still closed, Page said nothing.

"I'm intruding." Steve flipped over to tread water. "Signal me that you're okay, and I'll leave you alone."

Page lifted her hand and splashed him in the face.

Steve chuckled. "Message received loud and wet. Catch you later, Feisty."

She heard Steve swim away. Her musings returned, only with a change of subject. The repeated nudge came stronger. She could no longer postpone the next step asked of her. The sooner she solved this last piece of the mystery, the sooner she could devote more time to floating weightless. With long, steady strokes, Page swam to shore, oblivious as to whether Steve was watching her.

He was.

~*~

Before heading to the den, Page found an aproned Betsy chopping vegetables for an omelet. The jars of spices, like good soldiers, were lined up for inspection. Betsy's red curly hair was pulled up into something that resembled a ponytail. She waved hello to Page with the spatula.

"Can I bring you up to date on the investigation while you're in creation mode?" asked Page.

"If you can tell me in less than five, shoot. Sorry. Bad choice of wording. Want me to make you one, too?" Betsy sprinkled the multitude of spices and herbs over the array of vegetables.

"No, thanks, and I'll talk fast." Page went over the allotted time, but that didn't stop Betsy from tucking into her five-alarm fire omelet. "So, now you're fully informed. It's time I become Sherlocka and research foxglove before we leave for Honey Bees."

Betsy nodded while chewing. "I'll be quiet. I'm counting the hours until we wipe the suspect board clean, and it's back in the hall closet. Go prosper."

~*~

"Hey there. How's the dowager? Did she figure out who filled her perfume bottle with sherry?" asked a grinning Page.

Betsy closed the book. "Her grandson, Jasper, of course. He's such a little devil. Did you learn what you needed about foxglove?"

"I believe so. I need to ponder some things." Page stared off.

"No need to explain. After all these years, I know how you process. So, is it time to buzz? Since I fixed that cuckoo, time stands still." Betsy laughed at her joke.

"Aren't you the clever one and so early in the day?" Page glanced at the cuckoo's door, now covered in layers of packing tape. "Yep, and I thought we might 'buzz' to The Perk on the way. I've got a migraine trying to come in." Page massaged her right temple. "I need a mega dosing of espresso."

Betsy hopped up. "Sorry about your head. Let me grab my hat and tote. Want me to drive?"

For a brief moment, Page considered saying yes, but adding car sickness to her migraine prompted a fast response. "No, thanks. I've got the keys in my hand."

As Page drove, she noticed dark clouds forming over downtown. The inkling followed the observation. The pulsing pain above her eye canceled the desire to tell Betsy. "I need your parking karma right now." Page slowed her SUV as they approached The Perk.

Betsy's finger flew up. "There's an empty place. Yay, for Betsy's parking karma."

"It's the best," replied Page. She pulled into the extra-wide space.

As they approached the shop's door, Betsy spoke, "I bet Mickey will give me the business about the Mermaids' losing."

Page managed a slight grin as they entered. "Think of it this way. He's a man, and you do love all—"

"Not so. I do not love all men. Your migraine has you thinking loopy. Hey, Mickey," waved Betsy, leaving Page to order.

"All men," finished Page. Amused, she watched Betsy land on Mickey. She ordered both their coffees and scanned the area for a place to sit. Spying two empty chairs and the reason for her inkling, Page changed her expression to sociable and traveled the short distance.

"Hi, Page. Are you taking good care of my flowers?" Rosa lifted her coffee cup and stared off absently.

"I sure am. The edible flowers are such a huge hit with the customers. We received three custom cake orders yesterday requesting them. I'm so sorry about your father—" Page froze, seeing what was next to Rosa. She gulped for air.

Rosa scrutinized Page. "You know flowers have feelings.

They can even turn on you."

Page tried to act nonchalant. "I always learn so much from you, Rosa, about flora. Are you scheduled to work today? I need to swing by and have you recommend more edible petals for the three cakes." Page backed away.

"What time?" asked Rosa. A naughty smile turned up each corner of her mouth.

"Eleven, if that works?" Page saw Betsy heading over.

"You'll be there, right? Because people who make promises they don't—"

"Count on seeing me. I've got to dash. My cousin's waiting." Page hurried to block Betsy's arrival.

"Is that crazy, Rosa? What's wrong? You look like you've seen a ghost."

Page pulled Betsy's arm. "Let's get out of here. I'll explain everything in a minute."

"Hold on. I didn't get my coffee," Betsy complained while looking over her shoulder at their waiting order." Betsy followed Page outside. "This better be good. And what about your migraine needing espresso?"

"Get in the vehicle. My migraine can wait. We need to hurry and unlock Honey Bees for Ina and Daisy. They've got to cover this morning for us. I need you to do something far more important."

"What's more important that I have to do?" asked a confused Betsy.

"I need you to go to Hibiscus and make one of your magical honey cakes."

"I thought we agreed that I'd only create a honey cake if—" Betsy grabbed her fan. "Oh, my stars and garters, tell me."

"I know who was poisoning Jake and probably killed Bert, too." Page's mind had begun formulating a plan. She understood the nudge to return to Plant Hugger. The pieces were falling into place.

"Who was doing the poisoning? I swear I won't bake the special cake, and you know I mean it if you don't tell me," vowed Betsy.

"It's Rosa. She's a murderer." Page's fingers rubbed her temple.

"But, but how do you know it's that young woman? I mean, she's a loon for sure, but—"

"I know because of what Rosa was cradling to her chest. A pot with a foxglove flower."

Page double-parked in front of Honey Bees. "Great, the girls are waiting. Unlock the door and explain we've got something to handle this morning."

Betsy jumped out. Within a minute, she was back in the passenger seat. "They're good. Let's go."

"That's one less thing on my mind." Page headed toward her cottage.

"My mind is humming with things. Can you maybe elaborate a bit more on this foxglove? I won't renege on baking the cake, but I'm still confused." Betsy released a whoosh of air.

Page nodded. "After Steve told me foxglove was the poison found in Jake's system, I did some research. Rosa chose well since Jake had a heart condition. It's a plant that can cause damage to the heart and, of course, death. All parts of the plant are poisonous. When I recognized that the flower Rosa held was foxglove, a lot of blanks filled in for me."

"Give me an example of those blanks." Betsy grabbed her fan.

"For example, maybe that's why Rosa needed to get into Jake's house. I bet she was brewing him tea with it or something and had to remove the evidence."

They rode in silence while Betsy processed Page's words.

"Wow, Rosa. It makes sense now. She and Bert knew

plants. And, didn't we speculate she wanted Jake's money to become a world traveler?"

"We did."

"What else?" asked Betsy.

"I've got a hunch she killed her father with a strong dose of foxglove. We're home. I'll finish telling you the rest inside."

Betsy flew into the kitchen, pulling out the bowls and mixer. Winded, she sat on the stool. "Give me a minute. I'd like to hear the rest, and then I'll concentrate on the honey cake."

"Good plan." Page joined Betsy on the other stool.

"Continuing with this insanity, you suppose she poisoned Bert, too? Why? She had the inheritance?"

"Rosa's mentally twisted, so we can't apply logic to her actions. That's why I need the honey cake to open that warped door to Rosa's mind. The icing on the honey cake, so to speak, was I got a nudge yesterday to visit Rosa at Plant Hugger's today. The inkling to stop at The Perk answered the why."

Betsy returned to her bowls. "I get it now. You need the honey cake's special magic again. What time are we expected?"

"Eleven. How can I help?"

"Start by telling me if we are using Plan A, B, or C. I'm partial to B for this caper," grinned Betsy.

"Um, Betsy, we don't have a Plan B or C. You only discovered the Old-World Honey Cake recipe when we needed help solving our last case. All we have is Plan A."

"Well, as I recall, our Plan A got Dreamboat pretty fired up. I'd like to avoid his wrath, though it was kind of sexy from my side. Can't you conjure another plan?"

Page smiled. "I'm not worried about Steve. We'll stay with what worked, Plan A."

"Guess I'm destined to see another fireworks show soon. Grab the secret flour mix from the pantry."

CHAPTER 31

Betsy sat in the driver's seat at Plant Hugger's parking lot. "Can we please go over what I'm supposed to do once more? I don't like this setup one little bit. We're dealing with someone cracked."

"Stop fretting. Everything will go smoothly. Intuitively, I know this, and we can trust those feelings, right?" Page's success depended on Betsy playing her role perfectly.

"Yes, or I wouldn't be sitting here covered in perspiration like I'm in some sweat lodge."

Page grinned. "I'm going to find Rosa. It's time for you to call —"

"I know. Dreamboat. At least we saw his vehicle parked at home. He can get here in three minutes tops, dressed in swim trunks or not. Don't take any risks. The honey cakes will mellow Rosa and help her speak the truth, but that doesn't mean she can't go bonkers." Betsy reached for her cell phone.

"I promise to stay safe. See you in a few. As always, thanks for being my co-sleuth, Betsy."

It didn't take any sleuthing skills to find Rosa in the flower greenhouse. Page watched the young woman caress a flower and then squish it between her fingers. She'd need the honey cake's charms to act quickly. Tamping down her fear, Page moved closer. "Hi, Rosa. I'm here right on time. Your flowers look so cheerful today."

"They aren't cheerful. They're angry with me." Rosa turned to Page.

"Oh, dear. Why would the flowers get angry with someone that gives them so much love and care?" Page paused six feet away.

"I told them I'm leaving tomorrow and won't return ever. They'll die now." Rosa crushed another blossom.

Page touched a pot of yellow zinnias. "I love yellow."

"I don't." Rose dumped the pot with the crushed flower in the trash. "I'm going away."

"Well, yes, you're leaving on this exciting world travel adventure, right?" Page was treading slowly.

"With my boyfriend, now that I have all the money in the world," proclaimed a victorious Rosa.

"It all sounds so wonderful. And I brought something made, especially for your celebration. It's called a honey cake. Would you like to see it?" Page lifted the foil.

"I don't know. What's in it? You have to be careful about what you eat or drink. Did you know that, Page?" Rosa moved closer, trying to see the cake.

"Why don't I lay the plate on top of this bag of potting soil. I've cut slices and brought napkins. It's the most delicious cake I've ever tasted. The honey comes from special bees in Norway." Page took a slice for herself and then passed another to Rosa.

"I'm going to Norway." Rosa took a large bite.

"Oh, then maybe you'll visit the honey shop in Oslo. That would be fun."

"This honey cake tastes…I want more." Rosa grabbed another slice.

Page observed the unstable woman's countenance shift. She hoped Steve and Betsy were watching. She didn't dare stall much longer. "Have all you want."

Rosa ate another bite and smiled. This cake makes me feel happy. I like feeling this way more than how the Magics make me feel."

Page nodded, ignoring the reference to the illegal mushrooms Rosa and Bert had been peddling. "Happy is a grand

feeling, especially after you've just lost your uncle and father."
She placed the hook.

"I didn't lose them. I know where my uncle and father are.
Burned into ashes, and that makes me happy, too."

Out of the corner of her eye, she saw Steve's angry face,
and Betsy's frown directed her away from the side entrance to
the greenhouse. With Rosa's back to them, Page motioned for
Steve to stay back and listen.

"I'm eating a third piece. Do you mind?"

"Not at all. It's a compliment to see you enjoying this
special treat." Page placed another slice on Rosa's napkin.

"My dad would mind. He'd tell me that I'm a fat lardo."

"I don't think you're overweight. You're a pretty young
woman, Rosa. I think your hair braid is lovely. And, if your dad
spoke so cruelly, no wonder you're happy to have him gone."

"You think I'm pretty? My dad told me over and over that
I was plain in all ways, but he's ashes now. He can't say that
again. This cake makes me feel happier."

"Your dad was wrong. You aren't plain. Did your uncle
say mean things to you as well?"

"No. I cleaned for my uncle, but he wouldn't pay me
enough money to take my trip. He was stingy. People shouldn't
act stingy with money. I'm not. I'm paying for my boyfriend and
me to travel everywhere." Rosa broke off another piece of cake.

"That's very generous of you, but didn't you need to do
something for your uncle's money?" prodded Page.

Rosa nodded. The naughty smile returned. "I'll tell you a
secret. You know the plant I had with me earlier?"

"I do recall seeing the flower and thinking it unusual. Did
that flower want you to feel happy?" Page made her tone caring.

Rosa reached for the foxglove. "This is it. Want to hear
how it helped me?"

"Very much."

"It helped my uncle's heart stop beating, so I wouldn't have to ask him for money again." Rosa stroked the leaves.

"Did you brew him a tea? Or—"

"You're smart, Page. Yes, a tea. I've been worried about my plant because the police wouldn't let me inside my uncle's house to care for it. Besides, I needed more help from it."

Page smiled. "I'm so relieved you were able to get your plant back."

"Yes, that's why I keep it with me always now. I'm taking it on my trip in case my boyfriend needs tea."

"What other help did you need, Rosa? Maybe with your dad?"

"Most of all, him. He tried to cheat me out of half my inheritance by telling the attorney to dole out small amounts. I couldn't go to the Amalfi Coast with so little. My boyfriend wanted to break up with me when I told him."

"I imagine you felt a lot of anger but knew how to solve the problem. Am I right?" Page pointed to the foxglove.

Rosa smiled. "I realized the other night all I had to do was serve my father a meal with enough of my plant friend's gift to turn him to ashes with my uncle. So, I did. And voila, I have all the money now. My foxglove looks after me, and I look after her."

"I think I understand. You served your friend's gifts to your uncle and your dad so they wouldn't cause you unhappiness anymore. Now, with all the money, you're ready to begin a new life and see what the world has to show you. Do I have it right, Rosa?" Page slid the remaining cake closer.

Rose declined another piece. "I like you. You're nice. I would never serve my foxy to you, but I would my boyfriend." Rosa crushed another flower. "Maybe I don't like you."

The honey cake had done its job. Page got the signal from Steve to wrap up the talk. "Rosa, I still care about you. Perhaps it's time that you and foxy go talk with someone who knows exactly how to help you feel better and love all of your flowers again." Page stepped backward, adding distance.

"Love all of my flowers, not just foxy? Love all of my flowers. Love all of my flowers," repeated Rosa.

Steve and a female officer came up to Rosa.

She hugged the foxglove plant to her. "I'm going to love all my flowers," Rosa told Steve and the officer. "Isn't that so, Page?"

"It's true, Rosa." Page waved goodbye and collapsed on the bags of potting soil.

Betsy hurried over. "You were amazing. And, how you waltzed her into confessing was something to behold."

"Thanks, Betsy, but I had your magical honey cake's help."

"Speaking of cakes, if you ask me — and you should — I bet fruitcakes were named after poor Rosa's ancestors."

Page offered a weak chuckle.

Betsy sat down and draped her arm around Page. "You're exhausted."

"Yeah, I am. Take me home before Steve comes back. I'm not ready for his 'what the hell were you thinking, lecture?'"

"Sure thing, Toots. Don't forget we have an extra honey cake to enjoy later. Let's get you home, Page Wright, sleuth extraordinaire. Once you're tucked away with an ice pack for your migraine, I'll go to Honey Bees."

"Eating some of the cake took away my headache. That's not fair for you to work — "

"Of course, it's not fair," Betsy joked. "I get to do what I love while you recharge your emotionally spent batteries and hide from Dreamboat." Betsy looked at the greenhouse's main entrance. "Cancel the hide from Dreamboat part."

Page turned, seeing Steve's fast approach, and groaned.

"Miss Drew, would you care to accompany me to the station? I need another statement, and after that risky — "

Betsy planted her hands on her hips and puffed her chest like a strutting peacock. "Listen up, Dream…Tanner, you take Page straight home after she gives her report. Straight home. She's depleted from this ordeal. I want her sitting in the beach chair holding a bottle of…Page, what do you want to hold a bottle of?"

Page and Steve exchanged smiles.

"I'd like to hold a bottle of French sparkling water and—"

"And the hand of a detective who thinks you're the most remarkable woman he's ever known," finished Steve. He offered his hand to Page. "Your lecture, Miss Drew, comes tomorrow night when Carpi Diem and I have you all to ourselves." His eyes captured hers.

"And so does my list of stipulations," mumbled Page, feeling her willpower ebbing.

Betsy threw her arms in the air. "Why do I bother chaperoning you two? I want no hanky-panky," she hollered to their retreating backs.

"Exactly, what does no hanky-panky mean?" Steve grinned at Page.

"Let's ask her later."

"A lot later." Steve pulled her closer.

ABOUT THE AUTHOR

Multi-genre Author~Inner Explorer~Humor Chaser~Labyrinth Lover~Waterfall Wanderer

Author Tonya Penrose (pen name) is a storyteller who believes in the power of humor and narratives to touch her readers' hearts. She's always been moved by how a story can invite personal exploration and leave a lasting impression on those who read it.

When Tonya sits in her favorite writing chair gazing at a lake, she's all about creating beguiling characters that leap from the page and capture a reader's fancy. Her characters aren't just words on a page. They become real people with their own challenges and quirks. She enjoys sprinkling her romps with moments that offer readers grins or even bursts of laughter.

But for Tonya, it's not only about the characters or the humor. The dialogue is where her stories shine. As a multi-genre author, she feels that engaging dialogue provides the heartbeat for any truly wonderful tale. It breathes life into the narrative and allows readers to feel they're with the characters along the way.

Whether you're seeking an entertaining escape or a thought-enlivening journey of inner discovery, Tonya's books are waiting to whisk you away. Embark on a path where humor meets introspection, and unforgettable characters await at every page turn.

Tonya invites readers to explore the familiar and enchanted settings with her. To uncover secreted truths, share inspiring moments, and awaken to her deeper message—that living in the *now is how*. Tonya's fiction and non-fiction stories are published in numerous anthologies, e-magazines, local press, and literary magazines.

Find Tonya Penrose listed in the Poets and Writers Directory. If you enjoy Tonya's novels, please tell others.

VISIT:
Website: http://www.tonyawrites.com
X: @TonyaWrites
Instagram: @TonyaPenroseWrites
Threads.net @TonyaPenroseWrites
Bluesky @tonyapenrose.bsky.social
Substack @TonyaPenrose

BOOKS BY TONYA PENROSE
Old Mountain Cassie: The Three Lessons
A Secret Gift

Welcome to Charm
Venetian Rhapsody
More coming…
The Shell Isle Mystery Series:
Baubles to Die For
Red, White, and Boom
Murder by Numbers
Teatime Trouble

RECIPES

Betsy's Bright-Eyed Hashers (Pg. 37)
3 T organic salted butter
2 ¾ cups frozen hash brown potatoes
1 shallot minced
½ cup sliced kalamata olives
1 ripe mango chopped
1 tsp turmeric
¼ tsp cinnamon
Celtic salt to taste
2 tsp black pepper
4 organic eggs from those happy hens

In a seasoned and well-loved cast-iron skillet, melt the butter. Add the frozen hash browns, chopped shallot, olives, salt, pepper, and turmeric. Cook for about ten minutes until hashers are crispy on the bottom. Carefully, flip them over and brown on that other side. Now for the fun part. Time to make the bright eyes. Crater out four holes in the hashers and crack an egg into each one. Reduce the heat to low and cook three minutes until the eyes are bright. Transfer to a warm plate. Toss the mango and cinnamon together and serve on the side to add that needed sweetness. Serves 2 *healthy eaters like Page and me. Garner those compliments.*

Brunch Hash Browns*
2-2 ½ cups frozen hash browns
3 T unsalted organic butter

4 large organic eggs
¼ cup green onions chopped
1 yellow bell pepper diced
1 tsp fresh parsley chopped
½-¾ tsp sea salt
¼ tsp.freshly ground black pepper

In a nonstick skillet, melt the butter. Add the onions, pepper, salt, and pepper. Sauté for a minute or two. Add the hash browns and let cook on medium heat without stirring for approximately 7 minutes. Make sure the bottom is nicely browned and crispy. Flip over. Create four holes and crack an egg into each. Turn the heat to low. Cook eggs until the desired doneness. Top with fresh parsley. Serves 2-4.

Betsy's Sweet and Salty Chicken Thighs (Page 48)
4 organic boneless chicken thighs
½ cup quality olive oil
1 cup golden raisins
1 tin anchovy fillets, chopped
2 firm poblano peppers, sliced
2 garlic cloves, smashed
1 small white onion, diced
½ cup chicken broth
1 tsp allspice
1 T orange blossom honey
1 tsp cayenne pepper (Don't be stingy with it.)

Preheat the oven to 350. In a nonstick skillet, brown the thighs in olive oil. Place chicken in an oiled baking dish. Pour broth over meat. Top with the raisins, anchovies, onion, poblanos, and garlic. Sprinkle the allspice and pepper over the chicken. Add a bit more olive oil to the chicken. Cover with foil if desired.

Bake for 30-40 minutes or until done. Choose a colorful serving platter. Drizzle the honey over the chicken. I serve the dish over a lovely bed of jasmine rice. Have a bottle of hot sauce on the table. Serves 2.For a beverage, I brew a pitcher of flavorful iced licorice mint tea. *You know mint helps with digestion.*

Delectable Chicken*
6 boneless chicken thighs
¼ cup olive oil
1 large white onion sliced
2 crushed garlic cloves
1 envelope dry onion soup mix
1 cup dried apricots
1 cup water
½ cup white cooking wine
½ tsp allspice or to taste
2 T wildflower honey

Preheat oven to 350 degrees. Season chicken with salt and pepper. In a nonstick skillet, brown chicken in olive oil. Transfer chicken to a shallow glass casserole and top with apricots. In a bowl, combine soup mix with water and wine. Add onions, garlic, allspice, and pepper. Pour over chicken. Bake 30-40 minutes until done. Add more water if needed. Drizzle the honey over the chicken. Basmati rice makes a nice accompaniment. Serves 2.

Ina's Perfect Popovers (Page 7)
2 cups all-purpose flour
4 large organic eggs at room temperature
2 tsp kosher salt
2 cups whole milk at room temperature
6 T organic unsalted butter, melted
Honey Bees special honey

Preheat the oven to 400 degrees. Coat 16 muffin cups with melted butter. Place the muffin pans in the oven for 3-5 minutes to warm. (*Betsy never did this step, and her popovers flopped.*) Beat the eggs until fluffy and pale yellow. Slowly blend in the milk. Next, add the flour, salt, and remaining butter. Blend all the ingredients gently until the mixture is smooth. Pour the batter into the muffin cups. Don't jiggle the pans, taking them to the oven. Bake them until they turn golden. Carefully remove the popovers from the oven. Serve warm with a nice honey. *I let Betsy choose the honey flavor, so she feels important.*

Betsy's Feisty Fiesta Cakes (Page 65)
2 large organic eggs
1½ cups whole organic milk
2 cups all-purpose flour
2 T organic cane sugar
1 T organic baking powder
¼ tsp Celtic salt
1 T Red pepper flakes
1 tsp cumin
3 T fresh snipped chives
3-4 juniper berries crushed to smithereens
⅔ cup organic unsalted butter melted

In a glass bowl, mix the flour, salt, and sugar. Pour in the milk, 1/3 cup melted butter, and room temperature eggs. Stir until blended. Add the spices and baking powder. Mix everything nicely. Let the bowl rest undisturbed for a few minutes. In a medium-hot skillet or griddle, add the remaining butter to heat. Pour ½ cup of the batter for each pancake and cook until the top bubbles. Flip and repeat, making sure both sides are golden. Place the pancakes on a warm, colorful platter. Serves 4. *I top*

Page's Fiesta Pancakes with crispy prosciutto and crumbled gorgonzola cheese. Oh, and, of course, maple syrup. So good. Trust me.

Fancy Breakfast Pancakes*
2 cups all-purpose flour or gluten-free flour
1½ cups organic whole milk
2 organic eggs
½ cup melted unsweetened organic butter
¼ tsp salt
1 T baking powder
2 T organic sugar
½ cup shredded extra sharp cheddar cheese
¾ cup cooked and crumbled turkey bacon
½ cup organic sour cream
1-2 T fresh finely chopped chives

In a bowl, combine flour, sugar, and salt. Fold in eggs, milk, and 1/3 cup of the butter. Stir until the batter is smooth. Add the baking powder. Set bowl aside. Heat griddle with remaining butter. Pour 1/3 cup of the batter onto the griddle for each pancake. Cook one side until golden and the top bubbles. Flip over and cook the other side. Place the pancakes on a warm platter. Sprinkle crumbled bacon, cheese, and chives on top. Add a few dollops of sour cream around the platter. Serves 4.

Betsy's Enchanted Honey Cake (Page 236)
Betsy agreed to share the basic honey cake recipe but confessed what makes her cake enchanted is the special kind of honey she uses. That is her secret ingredient, and she won't divulge the source of this amazing nectar. It seems our Betsy can keep her yap shut when it comes to creating magic for garnering a confession and closing a murder case.

3 2/3 cups all-purpose flour

1 tsp baking soda
½ tsp Celtic salt
1 T baking powder
1 cup quality vegetable oil
1 cup of the honey bees' magical nectar
1½ cups organic sugar
½ cup dark brown sugar
3 large organic eggs from happy hens
½ cup orange juice
2-3 T Kentucky Bourbon (*optional*)
¾ tsp vanilla extract (*Don't dare use imitation extract.*)
1 cup coffee freshly brewed (*I prefer a dark French roast.*)

Set the oven at 345 degrees. (*I find most ovens run hot.*) Spray a 9x13 pan liberally with butter-flavored baking spray. (*Page likes a Bundt pan, but I don't. Too finicky to get my cake out.*) In a rainbow-colored ceramic bowl (*No eyebrow-raising. You are making magic here.*), mix the flour, salt, soda, and powder. In a separate bowl, combine the oil, ¾ cup of the honey nectar, sugars, eggs, coffee, vanilla, and juice. Mix. Add the wet mixture to the dry until everyone looks married nicely. Pour the magic into the pan. Drizzle the remaining nectar atop the batter in a lovely pattern. Bake until done. I start testing with a toothpick after 30 minutes. Let the enchanted honey cake cool before removing it from the pan. *I drizzle more nectar on top, but that's just me helping Page solve our latest caper.*

*These recipes inspired Betsy's culinary debacles.